# THE ENGLISH
# CATHEDRAL

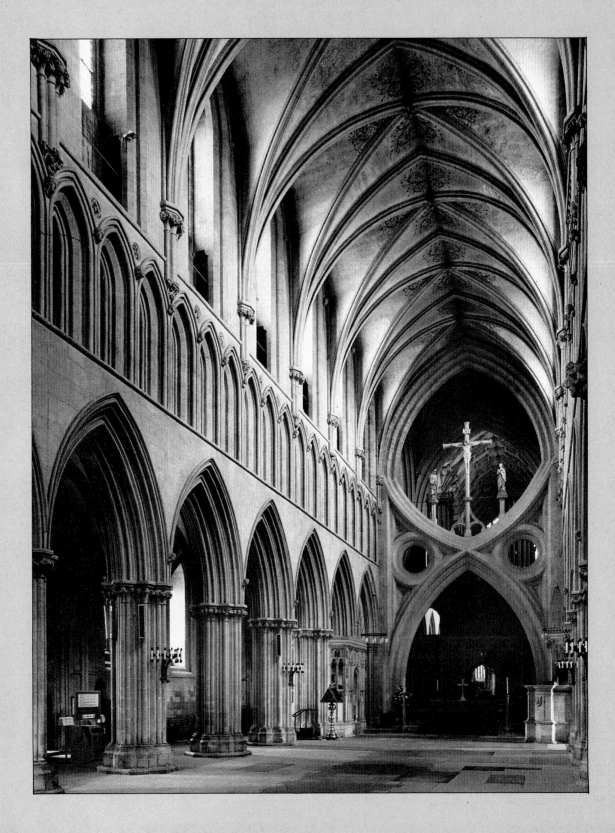

# THE ENGLISH
# CATHEDRAL

## RUSSELL CHAMBERLIN
## WITH PHOTOGRAPHS BY SIMON McBRIDE

*Webb & Bower*

MICHAEL JOSEPH

*This should be the ideal of the architect –
not to conceive a building but to conceive
an altar – and to create a building round it.*

Coventry Cathedral Reconstruction Committee
*Schedule of Requirements*, 1950

First published in Great Britain 1987 by
Webb & Bower (Publishers) Limited
9 Colleton Crescent, Exeter, Devon EX2 4BY

in association with Michael Joseph Limited
27 Wright's Lane, London W8 5SL

Designed by Vic Giolitto

Production by Nick Facer/Rob Kendrew

Text Copyright © 1987 Russell Chamberlin

Colour photographs Copyright © 1987 Webb & Bower/Simon McBride

**British Library Cataloguing in Publication Data**
Chamberlin, Russell
The English cathedral.
1. Cathedrals—England—History
I. Title
942   DA660

ISBN 0-86350-129-X

Typeset in Great Britain by P&M Typesetting Ltd., Exeter

Printed and bound in Hong Kong by Mandarin Offset

# Contents

# Introduction

Each cathedral has an overwhelmingly unique and distinctive personality. From the east, Norwich cathedral appears like some giantess wearing an exotic headdress. The feet of the buttresses at the west end of Wells resemble the vast hoofs of Assyrian bulls so that the whole building becomes a mythical monster advancing inexorably to the west. Close to, Salisbury seems to be a model, moulded by giant hands out of some plastic substance and unaccountably expanded: the spires of Lichfield seem in endless debate with each other: St Alban's is a vast humped figure, shoulders raised brooding on its green, green hill...

Like human beings, each belongs to a family group, identified by certain general characteristics even while it retains totally its own personality. And, like the human species, the family groups themselves fall into races. The Italian cathedral is dramatic, theatrical without: usually plain within, coming to life only on great festivals. The Germans compress their bases and raise their shoulders, striving higher and higher after ever more impossible heights emulating the titanic trees of their brooding forests: the French throw up a mass of living forms – animal, human, vegetable – in a great creative wave: the Spanish interior is fantastical, dark, brooding. The English ever preferred length to height so that you can be within a stone's throw of one of the great buildings and be visually unaware of its existence. Later, the builders would compensate, creating the unique English gift of the spire to Europe's unique contribution to the sum of cultural artefacts, the cathedral.

We take it for granted, but the cathedral is a deeply mysterious phenomenon, *sui generis*. Unlike its distant relatives, the mosque and the synagogue, it holds at its heart an unfathomable mystery, the located but invisible Deity. 'Conceive an altar and [then] create a building' the Reconstruction Committee at Coventry told their architect when commissioning him to build a cathedral to replace that destroyed by war. Unlike the temple of ancient Greece and Rome it is not the stage for the priest alone but also a meeting place for the commonalty. Unlike the parish church, it turns outwards towards the wide world. A century ago, the cathedral had almost wholly withdrawn from the mainstream of affairs, isolated by the rising tide of anti-clericalism and nonconformity, and was given over almost wholly to Barchester folk. But within the past decade or so the bishops have again engaged themselves in public, frequently political, controversy: the bishop of Durham launches an attack upon the social policies of a Conservative government, while in Liverpool the Roman archbishop and the Anglican bishop join forces to attack the extreme left-wing government of the city. The bishop of Malmesbury organizes a public meeting to discuss the social effect of closing down the railway works at Swindon: at Coventry the provost is urged by a leading trade-union figure to continue the attraction of tourists who generate much-needed local income. Culturally, the cathedrals have followed the same integrative role as they have in the political and economic fields: the great naves are again being used for purely secular purposes.

Most of our cathedrals are approaching their millenium. They are, perhaps, adolescent compared with the vast antiquity of the monuments of Greece and Egypt but these are, for the most part, masses of solid stone, decaying at the same rate as the hills decay, whereas the cathedrals are filigreed with glass, the whole object of their builders being to make them ever higher and lighter. They have not been cosseted, these delicate Titans. First they were the targets of iconoclastic fanatics: then they endured decades of neglect only to encounter the scarcely less destructive attention of the 'restorers' of the nineteenth century. The twentieth century adds its own peculiar hazards: first, sulphur from a million chimneys eating away more stone in a decade than hitherto in a century: then the onslaught of aerial bombardment when the distinctive monsters became aiming points (though it is said that the Kaiser threatened to hang any airman who bombed Westminster Abbey). And finally today, by day and by night, they endure the ceaseless vibration of motorized traffic. Yet, without exception, their custodians are confident of their future.

A study of cathedrals must touch on almost every aspect of civilized society, from problems of sanitation to the methods of restoring stained glass: from a consideration of the mechanical stresses involved in raising the spire, to a consideration of the effects of liturgical changes. Arguably, it is impossible for any one person to 'know' any one cathedral. John Harvey, the architectural historian who, more than any other, has demystified the story of our cathedrals by subjecting the techniques of medieval architects to practical considerations, unequivocally makes the point that 'Any one of the major cathedrals would provide work for an average lifetime'. He goes further: 'Indeed, those who know the cathedrals best, the resident architects, surveyors, clerks of the works and foremen can, from intimate knowledge and affection, speak most feelingly of the never-ending multitude of new facts constantly coming to their notice. There is no such thing as "knowing" the whole of a cathedral.'

On a personal note, the present writer can claim continuing acquaintance with one great cathedral, that of Norwich, since childhood. The first memory was of a wall of living fire, alarming to a seven-year-old, but later rationalized as the great west window in the setting sun. Later, too, is the memory of the spire standing up against the eerie beauty of chandelier flares during the so-called Baedeker air raids of 1942. Then follow the casual memories which build up into a mosaic: somnolent afternoons on the velvet green playing fields watching the cricket team of the cathedral school: the first glimpse of the 'head-dress', seen from the yard arm of a training barge moored precisely where the stone from Caen was unloaded for the building of the cathedral ten centuries before: the poignant, ever changing, ever the same cascades of notes from the great bells announcing the slow accumulation of the hours.... The number of times the close was used as a short-cut are uncountable: so, too, the number of visits made to the building itself, sometimes for ten minutes, sometimes for half a day. Yet on the last visit was seen something that had never been seen before because explicit search was made for it: the fragments of the Saxon bishop's throne. And, as John Harvey says, without doubt something new will present itself on the next occasion, and the next, and the next.

# Acknowledgements

The author is especially grateful to those members of cathedral establishments who put their time and expertise at his disposal. They are recorded here in alphabetical order, with gratitude. The interpretation of their information, together with any errors arising, is of course the responsibility of the author. Colonel T J Bowen, Administrator, Worcester; Canon Peter Brett, Canterbury; Anthony Bridge, Dean of Guildford; J Bridgewater, Administrator, Lichfield; Captain John Chillingford, Administrator, Wells; Linsey Colchester, Archivist, Wells; Peter Foster, Surveyor of the Fabric, Westminster Abbey; Canon Oliver Kelly, Administrator, Westminster Cathedral; Richard Marsh, Wells Conservation Centre; Patrick Mitchell, Dean of Wells; Father Philip Pargeter, Administrator, Birmingham RC Cathedral; David Rice, Master Mason, Wells; Canon Colin Semper, Provost, Coventry; Commander Charles Shears, Registrar, St Paul's, London; Canon Toy, Chancellor, York; Father Harry Wace, Administrator, Norwich RC Cathedral.

The quotation from William Golding's novel, *The Spire*, on page 72 is reproduced by permission of Messrs Faber & Faber.

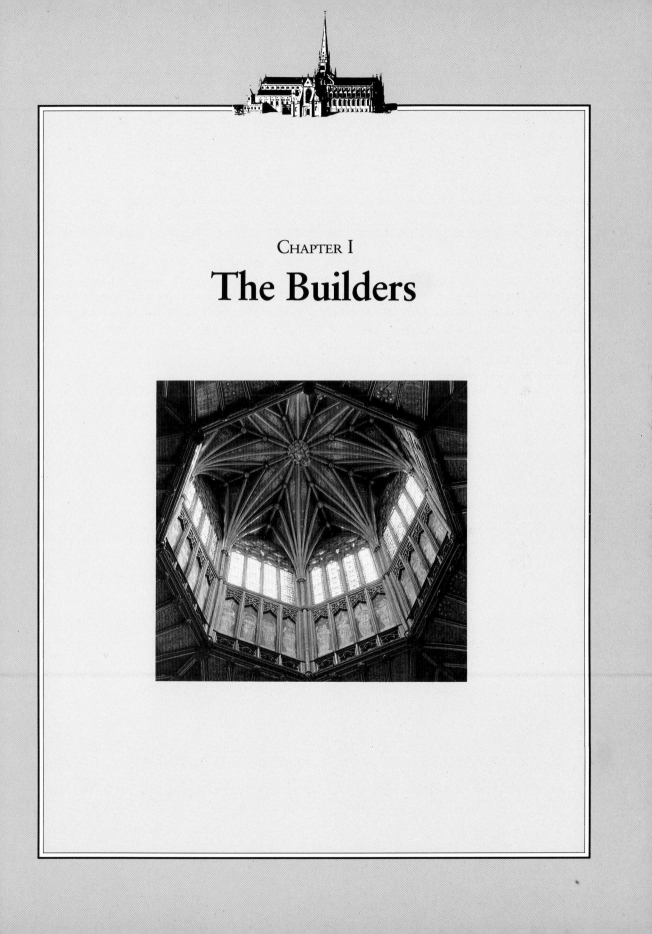

CHAPTER I

# The Builders

Shortly before dawn, probably on an early spring day, in the year 1070, a group of men gathered near the burnt-out ruins of a small Saxon church in the city of Canterbury. The group would have included a high ecclesiastic – a Frenchman called Lanfranc, an unknown master mason, a monk or some other learned person with at least an elementary knowledge of astronomy, and various important religious and lay folk. While waiting for daybreak, the group took part in religious exercises, leaving one of their number to watch for the sun's appearance. As the great disc appeared, this man thrust a stick to the ground, ranging it in line between what would be a high altar and the emergent sun, and in that manner the orientation of the first Norman cathedral was established. Work then began on the foundations.

It is not possible to say exactly which day the ceremony took place, for this cathedral was to be dedicated to Christ himself. Other cathedrals and greater churches, however, performed the rite of orientation on the day of the patron saint to whom the building was dedicated. The orientation of each was therefore unique, due to the varying position of sunrise from day to day, but all conformed to the east-west tradition until the twentieth century, when Liverpool cathedral broke the tradition.

Four years after this ceremony at Canterbury a similar ceremony took place in the ruins of the Roman town now known as Lincoln, and three years after that, workmen began plundering the ruins of another Roman city, that of Verulamium, to find material for the building of the abbey

*Opposite*
The manifest hand of the master mason. The choir of Canterbury, begun in the 'new style' in 1174 by William of Sens, finished ten years later by William the Englishman.

*Below*
Two of the identified master masons who created the cathedrals.

(*Left*) Henry Wy of St Albans – who seems to have given himself wings.

(*Right*) Thomas Witney of Exeter.

church of St Alban's. Nothing better demonstrates the incredible energy of the Norman invaders than that, within a generation of the Conquest, they had commenced building fifteen of these enormous stone structures, each one larger by far than any structure that had ever before been seen in the land, in addition to the innumerable monasteries and parish churches and the titanic castles needed to keep a resentful population in subjection. In some years they actually began two of the great buildings: St Alban's and Rochester were both commenced in 1077. The Norman vigour indeed was so great that in 1096 they not only began the building of Norwich cathedral but, dissatisfied with the hastily built structure in Canterbury, actually knocked it down, though it had only just been completed, and built afresh.

Some eight centuries after these Frenchmen had begun to place their impress upon England, another Frenchman – the resoundingly named Charles Forbes de Montalembert – launched one of the great romantic myths into history. In his magisterial work, *The Monks of the West*, he discussed the building of the vast abbey churches and cathedrals of the European Middle Ages. Who actually built them? His answer was unequivocal:

When we say that the innumerable monastic churches scattered over the whole face of Europe were built by the monks, the statement must be taken in its literal sense. They were, in fact, not only the architects but the masons of their buildings; after drawing up the plans, they carried them out with their own hands and in general without employing craftsmen from outside. While simple monks were often the chief architects of their buildings, abbots willingly condescended to serve as common workmen.

The myth thus launched rapidly took powerful flight. In 1905 the British scholar ES Prior took it a dizzy stage further:

One is often asked who were the 'architects' of the cathedrals? The reply must be that the function of architect as designer of buildings, and determiner of its forms of beauty did not exist in any personality.

Out of these two magisterial pronouncements there developed the legend of the cathedral developing spontaneously, virtually organically, as no other building had ever developed before, or since, in history. Unlike any other period before, or since, in history, it was deemed that the men actually at work upon the building did not do so through external pressure of force, as slaves, or of economics, as ordinary workmen exchanging their labour for money, but impelled by some internal impulse known as 'the greater glory of God'.

Both aspects of the legend are quite impossible to account for when it is considered that the identifiable portraits of master masons are scattered throughout the cathedrals of Europe; further, the builders they controlled belonged to a co-operative organization run on lines as precise and rule-bound as any modern trade union. English cathedrals are particularly richly endowed with the portraits in stone of their master masons. In Westminster Abbey, Henry of Reyns scratches his cheek with a comical expression of frustration – a gesture curiously echoed by William Wynford in Winchester. John of Gloucester, who followed Henry at Westminster, leans out eagerly, energetically, as though to address a recalcitrant workman. At St Alban's, Henry Wy, with his brow creased in thought, seems to be preoccupied with the rebuilding of the fallen bays of the nave. He has even had the confidence (or temerity) to range himself alongside portraits of King Edward and Queen Eleanor. At Exeter, Thomas of Witney looks like a playing card king with his sprightly, curled beard. Although the portraits of these master masons are separated from each other by many decades and many miles they bear a curious resemblance to each other – all are big men with broad, open faces, tolerant enough in expression, boon companions, one feels, but also very well able to keep a firm hand on the scores of men working under them.

As it happens, it is a monk, Gervase of Canterbury, who gives the clearest possible indication that the cathedral not only did not come about by some unknown means not far removed from magic, but that the men who built it were straightforward working masons. In 1174 the choir

*Opposite*
St Alban's provides dramatic evidence of change of style from the massive square pillars and rounded arches of the Norman period, to the elegance of the pointed arch of the twelfth century.

13

Architect and client in 'consultation' during the building of St Alban's as portrayed in Matthew Paris's *Lives of the Offas*.

*Opposite*
The great octagon at Ely, life's work of the sacrist Alan of Walsingham.

of Canterbury suffered an all too common fate and was destroyed by fire, leaving a vast, gaping hole in the very heart of the building. The choir was where the monks assembled to discharge their never-ending ceremonies based on the canonical hours, those ceremonies which ensured that the praises of God would rise, at fixed times of day and night, until the ending of the world. They were faced now with the same dilemma that was presented to Christopher Wren five centuries later: whether to try and restore the fire-blackened remnants, or whether to start from scratch and completely rebuild.

The work was put out to tender and so prestigious a project attracted the attention of a large number of leading English and French master masons. Most of them opted for total demolition and re-building, for the remaining pillars were so badly burnt that they could not be trusted. The monks objected because, as Gervase put it, 'they could hardly hope that in their days so great an undertaking might be completed by the ingenuity of man'.

The competition, for such it was, was won by a Frenchman, William of Sens, and one receives the very strong impression that Master William was as skilled in the arts of diplomacy as he was in those of architecture. Although he, too, was perfectly well aware that complete rebuilding was unavoidable he did not say so straight away because, says Gervase, 'he did not wish to shock them [the monks] in their depressed state of mind'. Eventually, however, he was able to persuade them that this was the only solution.

Gervase goes on to describe, year by year, the slow work of rebuilding the choir. It is a remarkably detailed account, considering the casual way monkish chroniclers tended to dismiss matters outside their usual sphere of interest, and from it one can see very clearly that William of Sens was following a carefully planned operation. The working year at Canterbury began at Michaelmas, 5 September, and continued until frost put an end to operations, resuming again in early spring. The entire first year was spent in demolishing the ruins, collecting stone from Caen (for which, says Gervase, William designed ingenious lifting equipment) and in preparing templates. These were the wooden patterns which the ordinary mason followed for the proportion and designs of the stonework. In the autumn of the second year two pillars were built on one side of the choir and in the spring and early summer two more on the opposite side. They were vaulted over, and the line extended the following year. Then disaster struck. In September 1178 William was working high up in the central vault when the scaffolding broke and he fell some fifty feet to the ground. He was lucky to survive not only the fall itself, but the shower of heavy timber and stones that followed. He was, however, seriously injured and took to his bed where gallantly he continued to direct the work, and two further vaults were constructed before a violent rainstorm put an end to the work for that year. By now, it was sadly evident that William of Sens had finished his active life: he retired to his home in France and another William, known simply as 'the Englishman', took over.

Work on Canterbury's choir had now been in progress for over sixty years and, very clearly from Gervase's account, there emerges the ancient, unending tussle between customer and builder. When was the work going to be finished? When could the monks move back into what they regarded as their surrogate heaven and which gave them their entire *raison d'être*? William gave what answer he could but the monks kept up the pressure, demanding that at least they should be able to celebrate Easter 1180 in the choir. William gave way and erected a temporary wooden screen 'with three glass windows', Gervase recorded proudly, between the choir and the still incomplete east end. Four more years were to pass before work was finished, ten years from the original decision to rebuild.

At the very heart of philology is the fascinating quest for the reason why words change their meaning over the centuries. When a word becomes totally archaic, or drops out completely from the language, posterity has to translate it into modern terms, and the essential meaning therefore remains unchanged. When, however, the word continues in common use but with subtly different significance, profound errors of interpretation can emerge. Such a transformation has happened to the word 'mason', a transformation which eventually produced the Montalembert and Prior myths. In twentieth-century eyes a 'mason' is simply a cutter and a worker of stone, a highly skilled craftsman certainly, but equally certainly, no artist. A 'master mason' therefore emerges, in twentieth-century terms, as the equivalent, perhaps, of a foreman. But throughout the great building period of Europe, 'mason' was interchangeable with 'architect'. Both William of Sens and William the Englishman were architects, whether the word is defined as 'designer' or 'creator'. Gervase the chronicler not only makes it very clear that the two Williams were controlling the workforce, but also that they had transcended their time to create an entirely new form of architecture.

Comparing the new design with what it had replaced, he emphasized the delicacy and elaboration of the details. In the old work, he said, what carving there had been was simply hacked out with axes: in the new work the men used chisels. The capitals of the old pillars had been plain and heavy: those in the new were decorated with delicate carvings, while the pillars themselves, though the same shape and diameter, stood a good twelve feet higher giving an impression of grace and lightness. Gervase was, in fact, describing the first appearance of a new architectural form which was destined to supersede the massive, unimaginative Norman.

Such a change did not come about accidentally or spontaneously: it was the conscious, deliberate work of one controlling mind, the 'master mason'. At Canterbury, the change in style brought about by an imaginative man is not immediately obvious: at St Alban's, it is impossible to miss, and unequivocal evidence is given as to the identity of the man who brought it about. The original, Norman, builders of the nave had used the plundered material from Verulamium to erect massive, graceless, square pillars, cheaply plastered over to give an impression of stonework. A century later, this nave was extended to the west by an unknown architect who introduced the entirely new form as had been adopted at Canterbury for two new bays of pillars, while leaving the great Norman pillars untouched. On a Sunday morning in 1323, however, five of the Norman pillars collapsed, bringing the roof down with them – and killing two monks and a boy. The master mason, Henry Wy, was given the task of rebuilding this collapsed section. No architect worth his salt would have deliberately copied the clumsy, ugly Norman pillars that still survived in the northern aisle. Wy followed the design of the unknown architect who had extended the nave, in his turn leaving the surviving Norman pillars, not so much from a sense of piety, for one medieval architect had not the slightest hesitation in demolishing the work of another, as lacking the funds to replace them. He added his own touches to the graceful new bays, and then finished with the boldest touch of all – placing his own portrait alongside those of the King, the Queen and the reigning abbot Hugh of Eversden. Modern guidebooks invariably describe Hugh as the architect while dismissing Henry Wy simply as 'master mason'. But abbot Hugh no

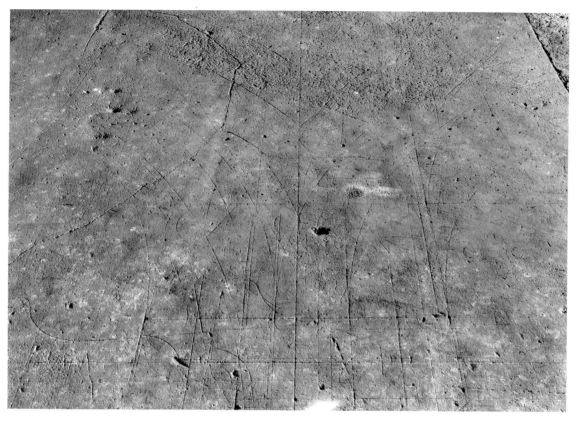

more 'built' the arcade than Dr Beeching personally tore up the railway tracks in the 1960s massacre of the British railway system that bore his name. He conceived it, ordered it, financed it and saw it to completion.

This, undoubtedly, was abbot Hugh's role at St Alban's, as it was the role of most of the powerful men whom history has credited with the 'building' of this or that great structure. In some cases, a powerful prelate with undoubted architectural – or, at least, artistic – skills would have had close and profound influence on the design of a particular building, thus reinforcing the later Montalembert myth. Such a one was Alan of Walsingham, sacrist and later prior at Ely at the time the great central tower crashed in ruins in 1322. The chronicler of Ely specifically gave him credit for the creation and erection of one of the great marvels of medieval architecture – the octagon of Ely:

With great labour and expense he caused to be removed from within the church the stones and timber that had fallen in therein: and at the place

*Tracing floor of York Minster. The incised lines are clearer than those at Wells, the only other surviving tracing floor.*

where he was about to construct the new tower, he by architectural skill measured out eight positions in which the eight stone columns were to stand.

The chronicler goes on to describe how Alan personally sought and found the eight, vast pieces of timber needed to stand above those eight towering columns of stone. Finding eight tall unblemished trees in a marshy area like that surrounding Ely could have been no easy task and points to an unusual degree of personal dedication. The chronicler's specific ascription of the work to Alan, unlike Gervase of Canterbury's ignoring of any contribution made by an equivalent figure at Canterbury, taken in conjunction with the known fact that Alan was probably a goldsmith of considerable skill, would point to him as that unusual combination, the contemplative and the man of action.

William of Sens, William the Englishman, Alan

17

Mason at work, depicted on the tomb of St William at York.

of Walsingham, Henry Wy – none of these were working in the dark, for they had as guide a long dead Roman architect, Vitruvius. Montalembert and Prior were elaborating their myth of magical architecture at a time when it was generally believed that Vitruvius's seminal work, *De Architectura*, had been totally lost until its 'rediscovery' in the Renaissance. Research since World War II has shown that, far from being the case, at least eighty medieval copies of the book were circulating in medieval Europe. Sixteen of them were written well before the year 1200, of which three survived in England. Bearing in mind their fragility and the fact that, as practical treatises they would have been in constant use under very harsh conditions, the implication is that a very large number must have been circulating.

The medieval, Christian architect was not in the slightest degree interested in the pagan Roman's idea of design for his theatres and villas and temples: they left that to their Renaissance successors who were to cover Europe with 'neo-classical' buildings. The cathedral architect was, however, deeply interested in Vitruvius's technical descriptions, a distillation of the Roman skills in handling great masses of stone.

A man like the sacrist Alan of Walsingham would have undoubtedly been working 'for the greater glory of God' or, at the least, for the greater glory of his priory, but even he drew heavily on outside, lay experts. As sacrist (discharging, roughly, the role of chief clerk) Alan kept the most meticulous records over the twenty years that the great work at Ely was in progress, and his humdrum record disposes, finally, of the romantic Montalembert myth. The octagon of Ely was a quite extraordinary concept for its time. It is, in effect, an enormous wooden tower or lantern, sixty-three feet high, which is itself suspended above eight stone columns towering up ninety-four feet from the floor of the cathedral, the whole being crowned by a bell chamber, so that the overall height of the lantern is 180 feet. Even finding eight trees which could be trimmed down to the requisite sixty-three feet was a major task, as the chronicler noted: 'Alan went searching far and wide and with the greatest difficulty finding them at last, paying a great price for them transported them to Ely by sea and land.'

But, having conceived the idea of the great lantern and acquired the materials to bring it into being, Alan was sensible enough to call in the experts to give form to his idea. An early entry in his Sacristy Roll notes: 'Paid to a boy for carrying a certain letter to Newport to Master Thomas, Carpenter'. The cost of the journey was charged to the general accounts, not to the later special account for the *Novum opus* and the 'certain letter' was evidently a preliminary enquiry as to whether the master carpenter Thomas would be willing to help in the work. The 'Newport' to which the boy

travelled was Newgate in London. Thomas was of reputation great enough to be in control of heavy timber work as a direct employee of the Crown and agreed to come to Ely if his travelling expenses of two shillings were paid. At Ely he received six shillings and eightpence for himself and two shillings and sixpence for his assistant – high payment, indeed, for his work at Ely was essentially advisory, as he returned soon after to his work in London. His major task was to design a great crane for lifting the massive baulks of timber nearly a hundred feet in the air, as well as designing the lantern itself.

As the *Novum opus* progresses, the stages of work are faithfully reflected in Alan's special accounts, the workforce both increasing and changing its composition as the great lantern slowly takes shape. At first there is a predominance of ordinary labourers and masons for digging the foundations and building the stone piers; then gradually other kinds of workmen are brought in: iron founders to make the windows, thatchers to put up temporary roofing, carpenters to construct the lantern and hoist it into position. The leaders of the workforce are identified both by their Christian names and by their professions (and one sees here very clearly how surnames come into being): there is a Master John Cementarious, a John Mason, a John Carpenter, a Peter Quadratarius. Alan identifies this latter man as being specifically skilled in the 'arte archetectonica' with much experience in the art of laying out buildings. His role, in modern terms, would have been that of surveyor, and payments to Peter the Quadratarius cease after a little while. John the Master Mason is so important that, in addition to his stipend (£31 18s 7d in 1326 out of which he had to pay his workmen) he is allocated a room of his own. It seems to have been a particularly cold year, for he and his fellow experts are given fur coats. Total expenditure for that year on the *Novum opus* was £123 5s 6¼d which included the laying down of waterpipes and the provision of baskets and barrows.

In 1340, seventeen years after work has commenced, Alan is able to make a kind of summary of the work at that stage. The campanile had been roofed in; the plumbers had finished; and the upper storey was completed although the windows were still only filled in with canvas. John of Burwell, mason, had carved a great figure for the central boss and other bosses had been carved by John Roke. He came from London, whereas the majority of the other workers were local. The glass worker was William of Brampton, the mason John of Burwell; Geoffrey and John Middliton were carpenters, and both from Ely itself. John Amyot had been in charge of the smithy and the tally of iron nails grew prodigiously towards the end. William Attegreene, another local man, had been gradually trained to take the place of the first master mason, John Ramsey, a 'foreigner' whose name then disappears from the wage rolls. In 1341 Alan is elected Prior of Ely, the accounts are taken over by another, less conscientious clerk and shortly afterwards the special account for the *Novum opus* is discontinued. The work was brought to a triumphant conclusion some twenty years after that terrible day, the Vigil of the Feast of St Eormenilda, when the great Norman tower had fallen 'with such a shock and so great a tumult that it was as though an earthquake had taken place'. Total cost for the work, including materials and wages, had been £2,408 19s 3¾d.

The consultant architect dividing his time between a number of sites was as much a figure in the medieval, as in the modern, world of architecture. The same William Ramsey who had made an appearance at Ely turned up a few years later at Lichfield. He was known as the 'king's mason', surveyor of all the King's Works in London, but he evidently found time, in 1337, to put in an appearance at Lichfield. There, the dean and chapter wanted to link up the newly built Lady Chapel in the east end with the main body of the building, but were faced with the problem that the new work was considerably narrower than the old. It would need very considerable skill to bring the two sections together so that the join was not obvious in the most important part of the building. Ramsey agreed to do the work for a fee of twenty-two shillings a visit, plus the payment of his travel expenses between Lichfield and London. These came to the very large sum of 6s 8d a visit, for the return journey took eight days. Ramsey would therefore have been spending considerable time on site, but even so, much of the work would have been done in his absence and his role was clearly that of consultant, brought in to solve problems as they arose.

The social status of the master mason is clearly shown in the famous illustration in Matthew Paris's history where a king is shown in conference with his master mason while building goes on in the background. The illustrator has not only drawn mason and monarch to the same scale, but given them the same attitude. That of the mason, for example, contrasts dramatically with the courtier, obsequiously standing behind the king. He is evidently arguing a point, and with such vigour and confidence, that the monarch has been obliged to raise a mandatory finger. Here, in this remarkably modern presentation, is no courtier, no cringing subordinate, but a free and highly intelligent man putting his case with confidence and skill.

In English social life, with its hairbreadth distinction between castes, the master mason ranked as 'squires of minor degree' and could even take precedence over gentlemen. Usually, he had worked his way up, frequently as a member of a family group. He was probably literate; certainly those masons who were more or less attached to one of the great cathedrals would have benefited in some degree from the education imparted in the cathedral school to boys destined for the choir. He would certainly have been numerate; as early as 1200 Euclid's geometry was in common use among masons. He would obviously have been a draughtsman of considerable skill, for it would be his interpretation of his employers' wishes that would be passed on to his workmen for them to execute.

But how would he, and those working for him, actually go about their work? Only slowly as research is carried out in physical spheres, rather than from historic sources with their theoretical interpretations, is this becoming clear.

In 1957 the architectural historian John Harvey was exploring the triforium of Wells cathedral, accompanied by its historian Linsey Colchester. Externally, the triforium of a cathedral is the second stage, or storey, of a nave – the repeated sequence of three arches (*triforium*) over the main arcade. Internally, it is simply the space below the lean-to roof of the aisle and, while it may lose something of the majesty of the nave, this area

*Opposite*
One of the many versions of the building of the Tower of Babel, showing techniques and tools. This is from the fifteenth-century Bedford *Book of Hours*.

gains in human interest; for here one may encounter the master mason and his employees at work through the inconsequential marks they made three or five or seven centuries earlier. At Wells, on the interior of the triforium arches are the straight lines incised by the master mason as guide for the lining-up of the false lintels. No ordinary member of the public will ever see these lines so they were simply left as clear as the day they were made. On one of the walls someone has sketched in, hurriedly, as though to explain a point, the sequence of the triforium arches themselves; elsewhere, there is an elaborate mathematical symbol based on spirals which, although resembling some arcane symbolism, is probably nothing more than the equivalent of a table of logarithms. Here, too, in the triforium, it is possible to see the pragmatic reason for Wells's unique feature; the great scissor arch below the central tower. The fact that the tower began to subside in 1330, and the scissor arches were erected in some haste to check the subsidence is now common knowledge. But only from the triforium, where it is possible to see with the naked eye the extent of the subsidence, by noting the difference in levels between one side of the tower and the other, does the observer become immediately and personally aware of the problem facing the architect and the means he adopted to resolve it.

In many cathedrals, the gallery high up behind the triforium arches is a deliberately constructed service passage. At Wells, the great ribs of the arches above the nave were exposed as late as the 1950s when they were filled in, partly as a way of strengthening the structure, but acting, too, as a useful passageway by creating a flat floor where, before, it would have been necessary to clamber over the ribs of the arches. About halfway along this gallery a narrow opening leads to a chamber some twenty feet square. It is, in fact, nothing more than the loft above the North Porch and the horizontal beams of the roof are little more than chest height so that anyone moving around this loft has to be perpetually ducking to pass below the beams. A narrow staircase leads down to the North Porch proper but, until the 1950s, this had been forgotten. The loft had become filled with the detritus of centuries – dust and rubble and odd beams – until on this occasion when the two visitors were investigating the long-forgotten cham-ber. Beneath the dust and rubbish was a floor paved in some friable material which proved to be plaster of Paris. When the rubbish was moved away and the floor cleaned, incised lines became evident and it was discovered that these lines were life-size sections of the building, sketched in by the master mason, from which templates would be made for the guidance of the ordinary jobbing workmen.

The 'tracing floor' or trasour at Wells cathedral has its counterpart in York and both are admirably simple and effective in operation. A line incised in plaster of Paris will display a stark, dramatic whiteness: a design thus traced will stand out very clearly indeed during the time needed to copy it. Within a week or so, however, the brilliant whiteness will fade until the line is difficult to distinguish from the background. It is thus possible for the floor to be used again and again and again, each new design standing out clearly for the necessary period, then fading away into the general background. The incised lines in the Wells tracing floor remained in a traceable form however – so much so that Linsey Colchester was able to identify the arches of the windows of the fourteenth-century house he occupies in Vicar's Close, one of the ancillary buildings of the cathedral.

In addition to the purely technical information conveyed by the Wells tracing floor, however, was the social information conveyed by its position. The modern access from the triforium is an accidental result of changing uses, but even the planned access from the porch, up the narrow stone steps, was not an easy approach. Quite evidently, this was the master mason's private domain, one to which the workers would have been admitted only on invitation or by instruction. Even the cathedral clergy, one feels, would have hesitated to have intruded here without sufficient cause. This was, in practice, the equivalent of the modern drawing office. Even in the twentieth century a modern mason lays out the shape of his work in full size, for there is no other way of obtaining the precise shapes needed, and from this small room – or its earlier equivalent – the workers would have taken away the templates made in thin wood for the mass production of components.

In cathedral after cathedral one can see these workers as they have portrayed themselves in stone or wood or, less frequently, as their colleagues have portrayed them in glass. On the tomb of St William in York Minster, a mason has depicted himself in stone, working in stone. It is probably a winter's day, or he is working in the chilly confines of the building, for he wears his hood up. His hands, heavily gauntleted, hold two tools which would be instantly recognizable to a modern mason – a long metal chisel and a heavy wooden mallet. He is braced against the incline, and the rather heavy, intelligent face has an expression of concentration with even a hint of strain about the mouth. This was the man who, under the direction of a master mason, and with the aid of carpenters and glaziers, made such a prodigious step forward. Working pragmatically, his only theoretical equipment being those treatises of Vitruvius and Euclid, using the actual stone upon which he was working as his drawing board, as in that logarithmic table at Wells, he transformed the dark massive Norman architecture, whose main characteristic was a brutal strength, into something soaring, elegant and new. Shaving down columns until they appeared as slender as plant growths, drawing the walls up ever higher, rearing up great areas of glass that somehow would survive immense wind pressures over centuries, the unknown medieval mason altered the face of civilisation as profoundly and as permanently as the vaunted artists of the Renaissance.

As a worker, the ordinary mason was in a curious position. He was a highly skilled specialist and no untrained man could walk in and do his job, for behind each seemingly casual blow of mallet on chisel lay years of experience, of precise knowledge of just how a given piece of stone will react to a certain kind of pressure in a particular place. But the very fact that he was a rather rare kind of specialist presented difficulties to him. An experienced carpenter or baker or cobbler could be reasonably certain of finding work in any fairly large community – especially if there were not many others of his trade about. But a mason, by definition, could find work only where some large stone-built structure was in course of construction. Even in the twentieth century masons experienced in restoration work of historic buildings are of necessity peripatetic.

There was no formal apprenticeship for a mason until the late fourteenth century but a young lad would probably follow an older relative into the trade. He might very well get his first taste of working with stone in a quarry, for the trades of stonemason and quarryman were virtually interchangeable: significantly, three of the masons working on Westminster Abbey in the late thirteenth century bore, as surname, the name of the village of Corfe in Dorset, a major stone-working community quarrying the famous Purbeck stone. After three or four years fetching and carrying the lad might begin work as a fixer – one actually engaged in laying the blocks of masonry – or, if showing particular promise, as a banker, working on a bank or bench carving out the shapes that originated in the tracing house. Unless he was very lucky, or working during a period of high employment, he would very probably be obliged to alternate employmnent between that of mason and any other available means of earning a living. The usual working year ran from March to October: he would therefore be laid off in autumn or winter when the workforce was reduced to the barest minimum of skilled men preparing work for the next season. Here, again, the position of a mason was anomalous and insecure compared to other trades, for the rhythm of construction was parallel to that of agriculture, the major source of casual earnings, and he would be unemployed at about the time that work on the land was also necessarily contracting. But England was still a rural, peasant economy and the young mason would probably be a member of a family to whom he could contribute cash income during the working season with whom he would hope to find food and shelter during the off seasons.

But once on site he was a member of a tightknit, purposeful community. Not until the establishment of the printers' guilds in the sixteenth century was there a similarly sophisticated body of manual workers, able to impose their terms on their employers, if necessary, through the weapon of a strike. And here is one of the clearest pieces of evidence that, far from working 'for the greater glory of God' the workmen had a very lively sense of 'rates for the job'. At St Alban's in the 1190s, abbot John de Cella employed a certain Hugh de Godelif as a master mason for the ambitious work of extending the nave and building a new west front. Hugh was recognized as being an outstanding technician, but financially he was either incompetent or dishonest. The money allocated to him for the work was frittered away, or diverted into unofficial channels, and the masons, after some weeks without pay, simply walked off the site. In vain the abbot pleaded with them, threatening them with heaven's displeasure, assuring them that money would be forthcoming: the men took no notice and the walls remained a few pathetic feet high for years until the abbot's successor scraped up enough money to start afresh.

The bogus 'Freemasonry' of the nineteenth century sought to turn the organization of masons into an occult society, ascribing its origins to the architects of the pyramids. A fourteenth-century manual of masonry, itself based upon much earlier compilations, went considerably further than that. According to that manual the father of the mason's craft was a man called Jabal, who lived before Noah's Flood 'and was the first man who ever found geometry and masonry and he made houses and is named in the Bible'. From there the manual, known as *The Constitutions of Masonry*, traced the evolution of the craft through an ingenious and colourful history, a garbled mixture of half remembered fact and outright legend. Naturally, it touched on the building of the Tower of Babylon (a perennial favourite among medieval artists whose depictions are a rich source of technical information). Abraham taught geometry to the Egyptians and among his students was a worthy clerk called Euclid. It was this Euclid who named the craft 'geometry' – 'because of the parting of the ground'. The unknown author then makes a remarkable leap of a millenium or so to contemporary France, lauding a certain worthy king called Charles the Second 'who was a mason before that he was a king'. The reader is then hurled back dizzyingly to the second century AD, to Saint Alban 'who well loved masons...and ordained convenient wages to pay for their travail' and the writer brings the story down to King Athelstan whose son ordained that all masons should meet in a great assembly once a year or so.

The history of masonry as outlined in the Constitution might be fanciful, but embedded in it were also very practical Articles, addressed to master masons, and 'Points of Masonry' addressed to the workforce. The master must be true to his employer 'and not give more pay to no mason than he wot he may deserve'. He must take only freeborn lads as apprentices - a very sensible

obligation for a mason 'born of bond blood' could be whisked off site at the whim of his lord. No master should ever displace another – an impressive example of union solidarity. The nine Points addressed to the workforce naturally touch upon their quality of work: each 'must fulfill his day's work truly that he taketh for his pay'. Two of the Points bear witness to the fact that, by the fourteenth century certainly, the craft of masonry was a closeknit fellowship: the mason swore to keep secret the deliberations of his lodge, and also promised not to covet the wife or daughter of his masters nor his fellows 'but if it be in marriage'.

The lodge was simply the physical building where work could be carried out in bad weather and where, naturally, the masons would gravitate in their hours of leisure. Over the years, it would become charged with a certain social significance, later becoming the pseudo-mystical concept of the Freemasons. The master mason, as the effective representative of their ecclesiastic employers, was in charge of the lodge and responsible both for the off-duty conduct of the men as well as their work. Hours were long, even by medieval standards, averaging some fourteen hours a day with breaks for meals. But the hard regime was alleviated not only by the innumerable 'holydays' which all workers enjoyed, but by the special festivals appropriate to the particular ecclesiastical body on whose behalf they were working – festivals which really were 'feasts', lavish banquets that could occupy the greater part of the day.

In all cathedrals and greater churches, and in a considerable number of parish churches, the alert visitor can spot certain enigmatic marks in inconspicuous places. These are the ordinary mason's equivalents of the proud portraits of the master masons, their means of identification. But where the master mason's portrait was his claim to immortality, the 'mason's mark' was for the humdrum but essential purpose of ensuring that he was paid for the work that he did, no more and no less. It is possible that a mason was allocated his mark on completing his apprenticeship but, as with so much relating to the building of the cathedrals, this is an uncertain area. At one stage, indeed, it was actually believed that the marks had mystic purposes – part of the romantic myth of the builders. Investigation has shown that a mason's mark usually appears on plain stone or simple

Another, simpler portrayel of masons at work, emphasizing the idea of the priest as builder: St Guthlac builds himself a chapel.

carvings; rarely, if ever, do they appear on any major piece of sculpture. The deduction from this is that the carver of a major piece of work would be very well known among his fellows, and there would therefore be no need to identify his 'piece', whereas a line of ordinary masonry could be attributed to almost any man. It follows, in addition, that the mason's marks would more likely be made by an itinerant worker. In Wells cathedral some 509 masons' marks have been identified, relating to a period stretching from approximately 1174, when work began on the choir, to 1465 when the cloisters were completed. Some of the marks are repeated many times as the mason moved from job to job and it is thus possible to obtain an idea – if tantalizingly oblique and indistinct – of the number of men working in a given area. There were, for instance, thirty-one masons working in the transepts, of whom five later worked elsewhere in the cathedral, and seventeen masons were employed in the chapter house, one of whom had worked in its distinctive undercroft and five of whom later went on to work on the Lady Chapel.

These, then, were the men who raised the stone miracles: ordinary men, working for money to feed themselves, their wives and children; ordinary men grumbling about the demands of their employees or critical of the master mason, the go-between inevitably coming under fire from both sides; the same kind of men who would build the power stations and motorways and airports of the

25

twentieth century. The same kind of men, but with two overwhelming, all-pervading differences: the attitude to time and the attitude to religion.

The advance of western civilization can be measured by its increasing precision of the measurement of time: as late as the fifteenth century Louis XI of France was unable to establish the time of his birth within two years even though it had become a matter of vital political importance. Very few mature people had any clear idea of their exact age. Everyday time itself was measured first by the rising and setting of the sun, and then by such elastic units as the length of time it took to say a paternoster or by reference to the canonical hours – 'about tierce', 'about vespers'. When a given span of time had passed, there were few aids to bring it readily back to mind for rarely were accounts kept so meticulously as those of Alan of Walsingham. There were no newspapers with their convenient printed dates; no flood of diaries at the year's end; and published works commenting on current affairs were not common. The law measured time not by some universal notation, but by the years of the reigning monarch. The compiler of the *Anglo-Saxon Chronicle* contented himself with an annual entry; the compilers of *Domesday* dismissed all before the Conquest as that which occured 'TRE' – in the time of King Edward. It is probable that after the first decade of building had passed there was no clear idea of when the work had begun. There might well be impatience on the part of the clergy, the paymasters, for work to be completed, as William the Englishman experienced at Canterbury, but rarely indeed was there any contract stating exactly when that work *was* to be finished.

And if it is difficult for twentieth-century man fully to understand his predecessors' concept of time, it is all but impossible save for a handful of contemplatives fully to understand their concept of religion. The twentieth century is far more in tune with classical Rome, or even with classical Greece, in regarding religion as being, privately, a personal moral code and, publicly, a matter of ceremonial designed to display unity. The historical battle between 'Church and State' ended in this country not so much with the defeat of the Church as with the Church drawing aside from the melee of daily politics (until the social upheavals of the 1980s that is, which again drew the bishops into the arena).

The average visitor to some great cathedral today, observing the mellow houses in the cathedral close occupied by a privileged body of people, and the ritual conducted in the vast interior for a tiny congregation, is hard-put not to class it with other examples of 'tradition', like the Beefeaters of the Tower of London or the gift of Maundy Money. They see the Church as a charming survival which ought to be protected for its own sake, but without any relevance to ordinary life, past or present.

For the builders of the cathedrals, 'ordinary' life and 'religious' life were indissoluble, a true symbiosis. At the highest level of their society they saw how the all-powerful monarch was himself subject to the disciplines imposed by a priest in an Italian city – disciplines which included not only the banishment from heaven as also imposed upon themselves, but also the absolution of his subjects from all allegiance – in effect, the possibility of turning the fount of law into an outlaw. They saw their social superiors paying for passages to heaven by setting aside vast sums for chantries or other church adornments. They saw how the power of the Church could protect even criminals with the iron law of sanctuary. In their own daily life the Church not only protected them from the (to them) very real, if invisible, powers of the supernatural, but also provided the only comfort and aid that existed in a society which saw no especial need to legislate for the weak. The rich assisted the poor only through the Church, again as a means of obtaining passage to heaven; the Church itself set apart some of its wealth for the provision of the sick, the endowment of girls and the education of boys.

Bearing these two attitudes in mind – an indifference to time and a lively awareness of the imminence of God as expressed through His Church – posterity can begin to obtain some idea as to why a mason might spend days on an exquisite carving which would never be seen by mortal eyes; why a bishop might launch a building project whose end could not conceivably come about before generations had passed; and why a rich man might virtually disinherit his heirs in order to contribute something to that vast project. These stone Titans were the physical expression of their civilization, just as electronics are the physical expression of our own.

Shortly after the turn of the millenium a certain

monk called Raoul, nicknamed the Bald, turned his attention in his chronicle from the wars of kings to remark upon this startling cultural phenomenon, the sudden upsurge throughout Europe of great churches:

It seemed as though all the world were throwing off its slumber to clothe itself anew in white sanctuaries. Everywhere, people began to restore the churches and, though many were still in good condition, they vied with each other in erecting new buildings, each one more beautiful than the last.

The reason, thought good Brother Raoul, was the universal sense of relief that the world had not, in fact, come to an end with the year 1000. But long after mankind had slipped back into its ordinary ways in other areas, masons, under the direction of ecclesiastics who might be saintly, or worldly or even actively criminal, but who shared with their humble workmen the same belief in the inevitability of the Second Coming, continued to clothe the world anew in white sanctuaries, building what they called the City of God.

# CHAPTER II

# The City of God

Looking back some three centuries to the world before the Conquest, the twelfth-century historian William of Malmesbury scornfully remarked on the Saxon preference for raising their cathedrals in rural surroundings. He put it down to the fact that they had been influenced by Irish missionaries 'who preferred to bury themselves ingloriously in marshes than to dwell in lofty cities'. The scorn was unmerited but the perception accurate: the Saxon builders were undoubtedly influenced by the Irish. The fact that the Irish contribution to the development of their great neighbour has been ignored is one of history's injustices.

The coming of Christianity is enshrined both in legend and history: the beautiful, blond slave-children who so stirred the conscience of the great Roman, Gregory; his murmured remark '*non Angli sed Angeli*'; his dispatch of Augustine to bring the light of Christianity to their country. All this is now as much a part of folk memory as of history. But the Christianity that Augustine brought in 597 guttered almost into extinction after the death in 616 of the sympathetic king Ethelbert, and it was the Irish monks of Iona who fanned the spark back to life a generation later.

Christianity had, in any case, put out its frail but indestructible roots in Britain centuries before Augustine's arrival. Archaeological evidence shows the Christian rite being celebrated as early as the second century: the elegant villa of Lullingstone in Kent undoubtedly had the equivalent of a chapel. And it was as early as 209, a half mile or so up the hill from the great *municipium* of Verulamium that the first British martyr, Alban, was beheaded on the spot where, in due course, one of the greatest of all

North Elmham, Norfolk: the only Saxon cathedral surviving above ground level.

the Christian temples would arise. The great gift that Augustine and his forty companions did indeed bring to Britain – or, to be exact, brought back to Britain – was the Roman concept of order. And in doing so they established, if only tenuously, the historic link between 'Roman' Britain, the outpost of an empire which came to an end when the legions withdrew in AD410, and the Britain of the unimaginable future.

Pope Gregory's intention was to create a complete network of ecclesiastical control for England – in effect, re-creating the control that had existed for four centuries in a different form and for a different and higher purpose. Augustine was therefore instructed to establish two ecclesiastical centres, one on the old Roman capital of Eboracum, and the other at the flourishing trading town of Londinium. And here, at the very dawn of the Church in England, was established that feud between York and Canterbury over the matter of seniority, a feud which would last for centuries,

The heart of the building: the choir (Canterbury). Work would have begun here before extending to the nave.

giving rise to many an unseemly brawl. The see of London was, in fact, founded in 604 with the pope's precise statement that York was 'in no way subject to the jurisdiction of London, but priority shall belong to the one that has been consecrated first'. But the see of York was not established until 625, whereas there was already a flourishing community in Canterbury, and Augustine had actually consecrated a ruined Romano-British church there as his cathedral, for Canterbury was the capital of the Saxon king who had welcomed him to England.

According to Gregory's edict, both of the 'metropolitans' were to consecrate twelve bishops, the twenty-six sees or dioceses thus formed approximating fairly closely to the old Roman military administration of the country. In fact, only three of the dioceses had been founded – those of Canterbury, London and Rochester – before most of the land relapsed into paganism. In 633, forty years after that mission of Augustine's, another Roman missionary called Paulinus converted a king of Northumberland and it was that king's successor, Oswald, who invited the Irish monks of Iona on to the mainland.

Ireland had escaped the Roman occupation and, in consequence, had no urban traditions, no existing civic centres towards which the first missionaries would naturally gravitate. The Christianity which rooted itself in Ireland remained rural but, obeying that fundamental human instinct towards gregariousness, the first Christians formed communities in the remote and hostile countryside. These early monasteries were humble enough affairs: a simple church as focal point for a number of poor huts, the whole surrounded by a primitive defence system. But it provided the dynamic for a system which would survive, and flourish, into the twentieth century. The Normans, following those Romans whom they so closely resembled, established their cathedrals in urban centres, brutally extinguishing all rural Saxon cathedrals in the process. But the monastic tradition which the Anglo-Saxons had adopted was also adopted, in due course, by the Anglo-Normans, creating in England a virtually unique tradition, the 'cathedral-priory' – the great church which acted as the chapel to the monastery or priory, but was also the seat of the bishop, the place where his *cathedra* was situated. Even those so-called 'secular' cathedrals

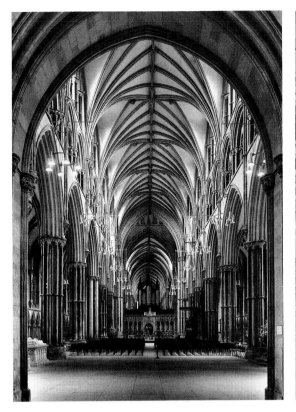

The 'secular' part of the cathedral, the nave, built after completion of choir: (*left*)Lincoln, (*right*)Exeter.

which came into being after the Conquest – that is, cathedrals administered by ordinary clergy and not by members of a monastic community – nevertheless adopted the prestigious monastic tradition for their architecture, adding cloisters, for example, even though they had no function.

By the time of the Norman Conquest there were twenty English dioceses. Despite the Saxon dislike of urban life, it is significant how many of these were established on Roman cities – Winchester, York, Worcester, Rochester, London, Exeter – the enormous shadow of Rome extending even over the new world. Most were to survive, in name at least, under the Norman administration though the vast building programme so promptly instituted meant that the small Saxon cathedral itself disappeared, usually even its foundations sealed off by the enormous bulk of its successor. Here is one of the greatest and clearest distinctions between the Anglo-Saxon and Norman approach to their religion, as exemplified in the physical church. The

Anglo-Saxons regarded the past with a deep piety, preserving the core of the church, adding to it if it needed enlarging until eventually it was a complex warren of chambers. The Normans had no hesitation in demolishing totally, rasing not only the work of their subject peoples, but destroying their own buildings when change proved necessary.

Anglo-Saxon culture was inferior to the Norman only in one field, that of architecture. In all others, it was the equal if not the superior. In literature, in particular, the exuberant Anglo-Saxon imagination wove aery clouds of fantasy – and not least in the description of their cathedrals. Judging by the poem which a certain Wolstan addressed to the bishop of Winchester around the turn of the millenium, the Saxon cathedral of Winchester rivalled, at the very least, the great basilica of St Peters in Rome. Describing how it had first been founded 'by the holy Athelwold, a great builder of churches...who built all the dwelling places with strong walls, covering them with roofs and clothing them with beauty' the poet goes on to paint an extravagant picture of the work carried out by the reigning bishop.

Bristol: the lady chapel.

You, Alphage, his successor, have diligently carried on the work begun. You have taken care to add the secret crypts so that whoever entered them would be at a loss which way to turn...You have constructed here such organs as have never before been seen. You have added a lofty temple, that is, a sparkling tower that reflects the first rays of the rising sun: the lofty peaks are capped with pointed roofs and are adorned with various and sinuous vaults. Above there stands a mighty golden cock which boldly turns its face to every wind that blows....

So continues the extravaganza, painting a picture that would not be out of place in the Arabian Nights. It comes therefore as a considerable surprise to discover, through the major archaeological excavations that took place for the first time in the 1950s, that the royal Saxon cathedral of Winchester, burial place of kings and site of one of the great popular shrines of England, was a modest little building, barely two hundred feet long which could be tucked very comfortably into about a

The cult of the Virgin Mary was of relatively minor importance in the early centuries of the Church. In the twelfth century, however, the cult expanded greatly with immediate effect upon cathedral architecture by the provision of 'lady chapels'. These were usually, but not always, at the east end of the cathedral. Those featured here and on the immediately following pages are Bristol, Ely, Lichfield, St Albans and Galilee chapel, Durham.

third of the present, Norman, building. Typically, the excavations showed that the Saxon cathedral remained unchanged for over three centuries: built about 647, it retained its original form until 971 when it was extended to the west. In that space of time a Norman cathedral would have been drastically altered many times.

The Norman cathedral at Winchester was built not on top, but to one side of its small Saxon predecessor but the close proximity of the giant meant that the smaller church was robbed of stone right down to its foundations, which alone survive today. By contrast, the Norman decree that all cathedrals should henceforth be sited in urban

Ely: the lady chapel.

Lichfield: the lady chapel.

St Albans: the lady chapel.

Durham: the Galilee chapel.

areas meant, paradoxically, the physical salvation of the Saxon cathedral of North Elmham in Norfolk, a genuine rural cathedral, for even today the village population is less than a thousand. In obedience to the decree, the new Norman bishop moved his *cathedra* first to Thetford and then, finally, to the flourishing Danish city of Norwich. (The remains of this most ancient throne were incorporated into the bishop's throne in Norwich where they are still visible, testimony to the enduring power of the concept of physical continuity of spiritual powers.)

After its demotion, the building at North Elmham served first as a chapel. Then, in the late fourteenth-century, that savage prelate Henry Despenser, bishop of Norwich, converted the place into a fortified manor house. Eventually totally abandoned, its ruins survived in sufficient detail to give some indication of the dimensions and form of a Saxon cathedral. A local antiquary made desultory excavations in 1785, but it was not until its acquisition in 1948 by the State, in the form of the then Ministry of Works, that a full-scale archaeological investigation disclosed its form and something of its history, adding a little further to our knowledge of Dark-Age England.

The first, and abiding, impression made by the building at North Elmham is its size. The word 'cathedral' has taken on connotations of grandeur through its application to those enormous buildings raised after 1066, but that at North Elmham could be a small country church, a little over 100 feet in length and about fifteen feet wide – less than half the size even of the small cathedral of Winchester. It had no aisles, no stately pillars to give a perspective of length: it was simply an oblong box made of flint, the prolific local building material, with another box at right angles to form the transepts. Beneath it, the excavators found traces of an older, wooden building that had been destroyed by fire.

Piecing together the scanty archaeological remains with the scarcely more detailed historical evidence it is possible to get some idea of the tragedy that happened here some time before the Conquest. The original Saxon cathedral, a wooden structure, was erected some time after the year 800. The savage advance of the Danes overwhelmed the area about forty years later when the wooden cathedral was put to the flames. The Saxons reconquered the area about 918 but, as the diocese was now being administered from London, in the characteristic Saxon fashion of preserving the status quo, the cathedral was not rebuilt until towards the end of the century. The new series of bishops of East Anglia commenced in 955 and a new church, in the dignity of stone, was built then or a little after, and remained in use until abandoned by the Norman bishops. The diocese of East Anglia was extinguished until the late twentieth century when the newly consecrated, first modern Roman Catholic bishop in Norwich took the style 'Bishop of East Anglia' to distinguish his office from the Anglican 'Bishop of Norwich' whose seat remained in that vast cathedral which superseded the modest Saxon structure.

The little building at North Elmham slumbered on, forgotten. And while its structure fell apart the Saxon concept of corporate worship continued not in a village but in the heart of Norwich, when in 1096 black-robed Benedictines began the construction of their cathedral priory.

There are three major elements in a monastic complex: a place to live, a place to work and a place to pray. Initially, all ingenuity, all wealth, all energy was directed towards the construction and beautification of the place to pray. Then followed the place to work, and only finally was wealth and energy expended upon the place to live. The monastic tradition developed on the pendulum system. At first, the monks embraced poverty and work, choosing the remotest countryside in which to establish their homes. A group of men, working for no individual return, putting all they earned into a communal chest would inevitably create wealth. Wealth, in turn would as naturally lead to corruption and those who wished again to embrace the austere ideals of their founder would abandon

their now too-luxurious home and, like a swarm leaving a hive, depart in a body to establish a new, austere centre. There, again, the cycle would begin with work creating wealth, wealth creating corruption and corruption creating reform.

The use of their church as an urban seat for a bishop tended to short-circuit the monks' natural progression so that the life-cycle of a monastic cathedral began, not in some harsh and remote part of the land, but in an already established urban community. But initially that impulse to adorn the temple before the palace was by far the strongest: one could indeed measure the progress of corruption by the gradual development of the living quarters, in particular the bishop's palace – not, perhaps, at the expense of the temple, but certainly parallel with it. In York, whose Minster took many years to complete, the sequence is particularly clear.

Today, the main entry into most cathedrals is by a door at or near the great west front. The visitor progresses naturally from west to east, eventually arriving at the high altar, and the impression is therefore given that this would have been the natural sequence of building. But, as far as the monastic builders were concerned, the nave was an afterthought, a later development. It was the presbytery, the section extending eastward from the great crossing below the tower, the section which contained, as the very heart of the place, the altar and the choir, that was the vital part of the building. This spiritual separation of the choir, where the monks gathered to chant their canonical hours, and the rest of the building, is physically emphasized by the great stone screen that is so dominant a feature of most cathedrals. The screen, together with the tombs and chapels on either side of the choir and presbytery, virtually make of the building a church within a church.

This spiritual separation continued even into the twentieth century. In 1925 the dean of Chester, making an impassioned appeal for the reintegration of cathedral clergy with the world outside, described a service:

I have actually been present at a diocesan service in a great cathedral where there was ample room in the stalls for all the clergy [of the diocese] who were present in robes. In the stalls sat three cathedral dignitaries (dreadful name!) and myself. With the congregation in the front seat of the Nave sat the

clergy from the diocese in their robes. The pathetic thing was that the cathedral authorities were wholly unconscious that such an arrangement was monstrous.

The dean is doubtless describing an extreme example: what he recommended, and what has subsequently come to pass, is not the abolition of the choir, but the inviting into the presbytery of the

Nineteenth century ecclesiastical thinking believed that the nave of a cathedral should be integrated with the building. The fact that the original builders viewed it as a separate, secular, entity is shown by the massive screens which divided the layman's nave from the clergy's presbytery. Those shown in this sequence are (*above*) Hereford, now demolished, (*opposite*) Exeter, and York, (pages 40 and 45).

38

The screen at Exeter.

congregation for such services as attract a relatively small number of people. The Victorians, by contrast, attempted to bring the choir into the nave by demolishing the great screen, turning the cathedral in effect into a great 'preaching house' – something for which it was never intended.

The choir and presbytery, then, were the first areas of the church to be built. Until the twelfth century, the next major development was probably the nave, the area intended for processions and thus, by extension, for ordinary layfolk. But from about the end of the twelfth century, however, there began to develop a quite extraordinary cult which was to have an immense influence both on the liturgy and on the physical structure of Christianity – the cult of the Virgin Mary.

In 1963 a group of Anglican scholars published a collection of essays that traced the development of this cult. Mindful of ecumenical trends, the majority of the writers were careful to limit themselves to historical observations, avoiding the possibility of giving offence by commenting on contemporary implications. One of the writers, however – canon John de Satge – boldly grasped the nettle. He wrote:

The evangelical has a strong suspicion that the deepest roots of the Marian *cultus* are not to be found in the Christian tradition at all. The religious history of mankind shows a recurring tendency to worship a mother-goddess (and) the cult of Mary may be an intrusion into Christianity from the dark realms of natural history.

The screen canopy at York.

Canon de Satge was voicing, in a cautious, courteous, twentieth-century accent, a belief that has been voiced – with considerably less courtesy and caution – over the centuries: the belief that the veneration of the human mother of God has again and again reached into forbidden areas.

During the first four centuries of the Church's history, Christians had paid no particular attention to the Virgin Mary, according her about the same degree of respect they accorded the other holy women in New Testament history. Even as late as the year 1000 the great mystic, St Bernard of Clairvaux, was attacking the idea that the Madonna was in some manner different from other humans, and the great Romanesque cathedrals that appeared about this time, and whose influence crossed the Channel, certainly made no special provision for her worship. But within a century of the Conquest the cult had rooted itself so firmly in England, surviving the rigours of the Reformation, that romantic twentieth-century Roman Catholics can still refer to the country as 'Our Lady's Dowry'.

The Lady Chapels that began to appear towards the end of the twelfth century bear physical and unequivocal witness to the depth and power of the belief. Usually they appear at the extremity of the eastern arm, though there was no liturgical reason

*Opposite*
Lichfield's three spires are delightfully known as the 'Ladies of the Vale'. The pool, one of two separating cathedral from town, was formed when a swamp was drained.

Statue of Charles II outside
Lichfield cathedral.

Lichfield's splendid chapter house.
Visitors or petitioners to the dean and
chapter waited in an antechamber.

*Opposite*
The lady chapel at Lichfield. Built long
after the main body of the cathedral, its
alignment required particular skill and a
special master mason was commissioned
to do the job.

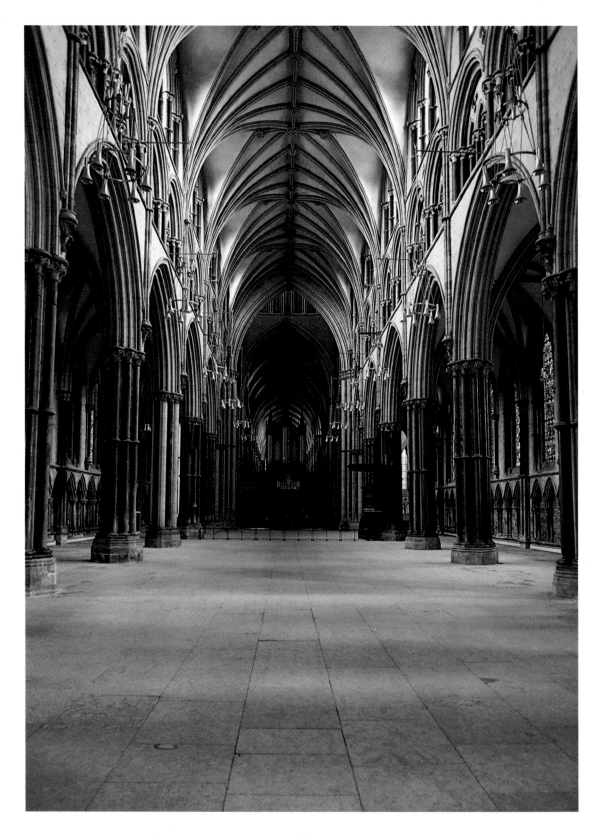

Details of the screen at York.

for this, and if lack of space forbade an eastern extension, the chapel could be built in any convenient place. At Durham, an extreme example of saintly misogyny resulted in the transference of the Chapel to the west end. In 1175 the reigning bishop, following the new fashion, began the construction of a Lady Chapel at the east end near the shrine of St Cuthbert, the patronal saint of the cathedral – overlooking the fact that the saint's hatred of women was supposed to be so great that the monks had inserted a line of marble across the nave beyond which females were not to pass. Cracks and settlements promptly appeared in the

walls of the new chapel until the builders gave up and built the chapel as far away from the irascible saint's tomb as possible.

Bristol, by contrast, boasted two Lady Chapels; the first, or Elder, was built on the north side, before its successor appeared, fifty years later, on the prestigious eastern arm. Canterbury possessed no less than three Lady Chapels while at Worcester the Lady Chapel built in 1224 exerted so powerful an influence that eventually the entire eastern arm of the cathedral was rebuilt to harmonize with it. The apogee of the Lady Chapel undoubtedly came in 1502 when, according to John Stowe's *Annales*, the old Lady Chapel at the east end of Westminster Abbey 'with also a tavern neere adioyning, were taken down; in the which place or plot of ground, on 24 January 1502/3 the first stone of our Lady Chappel was laid by the hands of Joh. Islip abbot of the same monastery...'. Abbot Islip might have laid the stone, but the impulse was provided by the king, Henry VII. As he later explained in his will, he

*Opposite*
The nave of Lincoln cathedral, uncluttered by chairs as it would have appeared in the medieval period when naves also did duty as secular meeting places.

45

had two objectives: to honour the Virgin and to provide a tomb for himself and his descendants. Money was poured out on the project, the king alone providing £8,000: Stowe calculated the overall cost of this one addition at around £14,000, a truly staggering sum whose result is clearly evident in the sumptuous finish of the Chapel.

It is perhaps unduly anthropomorphic to recognize a certain feminine delicacy and elegance about these chapels for, the majority being built over a span of fifty years or so, they would of necessity have conformed to the graceful architectural style prevailing at the beginning of the fourteenth century. But curiously, most would survive not only the changes wrought by the Reformation but also the fanatical hammers of the Puritan iconoclasts. The Lady Chapel of St Albans was badly damaged by the Cromwellians and was walled off for use as a school room, but the nineteenth century restoration has brought it back into the life of the church and one actually has to look for the depredations. The cooly rational seventeenth century abandoned the concept of a special chapel and Wren made no provision for such a chapel in St Paul's. But the supposedly iconoclastic twentieth century has revived the idea: Lady Chapels were included in the design for the new cathedral at Guildford, begun in 1933 and in Coventry, begun in 1951, and one was slotted, rather uneasily, into the east end of Wren's St Paul's in 1959.

The great screen or *pulpitum* that separated the choir from the nave in monastic cathedrals was the physical expression of the separation of the monk from the world, and emphasized the fact that the laity were permitted into the cathedral only as an act of grace. The screens vary as greatly as the building around them. Exeter's, built in the relatively light-hearted early fourteenth century, is elegant and graceful, seeming to act as a frame for the mysteries taking place beyond. That of Norwich is solid, almost forbidding, and quite definitely designed as much to exclude as to include: York's has a similar solidity but, built in 1475, its intricate filigree reduces the forbidding appearance, while the line of kings enthroned upon its face humanizes it. Screens became the target not only of early iconoclasts and reformers, but also of the nineteenth-century restorers. They formed a natural basis for a wall: at Exeter the screen was enclosed entirely in a brick wall that separated

choir from nave during the Commonwealth. In the nineteenth century, the desire to integrate clergy and laity led to widespread destruction of these beautiful and distinctive features. Hereford lost its original Norman screen in 1841; Chichester's went in 1859 (an event which some believe disastrously weakened the tower and so led to its collapse in 1861). Chester's was first moved, and then destroyed, by the ubiquitous George Gilbert Scott in 1868.

When Benedict of Nursia in 529 laid down the rules for the earliest of all monastic orders, that which bore his own name, he realized that unremitting contemplation and prayer would inevitably lead to psychological disturbances. He therefore decreed that one third of a monk's life should be spent in repose, one third in prayer, and one third in work. The Benedictine order became the model for all others which, though they might differ in detail, ordered their lives on the same general pattern. The monastery became a self-supporting organism in which each monk contributed his particular skill whether it was in cheese-making, carpentry or scholarship. During the early stages of building the cathedral church, the monks would have been living in more or less temporary huts scattered around in no particular order. Gradually, as the monastery took shape over the years, stone would be substituted for wood.

At the heart of the monastery was the cloister. Technically, this was nothing more than an arcaded walk which allowed exercise or some kinds of work to be pursued in inclement weather but, in time, it became virtually a synonym for the monastery itself. So prestigious was the cloister that, when Salisbury cathedral was moved from its cramped situation on Old Sarum down to the river, its canons set about making the largest cloisters in England. This was in spite of the fact that the cloisters had no function whatsoever, for Salisbury's was a secular cathedral with its clergy living 'in the world'. The canons of Salisbury were spared the expense of providing monastic buildings and so were able to devote both cash and time to the construction of their cloisters, so that these became a model for other, envious, ecclesiastic foundations to copy.

Salisbury's cloister, therefore, while the largest in England, was purely a luxury, used perhaps for the processions which formed so large a part of a church's life, but otherwise playing no part in daily life. The largest surviving working cloister however is that at Norwich, and its working parts are still clearly evident. This is the second on the site: much of the first was destroyed by a fire in 1272. Unlike most fires, this one was no accident, but the result of another common hazard – friction between townsfolk and monks. In the long run, in this case, the cathedral benefited, for not only did the heavy fine levied by the king on the townsfolk pay for a handsome new gateway, but the new cloister was built on the model of that at Salisbury. Scriptoria – the little wooden cells in which the monastic scribes produced their exquisite manuscripts – were established in many cloisters, those at Gloucester being the most famous. It is unlikely that Norwich had such a function on the lower storey, for the unglazed windows would have made such delicate work all but impossible for a substantial part of each year. The production of manuscripts, however, ranked very high in a Benedictine monastery, dedicated as it was to intellectual pursuits, and the scriptoria at Norwich, the only double-storeyed cloister in England, were probably situated on the upper storey.

Building of the Norwich cloister extended over 150 years, providing posterity not only with a textbook example of changing architectural styles that can be studied at close hand, but also an impressive example of the leisurely attitude to time itself so characteristic of the period. The change of style is all the more instructive in that the builders were striving to keep not only to the original dimensions as laid down shortly after the construction began in 1096, but also aimed for harmonization, if not homogeneity. The changes in style, therefore, exactly and subtly reflect the changing fashions of the generations. Even the most skilled copyist is hard-put wholly to expel the influences of his own time, and the masons who followed one another over some three generations would have had only a general directive to conform to what was already there.

Cloisters always lay south of the cathedral, the great mass of the building protecting the living quarters from the blasts of the north. In Norwich, the so-called Prior's Door is the main doorway of the monastic church. Through this the brethren would have made their procession seven times in twenty-four hours, starting at midnight with matins, returning again to the choir for prime at 6am and so on, every five hours or so, day and night, day after day, year after year, their praises of God ringing through the winter darkness, or the spring dawn, or the blazing afternoons of August. Immediately to the left on entering Norwich cloister book cupboards made of the universal stone are still visible. Below them, some frivolous brethren have scratched a pattern in the stone bench – an outline for some form of board game. Beyond is a doorway, now blocked, which led to the slyp, or passage to the cemetery; here was the parlour – the only place where talking was allowed. The chapter house at Norwich, along with that at St Alban's, is one of the few which has been destroyed down to its foundations, but the entrance to it was also in this arcade, which would have resembled a bustling, lively, but eerily silent, thoroughfare – the only human sounds being the rustle of robes and the slap of sandals on stone. Further on was the entrance to the dormitory; although there was a double door here, one side was apparently kept permanently closed, possibly in an attempt to maintain warmth, for only one side of the stone step is worn. Nearby is the lavatory – a simple but elegant trough for water with arches above for towels. The elaborate piping and taps which conveyed water to the trough have here vanished, but the supply of fresh water and disposal of foul seems to have been as sophisticated in medieval monasteries as in any Roman villa. At Canterbury, the great Norman watertower, built during the twelfth century, has not only survived but is part of the present-day water-supply system. The system is even more advanced than was that at Norwich, for the actual lavatory, or washing place, was here on the first floor and the water was raised to that level through brass pipes.

The guesthouse of Norwich cathedral was approached through the cloister and is identified by a carved boss showing an ever-open door. Logically, the locutorium was adjacent, for here visitors to the monastery were interviewed. And close by the guesthouse is the entrance to a chamber which, more than any functioning apartment, brings home to posterity the spartan life of a monastery, the level of sheer physical discomfort. This is the so-called warming house, the only room in the entire place, apart from the kitchen, which had the luxury of a fire.

The cloisters, originally simply a communication passage and working area, became more sumptuous with the years. Salisbury (*above* and *opposite*) started the fashion of a 'ceremonial' cloister; it had no function for Salisbury was a secular (non-monastic) cathedral. (*Overleaf*) Norwich rebuilt its cloister in a similarly grand fashion, followed by Worcester.

One of the most vivid evocations of life in a medieval monastery is made by a modern monk, Dom Hugh Aveling who, drawing upon his own first-hand experience, tries to enter the life of a monk living and working and praying in Westminster Abbey some time in the eleventh century.

We should be especially moved by the prodigious amount of church services and the midnight office, of great length and sung almost entirely in the dark. Yet, on the other hand we could hardly appreciate the ameliorating effects on the monks of an entire familiarity with it all – more habituated to physical discomfort and pain: tougher, less introspective...We should soon have to give up the unequal effort of trying to calculate the strain on such men and [on] moderns. We should undoubtedly be impressed by the fearful cold of the cloister and the church. The cloister arcades on the open side were still unglazed.

Cold. This, undoubtedly, would be the single dominant impression, a coldness almost beyond modern comprehension. The only way fully to appreciate it would be to emulate one of the devoted modern Friends of a cathedral and spend an hour or so seated at a table in the nave. But even this is only relative, for no cathedral today is without some form of general heating which reduces a little the terrible tomb-like cold of the vast stone building. At Westminster, iron chafing-dishes full of charcoal were brought in and left around the altar during the worst periods of cold and some such dispensation was doubtless followed in most cathedrals. But it would only be an alleviation and the fearful, all-embracing, rarely absent cold would make the monk's enveloping habit with its blanket-like material a very sensible and practical garment.

After cold, a guest unfamiliar with the routine of the monastery would most likely be afflicted by gastric discomfort, for extended periods of fast would be broken by a single gargantuan meal and

the feast days of the patronal saint, and other major feast days of the liturgy, would be marked by a banquet. The food would be good, not only because it was the product of the monastery's own garden, but because the cooks would be offering their gastronomic skills, in the exact same way the other brethren would be offering their different specialized skills, to the good of the community and, hence, 'to the greater glory of God'. Fatigue might perhaps afflict a guest or a novice, particularly as a result of rising for the midnight office. But, in general, the canonical hours established a sensible, humane pattern for, after four or five hours physical or mental work, the monk would need a change and a refreshment and this would be provided by the act of moving ceremonially into the choir, and there taking part in a series of ritualized actions and creating ritualized sounds.

The cloisters at Norwich (*left* and *below*) and Worcester (*opposite*).

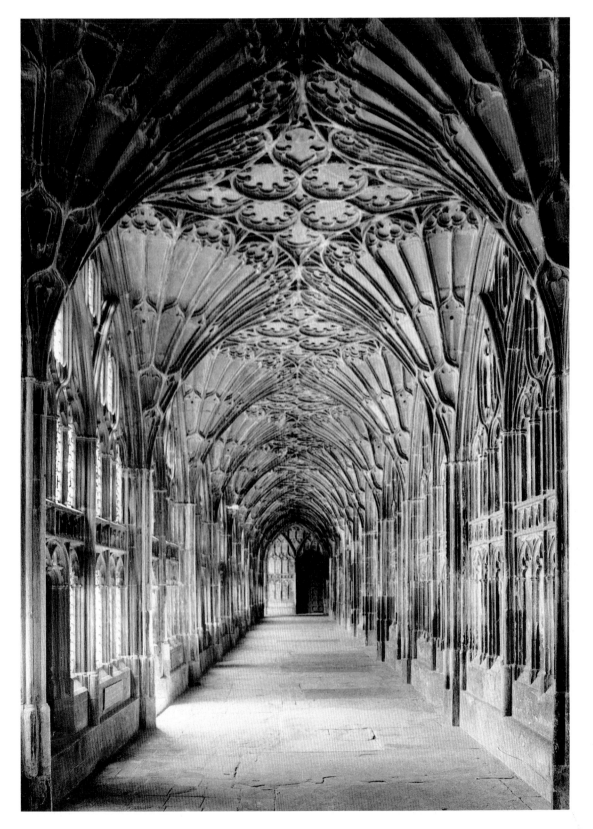

Allowing for variations between monastic communities, and changes of times over the centuries, a monk's day would start at around midnight. Woken by the clanging of the bell, he would dress rapidly (that convenient monastic costume could be slipped on, in the dark, in seconds) and make his way to the cloisters, joining the hurrying, noiseless throng whose black garments melted into the blackness of night. The cold draughtiness of the choir would be slightly alleviated in the later period by the elaborately carved wooden stalls. There, every night, he would stand, or sit upon a wooden seat, for anything up to two hours till around 1.30 or 2am. Much of the liturgy demanded a standing position and with the Christian Church's ability to temper rigorous ideals with sophisticated interpretations, the seat of his stall was so made that as an act of mercy (a *misericord*) it could support his weight while he was technically in a standing position.

Four or five hours sleep would follow until the bell clanged again calling the brethren to prime at between 6 and 6.30. This service lasted only about half an hour but almost immediately afterwards would come the morrow mass, the celebration of various private masses, one of which would be sung in the Lady Chapel. Still fasting, the community would then go to chapter.

The chapter house was the physical expression of the community's solidarity, and the sense of each member belonging to a corporate body, supporting it – but also being supported by it. Even today, some of the legal statutes governing a cathedral enjoin regular meeting in the traditional chapter house and though such usage is increasingly declining, the dean and chapter reasonably preferring modern if nondescript comfort to the chilly spendour of the traditional chapter house, their ancient home is invariably well preserved. Here was displayed the highest skill of the medieval mason, backed up by the glazier. The significant part the chapter house played in the life of the community is demonstrated by the widespread use of the polygonal shape, usually an octagon. This might give the impression of equality among members, much as use of a round table might do, for little architectural distinction is given to the bishop's or abbot's stall. Such an impression is quite misleading, however, the polygon being adopted because of its deeply symbolic meaning. It

is the form of the Rotunda on the Holy Sepulchre in Jerusalem, of the Dome of the Rock itself, and also the form adopted by Charlemagne for his own great chapel in Aachen. The Rotunda was rebuilt in 1048 and would have attracted the pious attention of the first crusaders which, in turn, seems to have had rapid effect in England, for a rotunda appeared at Canterbury in 1050. The oldest surviving chapter house using this form, however, is that of Worcester's, built in the early twelfth century.

The polygonal form created a problem whose solution created a unique and beautiful feature, the single central column from which the ribs of the ceiling radiate like the fronds of a plant. Most chapter houses are an integral part of the building, but their position can vary greatly: that at Wells is situated on an upper floor, approached by a flight of stone steps that seem to flow down like a frozen cascade. Although the chamber is, in effect, the business office of the monastery, it is quite bare, in startling contrast to the paper-producing twentieth-century office.

Surviving chapter houses are protected buildings and few opportunities are presented for the kind of thorough investigation produced by archaeological excavations. Such an opportunity did occur in St Alban's in 1978 when the dean and chapter decided to build a new chapter house on the site of the one destroyed in the sixteenth century – their decision, indeed, demonstrating in twentieth-century terms the vital role still played by the building, for the new chapter house acts as a social centre for the religious community. Professor Martin Biddle conducted an archaeological investigation which showed the development of the site not simply over centuries but over millenia: among the objects uncovered were a neolithic axe, Roman pottery and a heating system installed in 1937.

There were two chapter houses on the St Alban's site, one, the smaller, below the other, clearly demonstrating the growth of the monastery. The first chapter house was built at about the time that the church itself was being built, some time before 1088, and probably housed around forty monks. Both this and its sucessor were rectangular, not polygonal, and for the second building Martin

*Opposite*
The twelfth-century water tower of Canterbury, still in working order.

The endless rite: modern monks in their choir stalls.

Biddle calculated its length at ninety-three feet:

...If one allows about two feet per monk – and I imagine that not every one was a Friar Tuck – you will find that you can seat forty-five of the brethren on either side quite comfortably. This is just right: ninety monks and ten places for the officers along the east end; one hundred in all, which is the recorded site of the community at the height of its development...

A particularly moving discovery was the skeletal remains of monks identifiable by name, the chapter house being reserved as a place of burial for important members of the monastic community – not necessarily all abbots. Among them was Adam the Cellarer. He was responsible for the victualling of the monastery, but he was also its historian and was evidently buried with a book as a mark of this

role. In the older chapter house was found the grave of Robert the Chamber, father of the only English pope, Nicholas Breakspeare.

A monastery was not simply a community of bretheren, but also probably the largest local landowner and employer and the chapter house therefore had the additional role of estate office. To it would come a wide range of people with a wide range of interests and problems. The chapter house at Westminster Abbey was actually used as the meeting place for Parliament for some years. At Lichfield a handsome vestibule was provided for the petitioners, who were strictly separated according to rank. On the right-hand side was a plain stone bench for ordinary people while on the left were canopied stalls for magnates. A most unusual feature of these stalls was that a narrow gallery ran just above and behind them so that each magnate could have his serving man standing respectfully, literally, at his shoulder.

Into the chapter house, then, there filed each morning the members of the community. The chamber itself took its name from a *capitulum* or chapter of the monastic Rules. Each day a chapter of the Rule was read out so that eventually each monk would have been able to recite the entire Rules by heart. The Martyrology was read, commemorating the saint or saints of the day and then the Necrology, the obituaries of the deceased members of the community or its benefactors. Next would follow monastic discipline, the brethren owning to their misdeeds in public and receiving punishment – usually in the form of admonitions or verbal penances, but by no means infrequently including corporal punishment. The chapter then turned to business matters – the leasing of land, the receipt of rents or arbitration in disputes.

After chapter followed work, each according to his bent, whether it was farmwork, housework, or study. At about midday would come the only main meal of the day, in the refectory. Most refectories were destroyed at the Dissolution of the monasteries but that at Chester survived, together with the stone pupit on the wall used by the monk whose turn it was to read from some sacred book while the brethren ate swiftly and in silence. More work followed until 3.30pm, when the day began to wind down. There were two more offices to be sung, vespers at around 4pm and the beautiful compline, which 'completed' the day with its haunting invocation to the Virgin Mary, *Salve Regina*. There would be a light meal at about 5.30 and well before 8pm the monastery would again be dark and silent as the community snatched a few hours of sleep before the clanging of the bell again began a new day.

The Sacrists' Rolls or account books of Ely Cathedral give a fascinating insight into the domestic life of a great monastery. Before Alan of Walsingham took over and rationalized the accounts – in this, as with so much else, showing himself a very modern and organized man – the sacrists just entered items as they occurred which is confusing to read and use but gives a kind of cross-section of their daily life. The books ran from Michaelmas to Michaelmas – September to September – and the sacrist in 1291/2 was a certain Clement of Thetford. The frugal nature of society comes out very clearly in the accounts. Almost everything – food, clothing, tools, materials – was

wrested directly from the soil at great cost and labour, and was not only not to be wasted, but rigidly accounted for. Alan will himself later carefully tot up and record the price of eight hooks for a door, just as he will tot up and record the cost of twenty years' work. Clement does the shopping for the monastery, usually at fairs. On 2 November he buys rice and sugar at Bury St Edmund's fair; at Barnwell, wheels, axles and other equipment for carts. He goes to the sea port of Boston to buy good wine cheaply and sends to London for things needed for the vestry. In the spring he stocks the fishponds, that vital source of protein for the community. The king's tax, too, must be collected and paid – one-fifteenth of the monastery's income. There is an argument over arrears and it takes three journeys to London, at the large total cost of £10 17s, to settle the matter. A big monastery like Ely sees a lot of travel for its servants, and the sacrist conscientiously notes whether the costs of his journey are *cum stauro*, with food taken out of the storeroom, or *sine stauro*, which means the messenger must have money for food for the journey.

In the middle of all this domestic minutiae about

The chapter house was the administrative headquarters of the cathedral. Worcester's (*left*) is the oldest-surviving octagonal form; the rich details of the entry to Southwell's (*right*) emphasizes the importance of the place.

The 'frozen cascade' at Wells. The steps to the right lead up into
the chapter house. Lichfield's chapter house (*opposite*) is
approached through an ante-chamber.

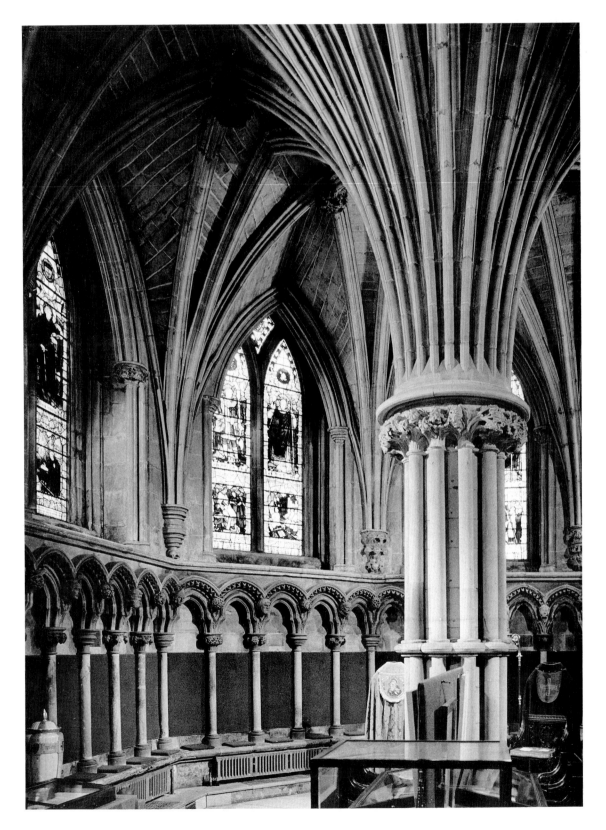

wines and cheeses and axles whose costs are measured in pence or even farthings, there appears a sudden massive sum – £66 13s 5d – over a quarter of the year's income, noted simply as 'Help for the Prior'. The monks had elected one of their number, prior Robert, as bishop of Ely but the archbishop of Canterbury had objected. It was necessary to send to Rome to get the pope's ruling – and most of this sum would have gone to grease the palms of a number of Italian clerics.

In 1530 there were about 1,000 monasteries in England of which twelve served a cathedral; in 1540 there was not a single monastic house. The cathedrals that had been served by monks, places like Norwich and Wells and Chester, had new constitutions given them, were called cathedrals of the 'new foundation' (though some were centuries older than those now known as the 'old foundation'), and all were now served by secular clergy.

The astonishing speed of collapse of a system which had endured for over eight centuries can be explained only by the existence of internal corruption and external exasperation. The system was ripe for collapse, and though the king started the process, the ordinary people helped it on its way through a mixture of genuine disapproval and considerable self-interest. The rapidity with which the actual monastic buildings disappeared argues that the locals must have queued up with wheelbarrows to help themselves to the expensively worked stone.

It is peculiarly difficult to obtain an objective view of monasticism before the Dissolution for the severity of the Dissolution either transformed the monks in the eyes of posterity into romantic figures martyred for their faith, or caused them to be regarded as a universal corruption whose cauterizing healed the State. The evidence of the commissioners carrying out the destruction is obviously prejudiced, but is not necessarily wholly inaccurate. Many a monk was himself perfectly aware of that internal corruption. A certain Richard Beerely wrote sadly to Thomas Cromwell, the king's jackal, admitting that 'the relygyon we do obser and keyp ys no rull of sent Bentt, nor yt no commandment of God' and goes on to give what is evidently a first-hand account of life in his monastery: 'Moncks drynk an bowll after colla-cyon tell ten or xii of the clock, and cum to mattens

as dronck as myss, and sume at cardes, sume at dyss'. One of Cromwell's own agents gives a hair-raising picture of the domestic life of one abbot – and, incidentally, of the violence used against many a monastery. The abbot's door was locked, and the agent 'dasshede it in peisses' with a poleaxe and so forced his way in:

...polax in hand for the abbot is a dangerous, desperate knave and hardy. His hore, alias his gentlewomman bestyrrede hir stumpis towardes her starting hoiiles and ther Bartlett [his assistant] towke the tendre damosel and after I had examynede hir, to Dover ther to the maire to sett hir in sum cage or prison and I browgt holy father abbot to Canterbury, and here in Christeschurche [cathedral] I will level hym in prison.

In its great days, during the twelfth and thirteenth centuries in particular, the monastery was a major dynamic in society, a generator as well as a reservoir of wealth, discharging locally most of the functions discharged today by the so-called welfare state. But by the year 1500 the dynamism was waning. There might have been 1,000 monasteries, but there were barely 10,000 monks and perhaps 2,000 nuns. Great houses which once had sheltered some one hundred men now perhaps had a dozen or so, while in many a small, poor house, perhaps half a dozen old men or women, cold, underfed, under-occupied, perfunctorily went through their rituals and were probably glad enough at last to abandon the hollow life, take a small pension and disappear into the community at large.

But though the system itself was at an end, the impulse continued, though directed into other channels. Nine centuries of self-governing and self-disciplining, nine centuries of living and working in communities could not be expunged overnight. The monastic system gave way to the collegiate system: canons took the place of monks, deans took the place of abbots and professional choristers occupied the monks stalls. But the cathedral lived on. There was even an increase in their number. Henry VIII, busily changing the shape of religion for his own purposes, found time

*Opposite*
Chester refectory: the pulpit. Here a brother would read aloud from some devotional work during meals.

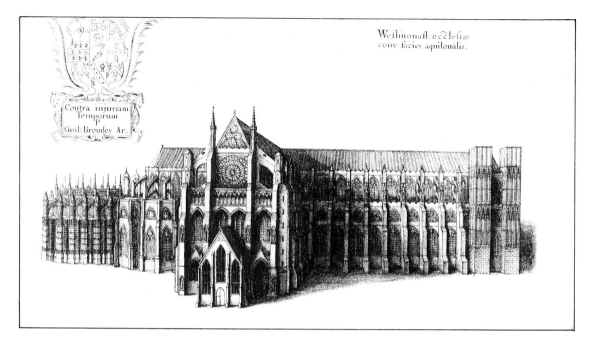

Westminster Abbey enjoyed the status of a 'royal peculiar' cathedral from 1542 to 1556.

to draft an injunction in his own hand: 'It is thowght therfore unto the kynges hyghtnes most expedient and necssary that mo bysshopprycys, colegyall and cathedralle chyrchys shulbe establlyshyd in sted of thes forsayd relygus housys.' Six monastic churches were promoted to the status of cathedrals – Chester, Gloucester, Peterborough, Westminster, Oxford and Bristol.

Westminster's role as a cathedral was both stormy and brief, extending only from 1542, to 1556 during the reign of Mary, when the monks returned. As a cathedral, the dean and chapter were granted £2,164 annually from the dissolved monastic estates, but this was by no means enough, and the chapter were reduced to selling the monastery's treasures, beginning with candlesticks, bells and 'angells of copper and gylte', easing their conscience by describing them as 'monymentes of Idlatre and supersticyon'. But this was not enough to keep the wolf at bay, the wolf in this case being the Lord Protector Somerset and his greedy Seymour relatives. At one stage Somerset threatened to demolish the deanery and use the stone for the splendid palace he was building himself on the Strand, but contented himself with extorting leases and rents from the cathedral's estates, so putting it ever deeper in the red. The

monks, under their abbot John Feckenham, indulged themselves to the full in the rites of the old faith under Mary. But Mary's half-sister Elizabeth was even more anti-Rome than their father had been. 'Away with those torches, for we see very well', she shouted when the abbot and his chapter came to meet her in all the splendour of canonicals, led by flaring torches and incensing and asperging as they came. The abbey was dissolved, finally, on 10 July 1559, the last abbot, John Feckenham, ending his days in prison. On 21 May 1560, Elizabeth granted the abbey a charter which gave it the unique distinction, which it shares with Windsor, of being a 'Royal Peculiar', that is, an establishment resembling a cathedral on all points but with the sovereign, not the bishop, as immediate head. That enviable independence enabled it to govern itself free of the ecclesiastical establishment. Looking at the mass of grandiloquent and graceless statuary that crowds out its transepts one wonders whether that freedom has always been used to good purpose.

CHAPTER III

# Ad Majorem Dei Gloriam

Some time before the year 1130 a French monk, Honorius of Autun, set down carefully and precisely what could be called a manual of symbolism. Every part of a great church, no matter how humble or how exalted that part, had a dual role: the physical function it was created to perform, and the symbolism it was meant to express. Beginning with the church itself, Honorius pointed out that it was set on stone foundations, even as the Church itself was founded on the sure rock of Christ. He then takes the reader on a kind of conducted tour explaining as he goes. The windows are to be seen as the learned Fathers of the Church: just as the glass keeps out cold but lets in light, so the Fathers keep out heresy and let in the divine light of the Church's teaching. The numerous columns of the building are to be seen as bishops supporting the organization; the very tiles on the roof, protecting the building from rain, are typecast as Christian soldiers protecting the faith. The pavements underfoot are the ordinary people themselves; the relics of saints preserved in the altar are the treasures of wisdom hidden in Christ. The great bell of the building is the Church speaking to her people, while the cock that crowns all, glittering high up on the steeple, stands as symbol for the priest calling the faithful to mass, even as the cock awakens sleepers in the morning. Every part of the cathedral, every action within it, is directed to a single end *ad majorem Dei gloriam* – to the greater glory of God.

Honorius inevitably touches on the dominant ground-plan of the building – the cruciform, in memory of the cross of Christ. Yet this was a relatively new development, for throughout the formative years of the Church it had been the Roman basilica, the ordinary law court of a Roman town, that inspired the ground-plan. The darkness of the Dark Ages has been rendered less impenetrable in recent years. Archaeologists and archivists alike have succeeded in throwing light over much of its course to show that, during the centuries-long period between the final extinction of the Roman empire and the appearance of nation states, though Europe had lost social cohesion, it had not slumped back into savagery. Art, sure index to a society's mind, shows an admittedly confused but immensely vigorous period whose vitalities were dispersed through many channels. Gradually, these channels found their way into one great stream, the Romanesque – that massive style of building which took its plan from the basilica but whose elevation perfectly expressed its time. Raoul Glaber's glittering white sanctuaries were as much castles as temples: Europe was still an embattled, fragmented society groping for unity through the universal Church.

Throughout the twelfth century Romanesque, that most suprahuman of religious styles, dominated. It was perhaps more truly international than the succeeding 'Gothic', even though its regional styles could vary from the mosaic-encrusted blaze of Venice's San Marco, to the dark, gloomy strength of Durham. It was not a style influenced by humanism. While the low doorway, enormous pillars and lack of windows were doubtless the result of architectural need, the decorations clearly reflected the philosophy. The elongated figures sculptured on the portals, with their remote, austere faces, inspire awe rather than affection. In His portrayal, Christ appears as Creator and as Judge: the Child is yet to come. In all its ramifications, from engineering to illumination, in stone, brick, vellum or glass, Romanesque art is the working-out of a theology more Oriental than Occidental.

The internationalism of Romanesque was essentially an expression of that great international institution, the monastery, which created it, but the cathedral came to express itself in 'Gothic'. This all-embracing term is of comparatively recent date. The Italian artist, Raphael, used it pejoratively in the sixteenth century, contrasting this 'barbaric' style with the sophistication of Greece and Rome. The term passed into England, still in the contemptuous mode, via Sir Henry Wotton. Evelyn followed him and the great authority of Christopher Wren established it firmly, still as an

The following pages show architectural styles according to Rickman. Although Rickman's system was an intelligent attempt to place order on a chaotic subject, in the long run it has probably done architectural studies a disservice as attempts are made to cram a building, whose construction may have extended over centuries, into one arbitrarily chosen phase.

*Opposite*
Norman style (Southwell).

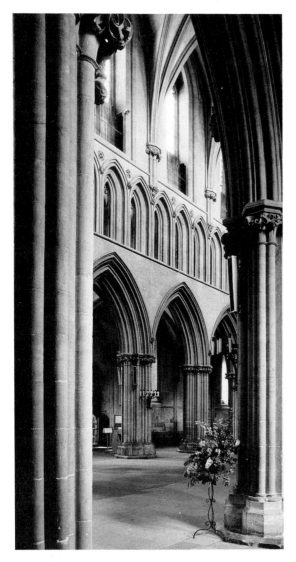

Early English style (Wells).

called Thomas Rickman, in a laudable attempt to bring some order into a confused subject, created a classification which has put the whole subject into a kind of straitjacket or bed of Procrustes. Discussing the admittedly botched attempts at repairing the ancient churches and cathedrals by builders who were ignorant 'of every real principle of English architecture' he proposed the following:

English architecture may be divided into four distinct periods of styles which may be named: first, the Norman style; second, the Early English style; third, the Decorated style and fourth, the Perpendicular style.

Rickman's useful piece of shorthand became, in timc, a tyranny whereby every guidebook felt it necessary to classify the described building as 'Norman', 'EE', 'Dec' or 'Perp'. The sheer naïvety of trying to find one label for a building whose construction covered perhaps centuries is summed up by Pevsner's comment on York Minster: 'Between about 1230 and 1475 every stage is represented so much so that the following description [of the Minster] has to be chronological by parts'. If a cathedral or great church could be photographed by some speeded-up camera, as is done to show some aspect of natural history, then the viewer would see it growing virtually organically, forms melting one into the other over the centuries. The fact that Rickman's classification ends with 'Perp', that is, around the 1550s, with nothing whatsoever to say about the intervening three centuries, much less the period extending down to our time, shows the severe limitation of this pedantic wish to cram a living, ever-changing structure into a pigeonhole.

Nevertheless, Rickman's classification was of value for it brought to the attention of his contemporaries the fact that ecclesiastical architecture, like all other intellectual activities, had its changing fashions and that those fashions reflected something of the contemporary world. It did this partly through the limitations imposed by that world, for example the fact that the Norman structures were massive because their builders had not yet learned the sciences of stress, and partly by the psychological bent of that world, as for example the richly flowing forms of the style Rickman called Decorated.

expression of contempt. But then, beginning with Horace Walpole, there began a reaction in its favour. The reaction obscured its essential nature as thoroughly as did the contemptuous assessments of the Renaissance, and culminated in the 'Gothic' of Victorian England when psalters were illuminated by chromo-lithography and produced on steam presses. Even as late as 1888 the great Ninth Edition of the *Encyclopaedia Britannica* was uncertain as to what term to use for the architecture, deciding at last, though hesitantly, on the non-committal phrase 'Pointed Architecture'.

Meanwhile, in 1835, an architectural historian

Decorated style (Angel Choir, Lincoln).

that William II, king of Sicily, has himself portrayed as a Byzantine emperor, while William I king of England is a home-spun Norman – despite these cultural differences, they were one race. In the words of the historian CH Haskins:

They did their work pre-eminently not as a people apart, but as a group of leaders and energisers, the little leaven that leaveneth the whole lump. Wherever they went, they showed a marvellous power of initiative and assimilation: if the initiative is more evident in England, the assimilation is more manifest in Sicily.

Scattered though they might have been, they retained their identity as 'Normans', so that the manifold influences flowed into one channel, in architecture producing that astonishing style called simply 'Norman'. It is a style which, at first glance, seems simply an expression of brutal strength, a style which the landscape historian Richard Muir likens accurately enough to the Nazi or the Stalinist. But it is one, too, with sudden extraordinary grace notes, such as the cool elegance of the nave of Norwich cathedral.

It was at Durham that, in the early decades of the twelfth century, some innovating mason took a step which, though simple in appearance, was to transform the whole world of architecture. Instead of making a curved arch, he sharpened the angle and brought into being the 'pointed arch'.

Romanesque builders had overcome the limitations of the barrel vault, which formed their round, shallow arches, by developing the cross vault. The substitution of panels of lighter masonry in the four triangular panels of the cross vault was a natural development, and the entire weight of the vault thus rested on ribs. But these, in their turn, still required massive, almost windowless walls to support them. The builders were still governed by the idea of orders rising one upon the other in order to achieve height – massive, enduring but still essentially earthy, the abiding characteristic of Norman work. The pointed arch, by contrast, took the weight of the vault straight down, to be supported by buttresses. It was as though sections had been cut out of the wall and placed at right angles to it, eliminating the appearance of solidity so that the building seems to be soaring up, weightless. The walls could now be pierced with

Perpendicular style (west front, Bath Abbey).

A capital of a column in the Norman crypt at Canterbury shows an extraordinary monster, a moustached winged creature holding a fish in its right hand, a figure more familiar in Byzantine than in European art. The carving hints at the mystery of the people we lump together under the title of 'Norman', and the blend of Oriental, Byzantine and Western European influences in their art is a summary of that people's achievement. The 'Norman Conquest' which, for the British, marks an epoch in their history was but one of several conquests. By the year 1098 the Normans were settled in the Middle East, at Antioch, throughout southern Italy and Sicily, as well as Normandy and England. But scattered though they were and influenced by such widely differing climates – so

Norman capital: Canterbury cathedral crypt.

more, and larger windows, flooding the interior with light which meant, in turn, that internal decorations could be far richer and more detailed.

The unknown mason in Durham was certainly not working in the dark. The pointed arch was one of the gifts of those Crusaders which, though utterly failing in their objective, were to alter the history of Europe by transmitting to it the genius of the Arabs. Certainly the idea of the pointed arch, travelling from the Middle East, had rooted itself in France in time for it to be adopted by Abbot Suger, the energetic, innovative man who, between 1132 and 1144, rebuilt the royal abbey of St Denis in the exciting new style. And here is a certain, if rare, instance of a cleric being truly the builder, for Suger recorded every detail of the work and its difficulties and triumphs in a vivid account that has an almost boyish excitement about it. He ran into difficulty with the construction of the towering new arches and breathlessly tells of the night of storm when it seemed that the work would come tumbling down. But the Arab mathematicians were vindicated, and the new arch stood the test though its mortar was still far from set.

After Durham the new style stood its fullest testing when William of Sens built the choir at Canterbury. Then, in 1175, the foundations were laid for the first purely English Gothic cathedral, the exquisite little cathedral church of St Andrew in Wells. Though one of the smaller of English cathedrals it dominated its host city, for even in the twentieth century Wells has a population of only 8,000 or so and the area covered by the cathedral and its ancillary buildings is about equivalent to the historic heart of the city itself. Bishop Reginald de Bohun is credited with the design of the building, and whether it was truly his work, or the inspired work of some unknown master mason, the plans were so detailed and fully developed that, though its construction extended over eighty-five years, and was not completed until 1260, the entire building is in one harmonious style. Much of this would be to the credit of the master mason, Adam Lock, whose powerful head is sculpted on the north wall of the nave. He died in 1229 and it is

Wells: the first purely 'English' cathedral.

therefore chronologically possible that he was indeed the original architect. The difference between Durham cathedral and Wells is the difference between two cultures: Durham overawes, Wells enchants with an atmosphere almost of gaiety, a delightful introduction of the style which would be known as Early English.

The building of Wells heralded two centuries of astonishing building activity throughout the country. One of the reasons that had tempted William the Conqueror to his adventure was that England was an extremely wealthy country and much of this wealth came into the hands of the Church. A substantial proportion of it was generated by wool but a lot, too, was the result of such humdrum activities as improved book-keeping, of the kind that Alan of Walsingham introduced at Ely, and more and more cathedrals and monasteries began

to run their estates direct, instead of fee-farming them. Salisbury's income nearly doubled in the thirteenth century. The new, so-called 'Decorated' style which began to supersede Early English in the middle of that century reflected the Church's exuberance and supreme self-confidence. It was now that the carver came into his own. The capitals of pillars became works of art; no longer were they simply stylized foliage, but now they were picture galleries in their own right, reflecting daily life. Stone window-traceries became filigrees, the windows themselves filled with immense areas of glass.

Then, in the following century; money grew tighter. The splendour of Decorated churches, a delight to posterity, was in fact a reflection of opulence and of arrogance which many found distasteful. The friars came into being, turning their back on the ostentation of monasteries and cathedrals, erecting their modest friaries and trudging on foot from town to town to preach the virtues of holy poverty. Money which would have gone to the embellishment of buildings was given to them for their work among the poor or for the building of parish churches. The economy of the country, too, began to stagnate. Between 1308 and 1340 the income of Durham cathedral declined from £4,526 to £1,931. Then, in 1348, came the appalling catastrophe of the Black Death when all life came to a standstill. When normality returned the mode had changed, the plainer 'Perpendicular' style ousting the exuberance of Decorated.

But through it all, the masons and their fellow craftsmen worked on. The master mason knew nothing of solid geometry, of blueprints, isometric drawings or any of the technical aids which the most humble builder of today instinctively draws upon. He posed and solved his problems in three-dimensional terms, making exquisitely detailed models for each part of the structure as work proceeded. His great problem was not labour but materials: in the fourteenth century population pressures forced rural workers into the cities and at Westminster for instance unskilled labourers formed fifty per cent of the workforce, but less than thirty-two per cent of the wage bill. There was no such easily tapped reservoir of materials. Where it was possible, existing buildings would be robbed and their material recycled; the almost total disappearance of Verulamium is attributable to the building of St Alban's cathedral. Elsewhere, the quarrying, shaping and transporting of the thousands of tons of stone required was a major operation, the responsibility for which lay at a higher level. Here the king might grant access to royal quarries; elsewhere the bishop, or some local lord desirous of obtaining heavenly merit, would arrange for the supply of stone. Again, where possible, quarries were opened up locally: the beautiful honey-coloured stone of Wells cathedral came from Doulting some six or seven miles away and the nearby Chilmark quarries supplied the distinctive stone for Salisbury. No such deposits of stone were available in East Anglia. Flint, the universal building material was not deemed suitable for Norwich cathedral and stone was brought from across the channel, from Caen, a canal being opened up from the river Yare up to the site.

A less obvious need, but one as vital, was the scores of thousands of feet of timber required for scaffolding and the frames for construction of

The fourteenth-century 'Great Wheel' still *in situ* in the tower of Salisbury.

arches and vaults. Later, builders would make a kind of cradle of the scaffold and erect their building within it. The master mason would have bankrupted himself before work started if this system had been adopted in earlier times. Then, the cathedral raised itself up by its own boot-straps. Scaffolding was built up to a certain height and then dismantled and re-erected on the wall itself, taking advantage of pre-arranged projections. The galleries that were built into the structure itself, either as part of the design or in anticipation of the never-ending task of inspection and maintenance, also discharged the function of scaffolding during construction.

Economy dictated that much of the building should be pre-fabricated. Stone was shaped in the quarries and the great beams were notched and

The spire of Salisbury, added thirty years after the completion of the cathedral,
threatened destruction of the tower under its 6,000 tons of weight.

Interior of Salisbury spire, showing the timber skeleton.

The spire of Norwich cathedral was also added after completion of the tower.

new-made roof as it was by its function, and enclosed by the projecting ribs of the vault, the removal of the framework without totally dismantling it was a complicated operation. One of the methods adopted was to stand the legs in drums of sand while the frame was being built. Plugs were pulled out of the drums when it was time to move the frame and, as the level of sand fell in the drum, so the whole structure descended until it was clear of the ribs.

A common hazaard of cathedrals was the collapse of the main tower. This was not so much the fault of the original builder as the impatience – or arrogance – of some later dean or bishop who wished to link his tenure of office with the building of some great tower or spire on foundations never intended to bear it. Spires and towers became an English characteristic in the fifteenth century. Norwich's spire appeared in the 1450s, Durham's great towers in 1465, Chester's in 1493. Canterbury doubled the height of the central tower in 1493 – a direct expression of a prelate's pride, for in that year Cardinal Morton got his hat. Usually, but not always, the ancient foundations stood the strain: sometimes it ended in disaster. The novelist, William Golding, took this hubris as the theme for his evocative novel, *The Spire*. In it the dean, overriding all technological and financial objections, has decreed that a spire shall be built on to their ancient cathedral. In the following conversation between the dean and the aged chancellor, emerges the difference between intention and reality, between practicality and the soaring ambition of a sedentary worker:

Opposite him, the other side of the model of the cathedral on the trestle table, stood the chancellor, his face dark with shadow over ancient pallor.

'I don't know, my Lord Dean. I don't know.'
He peered across the model of the spire, where Jocelin [the Dean] held it so firmly in both hands. His voice was bat-thin, and wandered vaguely into the large, high air of the chapter house.

'But if you consider that this small piece of wood – how long is it?'

'Eighteen inches, my Lord Chancellor.'

'Eighteen inches. Yes. Well. It represents, does it not, a construction of wood and stone and metal –'

'Four hundred feet high.'

made ready on the ground before being hoisted into place by windlass and pulley. Somewhere in the roof would be set the great wheel which discharged the function of crane: that in Salisbury still remains in the tower and was used until relatively recent times. Lacking the horizontal arm of a crane, the wheel could operate only on a radius of a few feet and had to be shifted every so often as the structure lengthened.

Prefabrication could not solve the problem of the length of time mortar took to set. A too-impatient builder could cause the collapse of the great vault: the ceiling of many cathedrals show here and there the tell-tale sag where the builder has removed the supporting framework before the mortar had completely set. The vault was constructed in sections, the massive framework being eased forward a little at a time. Jammed against the

Against all protests the dean succeeds in translating that eighteen-inch model into a towering structure weighing hundreds of tons, which brought sure disaster to all concerned, for it collapsed under its own weight.

Golding's novel was inspired by the story of the spire of Salisbury cathedral. That, admittedly, did not immediately end in disaster but the building was saved only by the ingenuity of later architects. Some thirty years after the cathedral was finished, in 1285, it was resolved to build the highest spire in England upon the tower. Eventually, the spire would reach a height of 404 feet, certainly the highest in the country and very nearly the tallest in Europe, that of Ulm alone exceeding it, at 530 feet. The actual design of the spire was practical. At the base of the tower, the walls are two feet thick but are shaved down to a bare nine inches as it ascends. The builders left the original stout scaffolding in as a brace, as well as the great wheel or treadmill used to hoist the building materials.

But the tower was never designed to support this additional 6,000 tons and the result can be seen by an untrained eye. The stone of the crossing upon which all rests has been warped out of shape by the enormous weight pressing down upon it, and immediately below the tower a datum mark has been placed in the pavement, showing the extent to which the spire was warped out of true. The builders had bequeathed a legacy of trouble to posterity that shows no signs of ending. In the fourteenth century, double or strainer arches were built at the entrance to the choir to prevent the pillars buckling in, and girder arches were added in the fifteenth century. Christopher Wren, Francis Price, George Gilbert Scott, all had a hand in strengthening spire or tower as the centuries advanced, each leaving his mark in the shape of iron tie-rods. Bronze rods were added in 1939, and in 1985 the cathedral announced a special appeal to deal with the perennial problem.

Wells had a similar problem when the central tower was increased in height in 1315. A few years afterwards the tower began to tilt westwards. (By standing at a certain position to the south of the cathedral it is possible to see the degree of tilt.) In 1338 large cracks began to appear. If the tower had collapsed it would have taken most of the nave and much of the choir with it. The solution gave Wells one of its most distinctive and beautiful features:

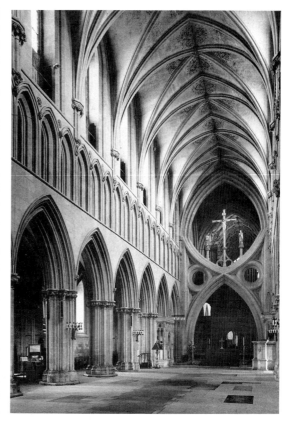

The 'scissor' arches at Wells were inserted to give added support to the tower after its height was increased.

scissor-shaped arches, rather like those at Salisbury, were built below the tower on three sides, the massive screen separating nave from choir acting as brace for the fourth side. The weight of the extension of the tower was not as great as the spire at Salisbury and the emergency work done in the 1340s has proved sufficient to check the danger.

One other frequent hazard was that of fire. Even in the twentieth century it is difficult to fight a roof fire in so enormous a building. Coventry cathedral was destroyed entirely by incendiary bombs in World War II, and an incendiary bomb can be smothered before it does any harm if it is tackled at an early stage. At Coventry, of course, the defences were swamped by the scale of the attack but at York in 1829, tremendous damage was done after a lunatic hid himself in the cathedral and at night after the cathedral was closed set alight its wooden structure. Again at York, in 1984, the roof of the

entire south transept was destroyed by fire following a presumed lightning strike.

If such devastation could be wrought upon buildings protected by modern equipment, how much more vulnerable were cathedrals until the nineteenth century. In the absence of water mains and high-pressure hoses, the only means of bringing water to the seat of the flame was laboriously, by sending buckets along a human chain. Access to the roofs of most cathedrals is by extraordinarily narrow and inconvenient stair-cases, whose steps are counted by the hundred, and along dark, low galleries. Even if a fire in these areas is discovered at an early stage, the possibility of extinguishing it with a succession of small buckets of water, each brought from a great distance, is remote. The surprise is not the frequency with which the cathedrals were attacked by fire, or the extent of the devastation, but the fact that any survived.

Although the art of glass-painting is largely French in origin, with its supreme culmination in the Sainte Chapell, York Minster possesses the world's largest area in stained glass. The design of the famous Five Sisters Window (*left*) is abstract in the restrained style known as grisaille while, by contrast, the immense Creation Window (*below*) is a riot of figures telling the Biblical story.

The mason provided the shape or shell of the building, in the Decorated period in particular enlivening it with a riot of figures, mythical and legendary, and everyday scenes. But, backing up the mason, filling in the details as it were, was an army of related craftsmen. Next to that of masonry, the art which most attracts attention is that of the glazier. The towering, glowing pictures in living colour that made an art form of the practical need to introduce light into the building, was the unique gift of Christianity to the world.

The use of coloured glass in windows was very ancient, but the combining of the two mediums of glass and enamel arose some time in the tenth century and reached its peak in the fifteenth century. Theophilus, a twelfth century monk and writer on art, specifically referred to glass-painting as being French in origin and, certainly, from an early period, identifiable schools of French glass-painters drew a luminous trail across Europe. The men who worked for Abbot Suger at St Denis, went on to Chartres, then to Angers and finally to York to create the earliest of the great windows of the Minster. Five hundred years earlier, the Venerable Bede had recorded that Benedict Biscop, abbot of Monkswearmouth, 'sent messengers to Gaul to fetch makers of glass till then unknown in England' and a few years later, in 709, Bishop Wilfrid of York repeated the invitation. But these 'workers in glass windows' were glass-makers: the trail of the glass-painters leads back to Limoges in France where, in 979, a colony of Venetian mosaic-workers had settled. They developed there the form of enamelwork known as *cloisonné*, in which strips of metal separate the areas to be filled with coloured enamel. The two techniques – the use of enamel and the use of metal strips to divide the areas – were the origins of the art.

The glass used was a special toughened substance which, for the greater part of its history, was produced in kilns in open country. The French called such glass *verre de fougère*, referring to the bracken or fern that was burnt to provide the necessary alkali. In England, the words *fougère* and *forêt* became confused and the glass was known as 'forest glass'. In its early period the glass was far from perfect, but these very imperfections increased the richness of the finished product as the light was deflected by the various angles of the imperfections. The colours were limited to the primaries and their composites – blue, red, yellow, green – and were produced by introducing different metals into the molten glass. The colours were called by the name of the precious stone which they most nearly resembled – red becoming ruby, green becoming emerald, blue becoming sapphire – a nomenclature still internationally used by the trade.

Theophilus describes in considerable detail the method of preparing a stained-glass window. A large, smooth board was whitewashed with a mixture of chalk and water which set into a glaze. Upon this the design was traced, the different colours being marked by letters. Sections of glass of the required colours were placed over a relevant part of the design, the outlines traced and the glass then cut to shape using a hot iron. The loose pieces of glass were then assembled and, upon this mosaic of coloured glass, the picture was painted.

The black or brown enamel used for the picture, though dull in itself, drew the coloured segments of the glass into a comprehensible whole. Theophilus meticulously describes the process of enamelling. To prepare the enamel itself:

Take copper beaten small, burn it in a little pipkin until it is entirely pulverised, then take pieces of green glass and sapphire paste and pound them separately between porphyry stones. Mix these ingredients together in the form of one-third green glass, one third copper powder, one-third sapphire paste. Grind them on the same stone with wine or urine and paint the glass with the utmost care.

Theophilus claimed that 'if you are diligent with your work, you can make the lights and shadows of draperies and of the human face in the same manner as in coloured glass'. The monochrome painting thus executed came to life when light passed through the glass, blending enamel and coloured glass into one whole. Dark lines had to be solid and heavy to stand up against the blaze of light: fingers were separated from each other by bands of enamel each as thick as a finger itself. After the painting, the glass was returned to the kiln and the enamel was fused on.

The next stage was that of leading. The artists of later centuries regarded the lead as a necessary nuisance, but those of the twelfth and thirteenth centuries employed its potential to the full. They saw it not simply as a device to hold the fragments together, but as an intrinsic part of the design, its solid blackness separating colours that would otherwise have mixed and blurred. The glazier used the lead to follow natural contours of the body or drapery so that it did not obtrude as a medium.

The ability to design and control huge areas of glass found its supreme expression in Paris in the Sainte Chapelle, built between 1245 and 1248 to house the Holy Thorn, a building which at first glance inside, seems to be composed almost entirely of glass, the massive supporting framework of stone seeming to melt into the general background. England has nothing quite so spectacular as this medieval 'crystal palace' but York, certainly, can show glasswork on an even greater scale. Seven years after the Sainte Chapelle the great Five Sisters window was constructed in the north transept of York, the harmony and balance of its components playing down the fact that each of the lancets is five feet wide and over fifty feet high: in other words, the window formed one complete wall of a building nearly thirty feet wide and four storeys high. But even this was surpassed a century later when the east end of the church was rebuilt. The then prevailing perpendicular style, with its emphasis on window spaces gave an immense area for the most important window in a church, that at the east. York had by then established its own highly skilled school of glass-workers but for this stupendous project the dean and chapter went outside it to find a man capable of solving both the technical and aesthetic problems involved. They chose a native of Coventry called John Thornton, a man who already had experience in the fashionable new style now called International at Oxford and Winchester, and they chose well. The famed Five Sisters window had been in the restrained style called grisaille – almost monochrome in colour – and with stylized figures. Thornton's east window blazes with colour and with a riot of figures telling a narrative story, with eighty-one scenes illustrating the Apocalypse. This, the largest single expanse of stained glass in the world is a technical tour de force, not least when considering the wind pressure that has steadily been exerted upon it for six centuries.

York, like most cathedrals, relied on foreign sources for its glass, native-produced glass being of an inferior quality, and though the material was heavy and fragile it was easily transported by water to within a few hundred yards of the site. Unlike much of the stone, and all of the superior glass, however, the timber used for the building was invariably a local product. The archaeologist, Richard Morris, points out that the Anglo-Saxon verb *getimbran*, to build and the noun *getimbro*, building, shows the overwhelming importance of timber before the Conquest. The work of masons and glaziers catches the attention in most cathedrals, but the probability is that carpenters far outnumbered them during the construction. It was they who designed the massive, but precisely accurate, supports which held the vaults in place until the mortar set; it was they who made the ceilings for the early cathedrals until the art of the mason allowed them to be made in stone (the ceiling at St Alban's is still composed of wood); it was they who designed the complex skeleton for the roof; and within the body of the cathedral itself, it is probable that, until the Reformation, theirs was the dominant art form, in quantity, at least. Elaborately carved stalls and screens were an easier target for fanatical iconoclasts than hard stone towering high in the air and, unlike aristocratic stone, timber could be rapidly utilized for a number of domestic purposes of a humble nature. It has been calculated that perhaps little more than ten per cent of non-structural woodwork survived the Reformation, and the prodigality of woodwork in a medieval cathedral probably accounts for the frequency and devastating nature of fires.

It is by one of the ironies of history that Manchester cathedral, situated in the heart of dissenting country, should have preserved almost intact its rich legacy of woodwork. It has not always been valued. As late as 1910 Filson Young, writing in *The Manchester Guardian* asked rhetorically: 'Do Manchester people really know and love their beautiful old Collegiate Church as the inhabitants of other cathedral cities know and love theirs?' 'I think not,' was his resounding answer to his own question.

It seems to me always, as the great tides go roaring for ever by and round it to stand there on Hunt's Bank as on an island, grey and sad and isolated in the mist and rain, calling with the voice of the departed centuries to men whose ears are filled with other sounds. But it would surely be well for Manchester if it brought up its succeeding generations to know and reverence the fine old building with its incomparable woodwork, the carved and painted glories of its choir, its ancient, misty chapels....

The great tides roar even louder round the cathedral today, a lethal traffic system having cut it off physically even more from its host city, but its interior is now recognized for what it is, a remarkable survival of a remarkable art form.

English woodcarving achieved its apogee in the fifteenth and early sixteenth centuries, and it is perhaps significant that Manchester's cathedral was a parish church until 1421. In other words, at precisely the time that woodcarving was achieving maturity, the building was benefiting from that swing away from the majestic but remote cathedral towards the parish church. It was promoted to the status of a collegiate church in 1421 and the following year complete rebuilding was begun. It became a cathedral in 1847 and a series of disastrously drastic 'restorations' were put in hand, but fortunately these were mostly confined to the stonework. The superb woodwork, particularly that of the choir, remains virtually as it was completed between 1485 and 1506.

Collegiate churches vary greatly and that of Manchester's was, in essence, a chantry college established to pray for the souls of a number of distinguished people, among them Henry V. To do this, it needed a permanent staff, or foundation, consisting of a warden, six fellow priests, four clerks and six lay choristers. The 'furniture' of the choir enclosed them from the world, assisted them in their tasks by providing desks, and gave some little comfort by enclosing them in stalls, provided with seats and canopied to reduce the draughts. The entire scheme was planned as a unit, under the direction, if not necessarily to the design of, the first warden, James Stanley. The fact that his step-mother was the mother of the reigning monarch, Henry VII, goes a long way to explain the magnificence of this work, conceived on so splendid a scale that the choir which had been so recently completed was drastically altered and widened in order to accommodate the furniture. In addition to the great screen separating nave from choir, there were sixteen other screens, of which the most notable is that in front of the Lady Chapel. This was first savaged by the Cromwellians and then by the scarcely less ruthless 'restorers' of the

Carved angel, Manchester cathedral.

nineteenth century, but sufficient remains to show its remarkable nature, in particular the delicate little statues adorning the front. Their faces and hands, where projecting, have been hacked off but because they were built as an integral part of the screen the figures survived. And high up in the nave roof, beyond the reach of all but the most dedicated vandal is the angel choir. Each figure is nearly three feet in length and shows a winged angel playing a musical instrument whose details both throw light on the actual forms of now obsolete musical instruments, and the way in which they were played.

So vast a project as a cathedral made it possible to establish on site specialist trades for the particular use of the building. Among these were the metalworkers, producing huge quantities of nails, ties, collars and the many other metal objects used to construct a building. But they produced, too, a considerable quantity of ornamental work which tends to be overlooked, or accepted by the casual observer as being modern work: the hammered iron grill at the base of Duke Humphrey's chantry in St Alban's was made in 1275, belying its extraordinarily modern appearance. The iron-work of the grill of St Anselm's chapel in Canterbury does not look quite so pristine but this, too, is of great age, being completed about fifty years after that at St Alban's. On site, too, would be the bellfounders. This was one of the most testing of all crafts for a large bell that represented a substantial financial investment could be ruined by careless handling. Bellfounders, like masons, tended to be itinerants, setting up shop for greater or lesser periods in or near the mason's yard, and then moving on once their commission was completed.

The builders and decorators of a cathedral were like members of a symphony orchestra, or members of a team assembling some gigantic mosaic. Behind the exuberant detail, behind the personal expressions made in stone or glass or wood by mason or glazier or carpenter, there lay an intellectual pattern for a specific purpose. 'Simple and unlettered souls find in the church what they cannot know through books', the international Synod of Arras pronounced. 'They see it in the plan.' The cathedral was, quite literally, the Bible of the poor. The wealthy had their books of hours in which God's plan for man was shown in gold and lapis-lazuli: for the poor, the blaze of painted glass, the endless ranks of three-dimensional stone or wooden pictures performed the same task, providing for earthbound man a mirror of eternity.

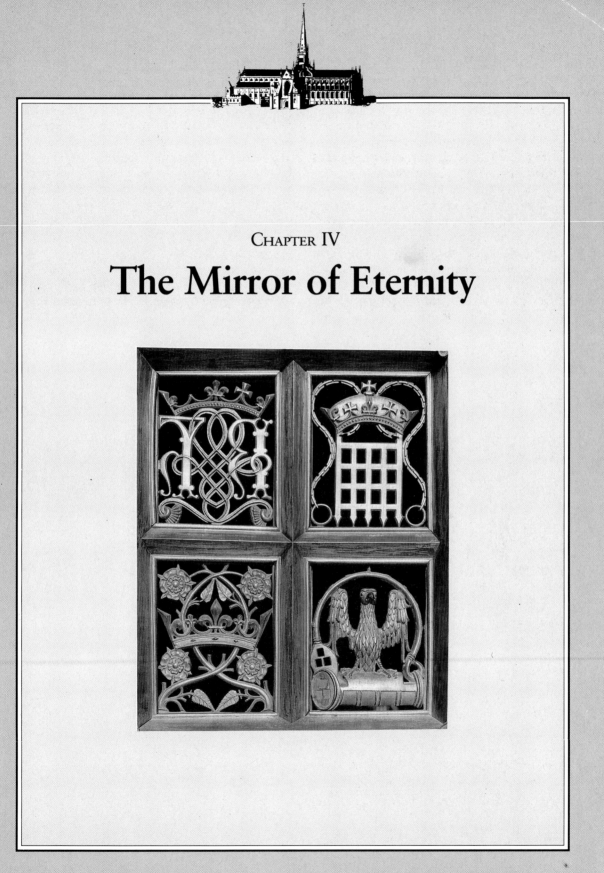

# CHAPTER IV

# The Mirror of Eternity

The central symbols of the Christian Church retain their potency even into the present century. The most casual, most irreligious tourist of European origins is well aware of the significance of the cruciform shape of the building itself. The dominant figures of the Christian faith are immediately and permanently identifiable: Christ cannot be mistaken among a group of figures; Peter will be recognized by his keys; the significance of Madonna and Child will remain unchanged as long as Christianity endures. From the Old Testament the symbols of Creation – Adam, Eve, tree, serpent – remain as immediately familiar in significance as the modern symbols of traffic lights or advertisements. Around these central symbols lie scattered other figures, minor or even mythical, which retain a recognized identity through some quirk of popularity: Jonah and the whale, St Christopher, Noah.

But these recognizable and readily identifiable symbols are, as it were, only the topmost leaves of a forest, much of which now defies interpretation. But it is probable, too, that much of the symbolism remained a mystery even to the contemporaries of those who created it. In Canterbury cathedral there still exists a scroll explaining the so-called 'Theological Windows' of the choir aisles, presumably originally hung beneath the windows to explain their complex story. The twentieth century, with its emphasis on the individual and, in particular, on the role of the individual artist, has an additional barrier through lack of understanding of the artists' motivation. The creator of the stained-glass windows and of the sculptures neither expected nor desired freedom in the modern sense. His approach was analogous to the role of an actor in a classical drama. No one expects a modern Hamlet to introduce new lines, or a new ending to the play: the course of the drama is utterly predictable in every performance, the actor's skill lying in the interpretation of detail. In the same way, the medieval artist was strictly limited by a tradition which had become sacred: each saint had to have his or her immediately recognizable attributes and even the colour of robes was specified. But, working within these ordained limits, the medieval artist produced work which is not noticeably inferior to many thousands of productions whose creators are conscribed only by their talent.

Few examples of medieval iconography have been subjected to so long, and so detailed a study as the incomparable west front of Wells cathedral. From 1655, when William Dugdale made the first authentic record of the still untouched front in his *Monasticon Anglicanum*, to 1985, when the reigning dean analysed the iconography as guide to the massive scheme of restoration, it has stood as the supreme example of fourteenth-century sculptural art in Western Europe. And as Dr Pamela Tudor-Craig remarked in her own study of the sculpture, 'It has long been recognised that the early to mid-thirteenth century stands to Gothic art as the Parthenon stands to Greek.'

The west front of Wells cathedral consists, in effect, of an immense screen twice as broad as it is high in which even the great west door is rendered insignificant, a mere break in the exuberance of

The west front of Wells cathedral has been described as the most important gallery of thirteenth century sculpture in Europe. Its iconography has been subjected to exhaustive study, but though most of the figures are obviously based upon living models, none have been identified. A general view (*opposite*) shows the astonishing wealth of subject while *above* shows in detail one of the figures, a deacon.

The fifty misericords in Exeter cathedral form the most complete surviving set in Britain. The three here display the immense range of subjects. They include one of the earliest known portrayals of an elephant. The extraordinary man-headed creature is a locust as described in the Apocalypse, while the Knight of the Swan illustrates a popular contemporary romance.

sculpture. But it is a controlled exuberance and though many hands were obviously at work – some of them men who would have been famous sculptors if they had lived in a world that identified its artists – their work fitted into an overall design. The designer of this screen or frame was probably Thomas Norreys, the master mason who took over on the death of Adam Lock in 1229. The work took some thirty years, between 1230 and 1260, and the mere statistical detail is overwhelming. There were 176 life-size statues, forty-nine Biblical scenes, eighty-five panels of a resurrection frieze, almost full-size statues of the apostles and archangels, quite apart from a riot of foliage and the formality of pedestals and canopies for the major figures. Altogether, there are 384 separate, identifiable works of sculpture, of which a very high proportion would be described as formal works of art if detached from their architectural background and viewed in isolation. The sculptors' skill with stone is little short of astonishing: the thin material of a fourteenth-century wimple as it lies on a woman's cheek provides the illusion of transparency; draperies flow, suggesting, not concealing, the human form behind. The figures – particularly those of real-life people – are frozen in lively action: a lady toys with the catch of her elegant cloak; a king leans forward energetically from his throne, left arm crooked impatiently, head bent with a frown of concentration. On the north side – the side facing the dark, cold, pagan northern world – are a row of sombre knights, each over seven foot tall, every link in their chainmail detailed, the eyes behind the great barrel-helm coldly glaring out. One of them has evidently been painted a chocolate colour and the face is distinctly negroid: he is probably St Maurice, the martyred Commander of the Theban Legion who is traditionally portrayed as an African. Biblical and mythological scenes are sculpted with the same loving attention to realistic detail: Noah building his Ark is an industrious Somerset carpenter; ecclesiastics are portrayed with every detail of their clerical garb; Eve spins with a fourteenth-century distaff in a manner taken from the life, for in her left hand she holds a mass of wool or flax and her right hand is stretched behind her as if twisting the thread with the spindle hanging from her finger; Adam, wearing only breeches rolled up to the knee, energetically digs. The sculptor, probably a local man and thus aware

of the wells and springs which have given the town its name and fortune, has made Adam strike a spring so that water is gushing from beneath the spade.

It is in this extraordinary admixture of the realistic and the fanciful, of fourteenth-century English people and Biblical allegory, that the west front of Wells cathedral can stand as an epitome of the whole vast and complex field of medieval iconography. From time to time attempts, more or less confident, have been made to identify the figures with historical characters. There was a legend that a key to the identification actually existed until the sixteenth century when Polydore Vergil, the archdeacon of Wells whose *History* of England has become one of our major sources of knowledge about Tudor England, destroyed it in a fit of jealousy. He was supposed to have 'committed as many of our ancient and manuscript historians to the flames as would have filled a wagon, that the faults of his own work might pass undiscovered', but this is all part of the small-arms fire of scholastic controversy. A nineteenth-century Royal Academician, C R Cockerell, published a work confidently identifying all the major figures: Pamela Tudor-Craig, a twentieth-century scholar, austerely dismisses the work: 'the plates, like the text, are imaginative'. It is impossible to doubt that there were living, human models for the gallery of observers and witnesses, for the deacons and ladies and kings and knights ranged below the great figure of the Christ in Majesty. The gently smiling Lady, with an expression as enigmatic as the Mona Lisa and known only as No 183; the supercilious deacon known as No 323; the rather skittish 'Young Queen' at No 198 – all must have stood in living, breathing form before the sculptor. But who they were, or where their bones now lie, no one will ever know.

The whole of Wells west front trembles on that borderline between real world and dream world that is one of the hall-marks of the fourteenth century. But the tendency continued throughout the Middle Ages, is to be found expressed in every church, and finds its most remarkable form, both in situation and in expression, in the decoration of those tip-up seats known as misericords. For, no matter how complex was the gallery of such a concept as Wells west front, it related to religion, whereas the iconography of the misericord paid only the most casual and offhand of salutes to the Bible. It was preoccupied not simply with everyday life, but everday life of the most down-to-earth kind, not infrequently approaching the obscene or the actually pornographic. In contemplating the undoubted art of the misericord – and some of the carvers achieved miracles of expression in impossibly cramped circumstances – posterity is made aware, more than in any other art form, of the gap between medieval and modern man.

The misericord permitted the monk or other participant in a lengthy ceremony to take the weight off his feet while being, technically, in a standing position. This simple fact established the shape in which the carver would have to fit his work. The front of the seat in its horizontal position terminated in a semi-circular bulge which, when the seat was placed in the vertical, became the ledge upon which the occupant could rest. The design was carved below this ledge or bulge, sometimes incorporating it. Even in a cathedral or church equipped with modern lighting, it is difficult to make out the details of a misericord. In addition,

The cathedral as theatrical stage: the aisle at Durham, designed for the progress of processions.

they are always in a cramped and awkward situation and to inspect them it is necessary to crouch down with one's back wedged against the back of the stall in front of the stall being inspected. The carver of a misericord, therefore, proceeded in the knowledge that few, if any, people could, or would, bother ever to inspect his work. This fact therefore at once explains the remarkable freedom of some of the work – and throws into deepest, impenetrable darkness the answers to why it was done and who paid for it. Contemplating them, one feels some sympathy for the old, romantic notion of the medieval workman working solely for 'the greater glory of God' as a possible explanation for their existence, though it is difficult to see just how God was supposed to be glorified in some of the depictions.

The fifty misericords in Exeter cathedral are the oldest, known complete set in Britain, carved some time between 1230 and 1260 and possibly all from the hand of the same carver. The stalls were mutilated in the late seventeenth century to fit into their present position but the actual carvings were spared and their variations, ranging from formal decorations to lively portrayals of monsters reflect the bizarre world of the misericord carver. Here is one of the earliest representations of an elephant – surprisingly accurate: the carver was almost certainly working from memory and may very well have seen the elephant which Louis IX gave to Henry III in 1255. But here, too, is an extraordinary creature – a human figure on all fours, though with hooves instead of feet, with a tail which terminates in a snake's head and is saddled. Improbably enough, this would appear to be a representation of a locust – to be exact, a locust as described in the Book of Revelation: 'The locusts looked like horses prepared for battle ... their faces resembled human faces ... they had tails and stings like scorpions'. The Devon carver made no bad job in interpreting the feverish imagination of the Hebrew prophet. His mermaid with a fish in each hand also has a marginally religious significance for it symbolized the soul gripped by earthly emotion; but in the depiction of the Knight of the Swan he

*Opposite*
The great west doorway of Canterbury, set in a gallery of sculptures.

Canterbury cathedral steps leading up to the long-vanished shrine of Thomas á Becket.

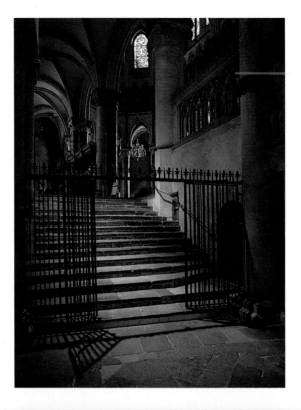

A hidden corner of the vast, rambling complex of Canterbury cathedral – a city within a city.

opted frankly for romance, for even a practical Devon man would have been familiar with the immensely popular twelfth-century romance, *Chevalier au Cygne*.

Manchester's misericords, like the rest of the woodwork, date from the mid-sixteenth century. And despite the three centuries that have elapsed between those of Exeter and of this northern church, hundreds of miles distant, the resemblance between the two is startling. The actual seats have become a little more elaborate, with a fluted edge given to the misericord ledge, but the carvings display the same phantasmagoric mixture. Here, again, is an elephant – not so well observed as that of Exeter's and bearing a castle, but in the same central position. At Exeter, a centaur is fighting a dragon: at Manchester two wild men (or 'wodehouses') are duelling, one mounted on a unicorn, the other on a camel. Manchester has a greater number of what can only be called illustrated folk-tales, many with animal heroes. The fox is a particular favourite, whether portrayed stealing the farmwife's goose or teaching its young; monkeys rifle a peddler's pack while he is wrapped in sleep; a sow dances on her hind legs playing the pipes while her litter dances beside her. The carver here has displayed very considerable skill in handling perspective, with the piglets lined up before the trough in the foreground while their mother struts in front of the sty which is receding into the background. This carver, or his colleagues, is particularly skilful in creating a miniature world beneath the misericord ledge: a woman scolds her husband who scurries away from her, while the pot of liquid which he has dropped, and which has aroused her displeasure, spills down the seat. A complete tavern scene features on one of the misericords: the observer is looking down at an angle at two men playing backgammon, while in the background one woman makes pastry and another draws ale.

The scenes of domestic life are immediately understandable, but the monsters and animals, both domestic and wild have a didactic purpose. Even though the carver of the misericord was obviously interpreting very freely and personally, he too was following a definite guide. The guide, in his case, was an enormously popular type of manual called the bestiary and the bestiary, in turn, provides posterity with a guide – though a tantalizingly oblique guide – to the workings of the medieval mind.

A bestiary's purpose was twofold: to give some account of the natural world and of the creatures inhabiting it and to draw a moral. The moral purpose predominated, even though it meant stretching out the characteristics of a given animal into unrecognizable form, and it employed a kind of circular argument in which a purely symbolic meaning became a supposedly real characteristic, thus providing more symbols. It was argued, for instance, that the breath of a panther was so sweet that it attracted all other animals in the forest: in this it was like Christ whose sweetness attracts all men. The religious interpretation buttressed the imaginary characteristic until the existence of the sweet breath of the panther is proved by the fact that it resembles Christ. The evidence of the few men who might have had the leisure to smell the breath of an actual panther would have done little to weaken the chain of such logic.

The animals that rampage, crawl, walk, gallop or wriggle their way across countless misericords are all linked to the central Christian tenets by equally bizarre chains of argument. The hedgehog, a harmless enough creature, is typecast as the Devil because, at the time of the grape harvest, the animal shakes the vines and impales the fallen grapes upon his spines. Thus the Devil impales the souls of men at the harvest of death and bears them away. Similarly, the lion is not the obvious choice of animal to represent Christ, usually seen as the Lamb of God. But the lion is the king of beasts and therefore is deemed to resemble Christ the Judge and its every characteristic is expanded and dissected in parable. Its square, solid front and slim flanks are symbols of the human and divine characteristics of Christ. Its great claws are to take vengeance upon the Jews. It effaces its track with its tail – a symbol of the incarnation, when God, to cheat the Devil, became man in secret.

The unicorn, a universally popular symbol, is the centre of a remarkably complex piece of reasoning. It can be caught only by a virgin who bares her breast. The unicorn is God, the virgin is Mary and her bared breast the manifest Church. The curious implications of the parable – that man is the hunter, God the hunted and that the Deity became incarnate after the Christian Church was founded – are all acceptable in the homiletic cause. Some of

Shrines became the particular target of iconoclasts, partly through religious fanaticism, but also because their wealth of dedicated jewelry made them worthwhile plundering.
St Alban's (*above*) was smashed to pieces in the Reformation, but restored in the nineteenth century. The wooden structure behind it is the 'watching chamber'. *Right* shows a detail of this shrine while *opposite* is the shrine of St Cuthbert at Durham.

the zoological characteristics have obvious, if colourful, applications – and incidentally provide evidence of a very wide knowledge of places far distant from Europe, much less England. The beaver, which severs its testicles in order to escape the hunter is an admirable example of the holy hermit who triumphs over temptation. So, too, is the ostrich which hides in the sand each year on the rising of a certain star, forgetting its eggs: on the rising of the celestial star of faith the holy man abandons home and family and seeks the desert. Beneath the occupants of the choir stalls, carved in the oak of England, the theology of an Asiatic religion underwent perhaps its most bizarre transformation.

The Reformation killed, in England, one aspect of the Christian Church which linked it to the great religions of the past – the element of the theatrical. Viewed objectively, the sacrifice of the Mass was, itself, a species of ballet with ritual movements proceeding towards a climax. The mystery plays performed on farm carts in inn yards were simply a vocalized and vernacular form of the great drama of Christianity, which used the entire cathedral as its stage. On the west front of Wells cathedral, a little above the doorways, are a line of portholes behind which is a gallery. Here, singers were stationed during great festivals, answering in antiphony other singers stationed below, outside the cathedral. The holes are not visible in the rich carving so it would seem almost as though the great building was itself raising its voice in song to praise its Creator. The vast size of a cathedral was primarily to allow processions, themselves a form of drama consisting as they did of great concourses of clergy, each in his distinctive robes, followed by the laity, and the whole held together with music.

In Manchester cathedral the 'Angel Consort' in the nave roof was high above the reach of iconoclasts and so maintained for posterity a priceless record of contemporary musical instruments, for each angel, visible from the waist up, has a particular instrument and is shown actually playing it. There are twenty-five different instruments, some like the drum and the bagpipes quite familiar in appearance though certainly unlikely to appear today in any ecclesiastical choir, while others have now entirely disappeared, or entirely evolved in form: the clavicymbal has become the piano, the psaltery – plucked and not hammered – became the harpsichord. The splendidly named symphony would have been recognizable to Victorian children as the hurdy-gurdy, a species of miniature barrel organ. On the evidence of Manchester's Angel Consort, a fifteenth-century procession would have been richly, not to say raucously, musical. Drums thudding, trumpets braying, the portative organ adding its rich note to the plangent sound of harp and dulcimer, with the deeper oboe-sound of the shawn, the entire cathedral must have become one vast sounding-box, as the seemingly endless procession wound itself round and round before achieving its ostensible objective, the depositing of the celebrant at the altar.

Second in importance only to the high altar was the shrine of the patronal saint. The Christian preoccupation with the human body, both in contemplating the physical tortures inflicted upon martyrs while living and its speculative destinations after death, led to an extraordinary cult of relics with which posterity finds it somewhat hard to sympathize. Whatever one's opinion of the fanaticism of iconoclasts, it is difficult not to feel some sympathy for the measured disgust of Bishop Barlow who, in 1528, wrote to Thomas Cromwell describing certain relics which had come his way: 'The parcels of the reliques are these: two heedes [heads] of silver plate enclosing two rotten skulls studded with putrified clowtes; Item, two arme bones, and a worm-eaten boke covered with sylver plate.' Early in the history of Christianity, the canny Romans realized that there was good profit to be made from the dead bodies lying in their sacred soil and shipped them out to the gullible northerners in large quantities without enquiring too deeply into their exact provenance. The

Wayneflete and Gardiner's chantry chapel, Winchester.

Fox and Beaufort's chantry chapel, Winchester.

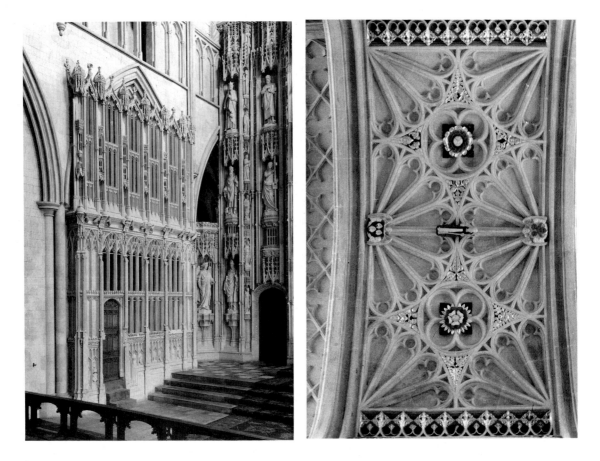

Chantry chapels: (*left*) Ramryge's, St Alban's; (*right*) vault of Nykke's chapel, Norwich.

opportunities for cheating were generous. That sturdy Christian, Geoffrey Chaucer, warned his compatriots in sprightly verse, with his portrait of the Pardoner peddling his sacred relics including 'our Lady's veil' and:

A gobbet of the sail
Thatte St Peter had whan that he went
Upon the sea, till Jesu Christ him bent ...

He carried with him, too, a glass of 'pigges bones' which would do service as the bones of this or that martyr. In 1535 one of Henry VIII's commissioners reported on one of these caches which he had uncovered:

Amongst the reliques we found moche vanitie and supersition, as the coles that St Laurence was tosted withall, the parings of St Edmund's naylles, ... divers skulls for the headache: peces of the holy crosse able to make a hole crosse of ....

But while English Christians would pay good money for a phial of the Virgin's milk or a feather of the Archangel Gabriel it was their own national martyrs and heroes who drew the largest crowds of pilgrims and, in doing so, contributed handsomely to their host church. Pre-eminent above all others was the cult and shrine of Thomas of Canterbury. Even as late as 1599, so sturdy a Protestant as the German Thomas Platter was aware of the significance of Canterbury even though Thomas's shrine had long since been plundered and destroyed and Platter thought that Becket was 'a Scotchman'. Pilgrims to the shrine followed an exactly worked out route, so great was the crush. They were met at one of the porches by a monk who arranged them 'every man according to his degree', sprinkled them with holy water and then led them to the site of the actual martyrdom, the Altar of the Sword Point. From there, they ascended steps (on their knees if

Henry VII's chantry chapel, Westminster.

physically possible) to the saint's chapel where the shrine reposed. A custodian first raised the wooden lid of the chest which actually held Becket's bones and then indicated, one by one, the jewels which encrusted the shrine, identifying their donors – evidently a high spot of the pilgrimage. About a generation before the shrine was destroyed a Venetian pilgrim described it (Becket was at least one English saint known to Continentals):

The magnificence of the tomb of St Thomas the Martyr is that which surpasses all belief. This, notwithstanding its great size, is entirely covered with gold but the gold is scarcely visible from the variety of precious stones with which it is studded. But everything is far surpassed by a ruby, not larger than a man's thumbnail, which is set to the right of the altar. The church is rather dark and particularly so where the shrine is placed and when we went to see it the sun was nearly gone down, and the weather was cloudy; yet I saw that ruby as well as if I had it in my hand.

From the shrine, the pilgrims would pass to the superb Corona Chapel which housed a bust known as *Caput Sancti Thome*. It held the top of Becket's skull which had been sliced off by one of his attackers, probably the knight Fitzurse, and the pilgrim would be invited to kiss the reliquary. As though this were not enough, at various stages the cathedral acquired other relics: the sardonic Erasmus and his friend Colet were offered the actual arm of St George – complete with flesh and blood upon it – to kiss, but declined. It was one of eleven arms the cathedral possessed, in addition to a piece of Christ's manger, another of His sepulchre and various parts of His garments.

All the major shrines had watching chambers, as much to place the rich offerings of pilgrims under surveillance as to do honour to the relic. Only two of these have survived, that of Christ Church, Oxford, and the magnificent two-storeyed structure of St Alban's. Built in 1400, the latter carries carvings depicting ordinary social life – rather reminiscent of misericord scenes – and the duty

Henry VII's chantry chapel, Westminster: detail of gate.

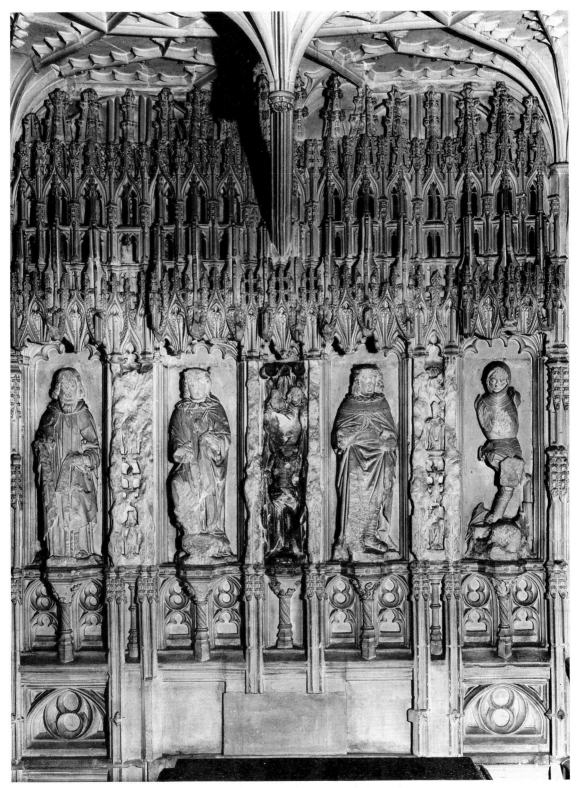

Prince Arthur's chantry chapel, Worcester.

monk would have sat in the upper half of the structure where he could oversee everyone entering the area. The shrine stood in the centre. Totally destroyed in the sixteenth century, the pedestal was painstakingly re-assembled in 1870 and appears now much as it would have done before its destruction. About eight feet high, it is carved with lively scenes of Alban's life and martydom and once would have been brightly coloured. Pilgrims placed their offerings in one of the four niches on each side and are believed to have thrust their hands into the holes along the base. These were said to have the power of healing. One of the wonder-working objects on view was a large Roman cameo, which almost certainly came from the ruined city of Verulamium, and was supposed to bring relief to women in childbirth.

The cathedral of Winchester, England's ancient capital, sheltered the remains of the Saxon bishop, Swithin, who was undoubtedly England's most popular – if actually uncanonized – saint, until his cult was overshadowed by that of Becket's. And where Becket's popularity was born of a political quarrel, exploited skillfully by the enemies of the king, Swithin's sprang from a genuine, grass-roots affection. He was born in 800 and so belonged to a generation destined to endure the full savagery of the Viking raids; even inland Winchester felt the fury of the Norsemen. Swithin acted as a father of his people. He was a statesman at the royal court but also aware enough of the plight of the common people to build the first bridge over the river Itchen in order to help the market folk – an act duly commemorated on the great screen behind the cathedral's high altar. At his death in 862 he asked to be buried among the humble folk he had always served – that is, in the common churchyard and not in the cathedral so glowingly described by the Saxon poet. In response to stories of miracles taking place around the grave, a century after his death his body was removed, or 'translated', into the Minster. The saint, apparently, objected to his wishes being overridden and caused rain to fall on the day of translation, 15 July, and for forty days thereafter, so beginning the legend of the effect of 'St Swithin's Day' upon the weather that has continued even into the twentieth-century. In due course his shrine was established in the Norman cathedral and, with that of Becket's established in Canterbury in the 1170s, provided a double pilgrimage very popular with continental visitors. Arriving at Southampton, they would go on to Winchester, make their offerings to Swithin's shrine and then, with the native pilgrims, travel along the so-called Pilgrims' Way (in reality a neolithic trackway) on to Canterbury and thence to Dover and so home.

The spiritual efficacy of a shrine (and, as a byproduct, its capacity for generating very earthly income for its custodians) depends upon the miracles wrought through its incumbent – and, in particular, upon miraculous cures of the chronically ill or crippled. Most shrines were prepared to accept claims for 'cures' at face value without enquiring too closely into the claimant's state of mind, but at Lincoln some attempt seems to have been made to establish a medico-ecclesiastical panel of the kind now established at Lourdes to check claims. The shrine was that of St Hugh of Avalon, the Frenchman who set about rebuilding the cathedral after its destruction by earthquake in 1185. And, unlike many an ecclesiastic credited with the 'building' of a cathedral, Hugh really did take personal, physical, part in the work. The hod with which he was supposed to have carried bricks as a common labourer became a sacred – indeed, a magical – object after his death, acquiring great significance for pilgrims to his shrine. The shrine was, curiously, in two halves, with the head of the saint kept in a silver reliquary in the superb Angel Choir, built as a memorial to Hugh. It was in the main structure of the shrine that cures were reputed to take place, the afflicted person bringing the affected part of his or her body as close to the shrine as possible – for instance by thrusting arm or leg through one of the holes – while reciting paternosters. On the occasion of a supposed cure, leading citizens of Lincoln were summoned to bear witness and, if necessary, to cross-examine the fortunate recipient of the miracle. On at least one occasion, the sub dean of the cathedral took the trouble to check with the person's home town that she really had been suffering from a supposedly incurable disease before coming to Lincoln.

The means of achieving cures seem dubious to say the least. The Venerable Bede records the

*Opposite*
Monument to Edward II, Gloucester.

procedure at the shrine of St Chad at Lichfield in unequivocal terms:

Chad's burial place is covered by a wooden tomb made in the form of a little house with an aperture in the wall through which those who visit it out of devotion may insert their hands and take out some of the dust. They mix this in water and give to to sick men or beasts to drink, by which means their ailment is completely relieved and they are returned to the longed-for joys of health ...

Or hastened on to their final end, must be the assessment of an objective mind. Chad's bones were destined to survive the destruction of his shrine, passing from hand to hand until the Catholic Restoration in the nineteenth century when they were at last housed in 1841 in the newly built Catholic cathedral of Birmingham.

The migrations of the remains of Durham's St Cuthbert were even more remarkable than Chad's, and were directly responsible for the founding of the cathedral. At his death in 687 Cuthbert was buried on Lindisfarne where miracles were immediately reported around the grave. Eleven years after his death, when the coffin was opened for some macabre religious purpose, the corpse was found in perfect condition – it had probably been mummified by the dry sand of the island, a fact which was to have considerable future significance. After the Danes raided the island in 794 the monks fled, taking the corpse with them together with other sacred items including the head of St Oswald and the Lindisfarne Gospels. They made their way eventually to Yorkshire and settled at Chester-le-Street where the saint's shrine gathered a remarkable collection of gifts over the 110 years it remained there. Again the Danes struck. Again, in 995, the monks moved on taking Cuthbert's remains with them, settling briefly at Ripon before coming eventually to a high bluff surrounded on three sides by the river Wear. Here, on this natural fortress, they finally settled and here in due course the great cathedral arose. In 1104, the body was moved into the splendid new shrine built for it – the eighth occasion it had been disturbed. The coffin was opened yet again and an extraordinary collection of objects disclosed for it appeared that, on each occasion that the coffin was opened in the past, something had been added. At one stage, indeed, a sacrist called Elfred Westou had

appointed himself the corpse's valet, trimming its hair and nails which he claimed continued to grow, changing its vestments and adding relics to the coffin – relics which included the authentic bones of the Venerable Bede as well as, eventually, the ivory comb Elfred himself used on the corpse's hair. It was, perhaps, this tradition of collecting relics around the major relic which accounted for the heterogenous jumble of objects which accumulated at the shrine over the following centuries. They included the elbow of St Christopher, yet another phial of the Virgin's milk, a piece of the True Cross together with a fragment of St Andrew's cross, a thorn from the Crown of Thorns, a griffin's egg and a fragment of the shirt of St John the Baptist, together with an immense collection of more conventional treasures in precious stones and metals.

At the Dissolution, when the shrine was destroyed, the corpse was found to be still intact and, in 1542, was buried on the site of the shrine. In 1827 it was yet again disturbed, ostensibly to kill a rumour that it had been moved during the reign of Mary Tudor. The excavators found three coffins: the upper was empty, the middle contained a miscellaneous collection of bones, the lower a complete skeleton together with an ivory comb (that they presumed to be the one used by Westou) and a pectoral cross known to have belonged to Cuthbert. This together with certain marks on the coffin which had been documented at the time of the 1104 translation, served to identify the remains. The cross and comb were removed (and are now on display in the cathedral treasury) and the skeleton reburied – only to be disturbed yet again when the grave was opened in 1899 for an anatomist to examine the bones. It is hard to imagine any other reason than idle and macabre curiosity for those pathetic remains had been 'examined' again and again over the centuries. They were, again, reburied and the grave sealed – presumably for ever.

The prestige bestowed upon a cathedral by a shrine was such that cathedral authorities would go to remarkable lengths to secure suitable relics. St Hugh of Lincoln, himself destined to become a relic, bit off two fingers from the supposed hand of Mary Magdalen when that relic was shown to him at Fecamp. In the crypt of York Minster is an imposing Roman coffin which held the remains of a bishop, St William, who was the centre of a cult after his canonization in 1227. This, almost certainly was due to the long feud between Canterbury and York. Becket's shrine had been launched into history just seven years earlier and the jealous canons of York promptly pressed for the exaltation of their own bishop, even though his life, though virtuous, had been undistinguished. His major claim to fame, indeed, seems to have been the negative one that he accepted his deposition with humility after a disputed election.

But St William of Lincoln had at least been a real person and his cult benign, whereas the Little Saint William whose shrine was established in Norwich after his supposed death in 1144 was purely mythical and his cult entirely malign. It was the product of one of the savage outbreaks of anti-Semitism and variants of the story of the boy 'martyr' are told in other places both in England and Germany, but only Norwich, lacking a respectable saint of its own, hastened to raise a shrine to him. The story first appears in the *Anglo-Saxon Chronicle*:

The Jews of Norwich bought a Christian child before Easter and pained him all the same pains our Lord suffered. On Good Friday they hung him on a cross because of his love for our Lord and afterwards buried him. They believed that it would be concealed, but our Lord revealed that he was a holy martyr. The monks took him, buried him solemnly in the minster and he made there for our Lord wondrous and manifold miracles. He is called St William ...

The story then developed with a wealth of detail, largely through the work of a monk, Thomas of Monmouth, who promoted the canonization through a hagiographical work *The Life and Miracles of St William*. The boy is identified as a twelve-year-old apprentice, lured by the Jews on promise of better employment. He was supposed to have been last seen alive entering the Jewish quarter near the castle and later a party of Jews are discovered with his body in a sack. The body is buried, the Jews are accused, miracles begin to happen and the cult is born. The evil little myth was strongly rooted, a version of it appearing in Nazi Germany in the 1930s. But Norwich has long since cleaned itself, the place where the shrine was housed now known simply as the Jesus Chapel, an attractive chamber but with no outstanding characteristics.

The saint's shrine posited a belief in a personal survival after death with the identified saint either interceding with the Creator in Heaven, or directly affecting the course of nature on earth. Chantry chapels owed their establishment to a similar belief, but where the incumbent of a saint's shrine was supposed to have gone direct to his eternal reward, the future in the hereafter of the incumbent of a chantry chapel was held to be so problematical that the chantry was established precisely to improve his chances by 'singing for his soul'. The founder — usually the incumbent — endowed a chantry priest or priests to sing 'soul masses' either in perpetuity or on a carefully planned system in the chantry chapel set aside for the purpose. Reading some of the wills setting up a chantry, one receives the irresistible impression of a planned assault upon heaven with so many scores or hundreds of masses, backed up by so many thousands of paternosters, hurled into the empyrean like so much artillery fire.

From its earliest days, the Christian Church had always held that 'It is a holy and a wholesome thought to pray for the souls of the dead'. In England in the thirteenth-century, however, this pious injunction became what can only be described as a major industry: in Lincoln cathedral there was one chantry chapel in 1290, but by the time of the *Valor Ecclesiasticus* in 1535 the number had grown to 36. Their number drastically altered the shape of ancient buildings, filling in bays that were intended to be viewed in perspective: at Manchester the chapels flank both nave and choir down the length of the cathedral. The old parish church of St Michael in Coventry, destined to become a cathedral in 1918, bears a similar picture. In both cases, these chapels were mostly guild chapels — corporate means of ensuring entry to heaven for people who were not financially able to build their own, personal chapel. In most other cases, however, the chantry chapels were not simply for important people, but for important ecclesiastical people: 19 of the 25 chapels in Salisbury were for ecclesiastics. Given that the whole purpose of a chantry was to secure forgiveness for the sins of the incumbent, it occurs to the observer that many must have been self-defeating both in their opulence and their arrogance: at Winchester, Bishops Gardiner and

Fox haughtily shouldered aside the common people come to the shrine of St Swithin, fencing it around with their chantries. Chantries diverted money not only from secular purposes but from the cathedral itself, more and more rich men preferring to set up chantries for their personal salvation instead of contributing to the overall good of the cathedral.

But they are, almost without exception, exquisite works of art, stone filigrees that conjure up the image of frozen music.

Between 1235, when the first recorded chantry was established in Lincoln cathedral, and 1547, when the last was built in a small country church, over 2,000 chantries were established. The Black Death of 1348 undoubtedly accelerated the trend, and in the more popular cathedrals there developed a species of traffic jam with perhaps dozens of chantry priests each anxious to say his mass and discharge his obligations for the day. Few people had anything good to say about chantry priests, most of whom led enviably indolent lives, certainly when compared with the life of an ordinary parish priest. Chaucer, with that beady eye of his, singled them out, holding up to scorn the parson who:

... left his sheepe accombred in the mire
And ran unto London unto Saint Paules
To seeken him a chantrie for souls ...

They became notorious for their lackadaisical and dissolute ways, perfunctorily discharging the light duties laid upon them – and sometimes not even doing that. Bishop Goldwell of Norwich sternly reminded them that they were charged with one of the most sacred tasks of all, administering the wishes of a dead man:

Seeing that a man's last will hath the force of law we therefore do strictly enjoin upon you that all foundations of obits and chantries for dead men be kept according to the force, form and effect of the original foundation ... Against all who contravene this we will fulminate the severest penalties reserving to ourselves the power of absolution therefrom or relaxation.

Bishop Goldwell perhaps had a personal interest in ensuring that chantry bequests were honoured, being about to establish his own chapel in the cathedral, but his complaint is echoed again and again from both lay and ecclesiastical sources. The

Lord Mayor of London complained to the dean and chapter of St Paul's that, despite the fact that much property in London had been bequeathed to finance chantries in the cathedral, 'We do see daily with our own eyes when we pass by your church of St Paul's that there are but few chaplains to sing there in proportion to the chantries which in the said church have been founded'.

The favourite place for the building of a chantry chapel was as near as possible to a saint's shrine or, in the absence of such a feature, the high altar. In its simplest form, the chapel was merely an adapted bay, or built between two buttresses of an aisle. In its most advanced form it was a miniature church, complete with its own altar, as with Prince Arthur's chapel in Worcester cathedral. Abbot Ramryge's chapel in St Alban's was actually two-storeyed with the upper floor used for a choir. The furnishings of a chapel could be as elaborate as any parish church. Thus, the two priests who served the chapel of Roger of Waltham in St Paul's had an extraordinary variety of equipment: two pairs of vestments – which included albs, amices, stoles and maniples, some of gold cloth, some of silk; a gold altar frontal; massive silver chalice and pattern; hand towels, cruets, bells, missal, even a brazier to ensure their comfort on a cold day.

The chapels of the kings outshone in splendour even those of abbots. Richard III planned an immense chantry in York Minster which would have occupied a very substantial part of the building for it was intended to have six altars served by no less than a hundred priests. Richard's death in battle at Bosworth put an end to the plan but his conqueror, Henry VII, had leisure to plan, and actually begin, what would be the most sumptuous of all chantry chapels, that in Westminster Abbey. It was virtually a monastery within a monastery with its own establishment, and all but physically separated from the main body of the building. Henry even planned a chantry within a chantry, because he ordered that a chantry tomb for his uncle, Henry VI, should be installed in one of the chapels radiating off the main structure. He died before he could bring the entire plan to fulfilment and though he left a rich endowment, together with the most minute instructions as to the completion of the building, his son Henry VIII fulfilled only part. Henry VI's tomb never came into being, but young King Hal did honour his

Black Prince's effigy, Canterbury.

father's memory sufficiently to commission Pietro Torrigiano to create the effigies of his parents in brass, so creating what has been described as 'the greatest portrait sculptures ever wrought in England'.

Chantry priests were attached to, but were quite distinct from, their host cathedral and bishops frequently thought it advizable to make the distinction physical by establishing colleges for the chantry priests. A college for fourteen priests was established in Wells by 1400, but undoubtedly the grandest of all was that of St William's in York, established in 1461 for twenty-four priests. The beautiful building around its quadrangle is today one of the city's major historical monuments but still maintains its connection with the minster, discharging the role of Church House for the diocese.

The frequency, duration, and elaboration of a soul mass was precisely related to the size of the financial endowment. One of the most lavish of all times was that provided by Edward I for his beloved queen, Eleanor. The Eleanor Crosses came into being to mark where her body had rested on its journey from Hardevy in Nottingham to London;

chantries were provided at each point culminating in a tremendous commemorative service at Westminster – and one which the king decreed was to be repeated in perpetuity granting the abbey twenty-two manors for the purpose. An indication of the size of the annual service is provided by the prodigal provision of that great luxury, wax candles – no less than 100 of them, each of twelve pounds weight. Throughout the year, thirty great candles were kept on the queen's tomb, two of them burning day and night.

Chantries felt the full onslaught of iconoclasts and, apart from the loss of architectural beauty, it is difficult not to feel some sympathy with the reformers. The point that the Lord Mayor of London made to the dean of St Paul's – that a large number of 'tenements and rents' were earmarked for the support of chantries – became in time a very real burden of complaint. More and more of the country's wealth was tied up, not for the good of the community as a whole but for the purely selfish desire of a rich man to ensure his own, personal, salvation. There was a certain spin-off: many chantries had almshouses or hospitals attached to them, the recipients of the charities paying for their accommodation by saying so many prayers according to a carefully worked-out schedule. (The 'bedesmen' of Sir Robert Marney were obliged to say five paternosters, five aves, one creed and hear Mass in his chapel, repeat the performance before his tomb and repeat it once more kneeling at their own bedside at nightfall.) But the bulk of the endowments were consumed by the chantry priests themselves, either in legitimate performance of their duties or for their own benefits. By the end of the fourteenth-century chantries were absorbing so much of the revenue of lands given to the Church – which themselves formed a substantial part of the national economy – that, in 1289, the Crown promulgated the Statute of Mortmain. Its purpose was to control the passing of lands and rents into, literally, a 'dead hand' and as such directly affected the establishment of chantries. Thereafter, before a chantry could be endowed it had to be shown that the king's revenue, at least, would not suffer. The Statute seems to have had little effect upon the proliferation of chantries in the next century and it was not until the coming of the reformer, with a Bible in one hand and a sledgehammer in the other, that the cult came to an end.

A twentieth-century visitor transported back in time to a cathedral before the Reformation would probably be startled by one dominant characteristic: that of colour. The whitewash brush of the iconoclast was accompanied or followed by the ravages of time itself; this was, in its turn, followed by the neglect of the clergy and finally by the sensitivity – perhaps the too great sensitivity – of the restorer and conservationist. The twentieth century, as much at the mercy of its own trends and inclinations as any other period, favours the appearance of the original stone. As a result, our cathedrals present a cool, sober, sometimes sombre appearance whereas their designers intended them to have a lively, if not a garish, display of colour. Even when colour was not directly employed, the builders were frequently desirous of covering the naked stone with plaster. At York and at St Alban's in certain protected areas can be seen the kind of stucco finish usually associated with eighteenth- and nineteenth-century private homes. The builders covered the original rough stone with plaster and then carefully drew lines upon it to give the appearance of impressive stone blocks.

It is difficult to comprehend the dramatic appearance the cathedral would have presented when fully robed in colour. During the 1980s' restoration of the west front of Wells it was confirmed that this enormous screen would have indeed been a blaze of colour: angels robed in red or yellow, arising from white clouds and backed by blue sky; ladies whose flowing robes would be picked out in their fashionable colours thus identifying each garment; knights in metallic silver; flowers in red or green or blue or yellow. The carvings on the front would have stood out with remarkable clarity in particular when the westering sun shone full upon them. At St Alban's sufficient of the original ceiling colouring in green and red remained to allow the ceiling boards to be reproduced in full colour during a recent restoration.

Most restorers still avoid the controversial repainting of major areas. In recent years, however, there has been a tendency to restore the colours on funerary monuments, most of which have retained some part at least of their original pigmentation. Southwark cathedral has transformed itself in this manner and some of the monuments have achieved a startlingly lifelike effect. The sour, disapproving expression of John Trehearne's wife contrasts dramatically with the monument's pious purpose; John Gower's monument is of an almost fairground garishness. In Canterbury, the Victorians actually daubed black paint all over the superb copper-gilt effigy of the Black Prince – an extreme and disastrous form of the romanticizing of history. It was only an accidental discovery, made when the paint was scraped off, that led to the gleaming restoration of the monument in the 1930s. The dean and chapter have carried this approach to its logical – if controversial – end by hanging up over the Prince's tomb replicas of his surcoat, helmet and gauntlets, all in the strident colours of heraldry, while placing the time-worn replicas in a cabinet nearby. In contrast is the undoubtedly authentic colouring of the tomb of Archbishop Henry Chichele in the north choir aisle of the cathedral. The tomb is restored every fifty years by Chichele's Oxford foundation, All Soul's College. It was last done in 1947, is due to be done again in 1997 and, allowing for the change in the composition of pigments, looks now as it did when it was completed – under Chichele's personal direction – in 1425.

*Above*
The west front of Wells. Originally this would have been
brightly painted, with every figure picked out.

*Overleaf*
Some of the 384 figures on the west front of Wells. David
Wynne's newly sculptured 'Christ in Majesty' is just visible at
the top, flanked by cherubim that have also been recently
sculpted.

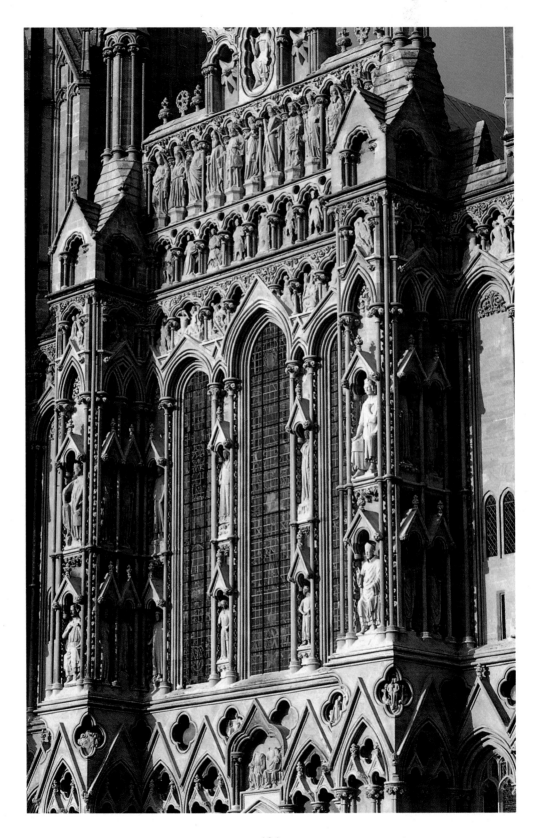

CHAPTER V

# Battle of the Bishops

We may, in the twelfth century, consider the Chapter and the Bishop together as an intellectual centre – rich, powerful, well-educated and always established in an urban community rather than in the rural isolation of most of the monasteries. The cathedral library, the cathedral school, the cathedral archives, the *gesta* of its bishops, the writings of its canons, the bishop's jurisdiction, the bishop's patronage of learning, play a large part in this age, intermediate between the monastery on the one hand and the princely courts on the other ...

Thus wrote the historian CH Haskins in his epochal study *The Renaissance of the Twelfth Century*. By the end of that century, the 'shape' of the cathedral, both in its physical and social sense, was established. As with all institutions, it would change a lot over the following centuries, the social

Lambeth Palace gatehouse, London.

side waxing and waning, responding obediently to changes in society, being itself an integral part of that society, even as its physical shape would change in response to changing fashions. But it would remain, always, instantly identifiable, just as an oak tree will change over the seasons and over the years yet always, instantly, be identifiable. The vast building set in its close, with its ancillary buildings – palace and deanery, chapter house, school, gatehouse, mellowing over the centuries even as its clergy became ever more integrated with its community, forming at last the proud heart of the most ancient and beautiful cities of the land. Quintessentially English.

Quintessentially English? In 1713, Christopher Wren made that bold leap of his, tracing the origins of Gothic, that 'quintessentially European' art form, to the architecture of the Middle East – specifically, the pointed arch evolved by the Saracens. Three centuries later, the architectural historian John Harvey made an even bolder leap,

tracing the origins of the entire cathedral complex, that flowering of Christian art, to the fiercest of all enemies of Christianity – Islam. He brings forward as evidence the contemporary account of the activities of Geoffrey de Montbray, bishop of Coutances in Normandy. According to the chronicler, Geoffrey made a pilgrimage to southern Italy sometime about the year 1050 to study at source the remarkable civilization that had come into being when the Norman conquerors of Sicily came in contact with the Saracens. The two cultures had fused, creating a wholly unique third, inspiring Bishop Geoffrey to emulation. On his return to Coutances:

... He brought from William the most glorious duke of the Normans, afterward also the most glorious king of the English the better half of the city suburbs ... He built the bishop's hall and other offices and planted a considerable coppice and vineyard. He also made two pools with mills; he won part of the site of the park from the Count of Mortain and surrounded the park with a double ditch and a palisade. Within he sowed acorns and took pains to grow oaks and beeches and other forest trees filling the park with deer from England.

Through the stilted words of the Norman chronicler, struggling with a new concept, can just be discerned a pattern which, passing to England with the Conquest a few years later, swiftly spread throughout the whole country. What Bishop Geoffrey had created was what the Persians had long known as a 'paradise' or park (*pairidaeza*), a pleasance where noble architecture blended with landscaped gardens. The Saracens had taken the idea to Sicily; Bishop Geoffrey transported it to Normandy and it entered England like some benign bacillus through the Norman Conquest.

But Geoffrey de Montbray did more than create a 'paradise', a physical setting for his church. The chronicler emphasized the fact, as though it were a novelty worth knowing, that Geoffrey also created a complete governing body for his cathedral, a formal establishment. This, too, crossed the Channel and, fusing with the Anglo-Saxon tendency to monasticism, created a unique institution. It would be subjected to enormous stresses over the centuries; it would even be legally abolished but the structure consisting of bishop, dean and chapter would survive alike the trauma of the Reformation

and the tide of nonconformity and dissent so that the statutes that govern a cathedral in the twentieth century would be recognizable to any member of a cathedral establishment from the Norman Conquest onwards.

It provided the dynamic for one of the most extraordinary figures in European history, the bishop. Like the cathedral itself, the office is taken for granted in the twentieth century, part of the larger 'establishment' which runs the country. But, like the cathedral, in its combination of roles it is unique, sui generis. In it there survived something of the *propraetor* from that vanished Roman world; in it there flourished the territorial baron hacking out his fief from other powerful men; in it there would develop the aristocrat eventually taking his seat in the House of Lords with peers of the realm. And in it was the spiritual leader, the father in God. Some few bishops were saintly men – or, to be exact had certain qualities which were rewarded with canonization. Most were honourable men. But the skills which would propel a man to this high level, fighting his way to the top, would rarely include the prime Christian virtues of humility and self-abasement. The fighting bishop was a medieval commonplace: with the medieval skill of chop-logic it was argued that he would not be transgressing the Founder's pacific injunctions provided he did not spill blood. He therefore used a mace. In East Anglia, the ferocity with which Henry Despenser, bishop of Norwich, pursued the wretched peasants in their hopeless revolt made his name a byword even among the savage lay nobility. In the north, the full and formal title of the bishop of Durham was 'Prince-bishop' and what others would call a diocese he knew as his principality.

The one place where the bishop was uncertain of his power was his cathedral. Here, the supreme governing body was the dean and chapter and the chapter-house became, in consequence, a sacred symbol of power. St Hugh of Lincoln was actually elected in London but refused to accept the title of bishop until it had been confirmed in the chapter house. 'Not in a royal palace, or in a pontifical council, but in its own chapter house must a church bishop be elected', he said unequivocally. The bishop was, by definition, pre-eminent: when he entered the church the bells rang in his honour and the dean yielded precedence to him. But his rights had to be spelled out in the statutes, defining

exactly the circumstances under which he was permitted to enter the church, exactly what his rights were in chapter. New statutes were framed by bishop and chapter working in concert, the chapter of Exeter cathedral saying very firmly 'No instrument has ever been allowed to be of any force unless ratified by the bishop and chapter, and authenticated by the seals of both'. Tension between bishop and dean was inevitable. Some bishops resolved the problem by simply keeping away from their cathedral. William Barlow, bishop of Lincoln in the seventeenth century was 'never in all his life at Lincoln but lived in Huntingdonshire, whence he was sarcastically styled "Episcopus Buckdeniensis"'. A plurality of palaces, many very far from the bishop's seat, was a commonplace. In addition to the palace in Huntingdonshire Barlow could have had access to mansions in Woburn, Sidington in Rutland and Banbury Castle, Oxfordshire. This was surpassed by the archbishops of York who possessed no less than seventeen manor houses. London was a natural choice for a permanent residence. Cardinal Wolsey, archbishop of York, lived like the prince he was in York Palace until evicted by Henry VIII, who turned the splendid palace into Whitehall Palace. The bishop of Exeter had his London residence in what is now Exeter Street – as well as thirteen other mansions scattered around the country, only nine of which were in Devon. The bishop of Winchester gave both a name to a street in Southwark, Winchester Street, and the prostitutes who plied their trade nearby: they became known as 'Winchester geese'. Lambeth Palace still survives as the official residence of the archbishop of Canterbury while the chapel of St Etheldreda in Ely Place is the last surviving piece of the palace of the bishop of Ely in London. Conversely, and perversely, the bishop of London had palaces in the manors of Fulham, Stepney, Bishop's Stortford, Whitham and Chelmsford, in addition to his palace adjoining St Paul's.

Tension between an autocratic dean and a resentful chapter could be as frequent as tension between dean and bishop. In 1440, as a result of prolonged strife in the chapter at Lincoln cathedral, the statutes – some of which went back to the year

1000 and were derived from those of Rouen cathedral – were re-defined by the forthright Bishop William Alnwick in a masterly New Register. They give, in their sum, a bird's-eye view of the life and work – and, above all, the cultural influence – of a great cathedral and, allowing for local variations, can stand as exemplar of cathedrals throughout the country. There were fifty-two canons at Lincoln most, but not all, of whom were in Holy Orders. Each held, as was customary, a prebendary – that is, an estate belonging to the cathedral which yielded him an income, and towards which in turn he had very real responsibilities. There was a perennial complaint, indeed, that canons put in far more time administering their prebendaries than they devoted to cathedral affairs. Each canon took the principal role in cathedral services once a week in turn, and each was supposed to be in residence for a certain number of weeks each year: if he undertook to reside for thirty-four weeks a house was provided for him. The whole business of 'residentary' canons was a running battle over the centuries, many a canon picking up his prebend without troubling to satisfy the residentary qualifications. Lincoln was an outstandingly intellectual chapter and its canons were much in demand both at the royal and papal courts, and thus unavoidably absent over long periods.

Membership of the Lincoln chapter was certainly no sinecure, for the cathedral was an intellectual dynamo. The chapter controlled the outstanding School of Architecture, consciously maintaining contacts with their opposite numbers on the Continent. The School of Music and the School of Grammar both had responsibilities far beyond the cathedral itself. The chancellor, who ran the grammar school, was responsible for all the grammar schools within the diocese and was, in miniature, a minister of education. Under the chancellor was also the School of Divinity. In addition to hammering out the doctrines of Christianity, the School also handled all the cathedral's correspondence, ran the library and was, in general, responsible for its intellectual life. In due course the universities would adopt the idea and title of this 'principal literary officer'.

The library formed the very core of the cathedral's intellectual dynamism. Most cathedral libraries have survived in some form or another,

*Opposite*
'Not in royal palace, or in pontifical council, but in its own chapter house must a bishop be elected'. Chapter house, Wells.

but that which gives the clearest possible picture of medieval working conditions is undoubtedly the Chained Library at Hereford. The room itself, above the north transept aisle, was built in 1268 and though the book-cases and desks were made in 1611 and add a certain element of comfort, the first impression that strikes the visitor even on a summer's day is darkness and cold. An indication of the sheer precious nature of books is provided by the fourteenth-century chest in the library: it has three locks as though it were a treasure chest, and the locks could be opened only when three of the clergy were present. The library has migrated a number of times and that in this room is only a part of the whole but contains about 1,444 chained books, the largest known collection of its sort in the world. Hereford holds, too, that other treasure, the *Mappa Mundi*, drawn about 1300 by a prebendary of the cathedral. It is, as it were, a theological rather than a geographical view of the world. Jerusalem is at the centre, Asia to the top, Africa to the right and the British Isles on the left, the whole surrounded by an uncrossable ocean. Adam and Eve, Noah's Ark, the wanderings of the Israelites and Moses on Sinai are given precedence over such humdrum details as topography.

Hereford also possesses one of the surviving colleges of Vicars Choral. The entire purpose of the cathedral was the 'cathedral service', the never-ending praise of God ascending from the choir. Each canon provided a 'vicar choral' to deputize for him in the choir, an indication of the prevalence of absenteeism from whatever cause. Many vicars simply occupied the house supposedly supplied for their canon but Hereford and Wells provided colleges. Hereford's is in the form of a quadrangle, but Wells's, built in the early fifteenth century, takes the form of a street, giving a most unusual picture of what a medieval street resembled. It is a cul de sac approached through a gateway. At the far end is the vicars' chapel and at the entrance is the Common Room which communicates, via a bridge, with the chapter house and the cathedral itself. Vicars choral were laymen: at Wells, each was paid 'stall wages' of two marks by their respective canons, and seem to have been a remarkably unruly and irreligious lot, judging by the prohibitions placed upon them in the early thirteenth century by Bishop Jocelyn. He threatened them with suspension for two months:

The embattled bishop: the fortified palace of the bishop of Bath and Wells, with (*right*) the moat surrounding the whole complex. Even as late as 1831 the drawbridge was actually used to cut off the palace from potential rioters.

... if they were slovenly in their office or talkative in choir; if they were hawkers, hunters, or anglers or idled about the streets or indulged in noisy singing abroad; if they were tavern haunters, secular traders or public players with dice or games at hazard ...

Evidently the vicars choral of the cathedral church of St Andrew in Wells considered that they had hired out only their voices.

Shortly before the outbreak of World War I the dean and chapter of Salisbury ordered the compilation and publication of the cathedral's statutes. They appeared in two massive volumes in 1915, unconscious testimony to the church's continuity of history and, covering all statutes from the Foundation Charter of 1091 down to Bishop Wordsworth's Visitation (Report) of 1890, they provide a lively insight into nine centuries of history, all the more valuable because of their idiosyncratic nature. Outstanding among them is the immensely lengthy

Code of Roger Mortival, bishop from 1315 to 1330: even through the formal Latin there comes something of a flamboyant tone and of a man who had something to say on an extraordinary range of topics.

The origins of Salisbury cathedral were unusual even among English cathedrals. It had originally been founded on a steep hill about two miles outside the present city on the site now known as Old Sarum. Although barely a third of a mile across, the hill has that concentration of history so characteristic of Wiltshire. There was an Iron Age settlement here; the Romans built here; and the Saxons here founded an entire town called Searisbyrig. In their turn the Normans built a castle, a cathedral and a palace all within the ramparts. The cathedral was largely destroyed by storm within five days of its completion in 1092 but the nave survived and a new church and cloister was added on. Then, in 1220, the reigning

Bishop Richard Poore made an astonishing decision: he would move the cathedral lock stock and barrel to a better site down by the river Avon. The reasons given for his doing so are conflicting. The official mandate from the pope gave as reason, 'Forasmuch as your church is built within the compass of the fortification of Sarum it is subject to so many inconveniences and oppressions that you cannot reside in the same without corporal peril'. Among the inconveniences and oppressions cited by the pope was the cathedral's lofty position 'where it is continually shaken by the collision of the winds' and the fact that access could not be gained to the church without permission of the warden of the castle. Another reason later given

The chained library of Hereford cathedral, the most complete surviving example of the medieval cathedral library. The actual book cases are seventeenth century.

Vicars' Close, Wells; the Close has been described as the oldest residential road in Europe for it had been in continuous occupation since its construction in the fourteenth century. Originally intended for deputies (vicars) of the canons, it is now, in effect, a 'grace and favour' residence.

*Left* Detail of the chapel.

*Below* General view.

was that the site had no water – the Saxon name indeed deriving from that fact. The probability is that, as the establishment of the cathedral and the garrison of the castle increased, so tension increased in the cramped and claustrophobic area and this, added to the undoubted inconvenience of the site, led to the unprecedented move.

Bishop Poore moved with speed. He made his petition to the pope shortly after becoming bishop in 1217; work began on the new site in 1220, thirty-eight years later, in 1258, the completed church was consecrated, a rare example of a medieval cathedral being built within a single lifetime. Bishop Poore was himself translated to Durham in 1229 but before doing so he laid out his new town of Salisbury, again an all but unprecedented act, for planned towns were rarities in England. Salisbury was the first post-Conquest cathedral to be built on an absolutely unencumbered site so that the architects, instead of endlessly adapting the new to the old, could plan the whole as a unity, even down to the vast close. The cathedral at Old Sarum provided the stone for the encircling walls – a fact which can be deduced from their shapes and markings – but the quarries of Chilmark provided stone for the cathedral itself, the curious, distinctive stone which close to seems almost drab but from a distance gleams like marble.

By the time that Roger Mortival became bishop in 1315, the maintenance of the cathedral was evidently causing a problem though it had been completed less than half a century earlier. Fulsomely, Roger praised his predecessor 'Richard [Poore] of blessed memory who did remove our Church from a cramped Sarisberie (or Caesar's burgh) where it had seemed for long years to be domiciled in the lowly guise of a handmaiden, and brought it even to the larger room of a fair maid of exceeding beauty', and then goes on to chide the lack of faith of the present generation, citing an all-too common reason: 'Among the laity, charity is waxing cold and devotion waning while they, withdrawing themselves from the Cathedral, devote themselves and their property to the creation of numerous oratories.' In order to encourage people again to give money to the cathedral instead of selfishly raising private chantries, Roger proposes the usual panacea, the granting of indulgencies – the remission of so many days punishment in Purgatory in return for so much contributed to the cathedral.

It was not only the laity at Salisbury who were failing in their duties: 'Many canons (we say it with pain) after receiving a benefice care little for the performance of the duties laid on by it'. Roger goes on to insist, at great length, that the new canon's duties must be fully impressed both upon him, and upon his proxy. The vicars choral of Salisbury seem to have been as violent and dissolute as those of Wells, judging by the stringent code drawn up to govern their behaviour. They would be fined twelvepence for laying violent hands on each other – fortypence if any vicar should draw blood with a knife.

Roger Mortival also took a particularly jaundiced view of the strolling players who brought a little breath of a larger world into the enclosed society of Salisbury:

Albeit sturdy fellows, despising to undergo the toil which man is born and choosing to look for a living in ease and laziness amid the foolish pleasures of the world, the which are called in the vulgar speech *minstrels* and sometimes *players* are ofttimes (not because they are such but because we see in them God's work and our nature) allowed by us in our houses and given refreshment'.

Nevertheless, says Roger with the equivalent of a deep breath, they are not to be given any money, or anything that can be turned into money. He then turns a stern eye on the canon's drinking habits. It was customary for canons to entertain their vicars 'for the sake of fostering greater mutual love among them'. But this had gone beyond bounds, Roger says sternly: 'some undesirable persons forced an entry, not without ribaldry ... and it is now ratified by Us that both Canons and Vicars being satisfied with the fixed distributions which they enjoy from the Church should abstain from such drinkings'. The fixed distributions to which the bishop referred probably includes the sums paid to the canons on attendance and so very carefully calculated that they were withheld during their absence.

Roger turns to the well-being of choir boys, who were resident in the cathedral:

To the end that the children, who should be trained in their tender years in morals as well as in learning,

Old Sarum, Wiltshire. The foundations of the cathedral alone survive.

be withdrawn from unlawful pursuits, we ordain that all the Choristers alike do live in houses in the Close appointed for this purpose under the perpetual ward of some Canon actually resident in our aforesaid Church ...

He then goes on to discuss the correct behaviour for one of the most extraordinary figures of the medieval church, the Boy Bishop. Only Lincoln, Salisbury, Old St Paul's and York seemed to have fully developed this custom and the *Sarum Processional* actually lays down the mock episcopal ceremonies the Boy Bishop conducted. The boy was elected, by his fellow choir boys, on St Nicholas Day – 6 December – and from then until

Childermass (28 December) he and his fellows parodied the solemn customs of the cathedral. Dressed in miniature episcopal robes, attended by his fellows in the roles of dean and canons, he occupied the great episcopal throne while his 'canons' took their place in the stalls. The Boy Bishop preached a sermon, all the offices were fully recited except for that of the Mass, and on Childermass Day the miniature parodists took part in a grand procession through and around the church. It was this part of the custom that exercised Bishop Roger. Crowds turned up to see what was regarded as an entertainment and the press was so great that, in some years, injuries had resulted. The problem was such that the bishop even threatened excommunication, the ultimate weapon of the Church, on those who 'pressed upon or in any way impede those boys in the aforesaid procession or otherwise in their ministry'.

All cathedrals had schools attached to them for the training of their youthful choristers. Some survived the changing fashions of centuries, evolving into standard grammer schools. *Left,* St Peter's, York and *above,* Wells Grammar School, are two which sucessfully made the change.

The cathedral school was one of the institutions which, founded in Anglo-Saxon England, would not only survive the Conquest but be strengthened by it, forming the foundation of what would be a national system of education. The cathedral school of York was internationally famous in the eighteenth century: one of its pupils and later master, Alcuin, becoming the right-hand man of Charlemagne when the emperor wanted to set up his own educational system. In his rather flowery prose, Alcuin left a description of Archbishop Albert who personally taught in the school, presenting an incredible range of subjects: 'He moistened thirsty hearts with divers streams of teaching: to some he imparted the arts and science of grammer: to others the skill of tongues. These he

polished on the whetstone of law, those he taught to sing in Aeonian chants ...'. He also taught playing the flute, astronomy, geometry, biology, geography, theology – the boys who attended Albert's school at York could claim to be well-rounded men. They were even taught to ride and fence and the art of archery. The grammar school of the cathedral of St Peter in the city of York was so well founded that it would survive into the twentieth century, endlessly adapting but still identifiable over 1,300 years. Hereford's school came into existence much later, in 1381, but this too was destined to survive even the vicissitudes of the Reformation; in London in 1509 Dean Colet founded one of the most famous of all, that of St Paul's. Wells, Lincoln, Norwich, Winchester, all had their grammar schools born of the cathedral and flourishing under its shadow.

Relationships between the bishop and the monks of a cathedral-priory could be particularly delicate. In the late twelfth century Archbishop Baldwin of

The chain gate, Wells, connecting the chapter house with Vicars' Close.

Canterbury wanted to set up his own college of secular canons in the village of Hackington. The monks of Christ Church cathedral interpreted this as an attempt to remove the archiepiscopal throne to Hackington and appealed to Rome. Baldwin, a high-handed and hot-headed man promptly attacked them, seizing their possessions. Writs flew back and forward between Rome and Canterbury and the king intervened, but to no avail. In 1186 Baldwin actually blockaded the cathedral and for over a year the monks were besieged and would probably have died of starvation had not citizens, in defence of 'their' cathedral, smuggled in food. A similar quarrel broke out in Worcester. This, too, was a cathedral-priory and the bishop, too, tried to establish a collegiate church where, he said frankly 'among whose canons he would feel more at home

than in his own house at Worcester'. But the reigning king ruled against it, and the reigning king being Edward I his ruling was accepted for few cared to oppose the Hammer of the Scots without very good cause.

But if tension between bishop and establishment could flare into open conflict, rivalry between bishop and bishop could be as great. None was more bitter, or more ludicrous in its operation than the long-standing battle for precedence between the archbishops of York and Canterbury. That rivalry went back almost to the foundation of the Church of England, and it became ever more bitter immediately after the Conquest when everywhere the conquerors of England were jostling among themselves for precedence. It produced an almost comically undignified incident when, in 1176, both archbishops were summoned to a conference by the papal legate. Archbishop Roger of York arrived late, to discover that his hated rival Archbishop Richard of Canterbury was already in the seat of honour on the right of the legate. 'Disdaining to sit on the left, where he might seem to give pre-eminence to the Archbishop of Canterbury' Roger strode forward and, according to some accounts, either attempted to sit in Richard's lap, or force himself between the archbishop and the legate. Richard's supporters fell upon him before the scandalized gaze of the legate, beating him up, shouting 'Away, away betrayer of St Thomas; his blood is still upon thy hands'.

That action marked the opening of a particularly violent period of confrontation by both archbishops. A successor of Roger's, having been consecrated at Rome, announced his intention of landing at Dover and going in procession through the diocese of Canterbury, bearing his archiepiscopal cross erect. This was an outright challenge to the supremacy of Canterbury, and the Canterburians responded in like manner. The archbishop's chief justice personally led an avenging party who beat up York's companions, smashed his crozier and forbade all clergy from giving him or his party any form of supplies as they travelled through the diocese. The dispute was not resolved until the late fourteenth century when a formula was devised describing the archbishop of York as 'Primate of England', but the archbishop of Canterbury as 'Primate of All England', a piece of chop-logic which leaves posterity bewildered but served to heal the breach.

In a brilliant analysis of the medieval economics of York Minster a modern writer, Henry Kraus, argues that it was this dispute between York and Canterbury which accounts for the unconscionable delay in completing the building of York Minster, extending over some 250 years from its beginning in 1220. The reason, argues Henry Kraus, is that money drained off steadily from York to Rome: in order to avoid seeking confirmation at the hands of the archbishop of Canterbury, the newly elected archbishop of York made the long, dangerous and highly expensive trip to Rome to receive consecration from the hands of the pope himself. And every trip to Rome meant a dispensing of gold either to grease Italian palms, or to pay straightforward but highly expensive 'dues' to the Curia. The Gaetani pope, Boniface VIII, demanded a sum of £3,667 to permit the consecration, in York by proxy, of Henry of Newark. The archbishop who actually began the rebuilding of the Minster in 1220, later

complained that his trip to Rome and consecration had cost him the incredible sum of £10,000 – the equivalent, perhaps, of at least £6 million in current value. The Italian benefited twice, for most of the money had to be borrowed at immense rates of interest from one or other of the great Italian banking houses. Each new consecration increased the load of debt, the need to scrape the money together invariably coinciding with a suspension of building activity. The most extreme, and pathetic, of all was the case of William of Greenfield. He was threatened with excommunication if he did not pay a debt of £4,000 he had borrowed from a Florentine banker 'in order to expedite his affairs at Rome' and to get the money together he almost literally begged it, even 'borrowing' £40 from his personal servant.

Consecration fees were only one, though a major, drain upon York finances: the loss of prebendal incomes was almost as grave. As with all other cathedrals, many of the canons of York were not simply absentee but were not even ecclesiastic, the fat pickings of a canonry attracting the attention of greedy and powerful men. But York seems to have been particularly vulnerable, probably due to that long-drawn controversy with Canterbury. In the thirteenth and fourteenth centuries probably half the canonries were in the hands of 'aliens' of whom a very high proportion were Italian. There was an extraordinary occasion in the mid-thirteenth century when three total strangers turned up at the Minster and asked to be directed to the dean's stall. On arrival at the stall, one of them was seated in it while a ceremony of 'installation' was performed by the other two, finishing with the words 'Brother we install you by the authority of the pope'. The reigning archbishop, Sewall de Bovill, furiously protested and was excommunicated for his trouble. John Wycliff, the great fourteenth-century anti-papist reformer made the point that when a native was appointed to a prebend, the money at least stayed in England even if the man was a layman: when a foreigner was installed, the money flowed out – usually to Italy and he calculated that at least £100,000 went out annually in this manner. Two centuries before Henry VIII came to the throne, Rome was preparing the mine which exploded in its face.

But the greed of Italian prelates could, on many

The world within a world: Salisbury cathedral close with Mompeson House (now belonging to the National Trust) on the right.

an occasion, be matched by the greed of the English counterparts and in his study, Henry Kraus demolishes yet a little more of that myth of great churchmen building for the love of God. The accounts of York Minster show that Archbishop Giffard's household expenses towards the end of the thirteenth century ran at around £900 a year, but he contributed nothing whatsoever to the cathedral building fund. One of his successors, William Melton, actually gained the reputation as a 'munificent benefactor' because he contributed £400. 'Averaged over Melton's twenty-three years, they would have sufficed to pay for the hire of three or four workmen', Kraus points out and goes on to describe how, during his episcopacy, Melton showered rich gifts on his brother's family – gifts totalling more than £2,000, all ultimately derived

from the Minster's income – and at his death in 1340 left seven rich manors to his nephew to maintain the family's prestige. It is scarcely a coincidence that, five years after his death, came the famous report describing how the neglected unfinished building was in danger of collapse. Fifty years had passed since the nave had been commenced, and it still possessed no vault, while those responsible for the workforce were so negligent in their duties that the cathedral was robbed wholesale, both directly through theft of material and indirectly through a grossly over-manned labour force.

The account rolls of York point up an English peculiarity: the way in which the cathedral establishment distanced itself deliberately from the city, even to the extent of turning down a lucrative chantry bequest from a wool merchant. The townsfolk, in their turn, ignored the cathedral, preferring to make their donations and bequests to their own parish churches. The separation of cathedral and city is made tangible by that peculiarly English institution, the close, and it is here that the English cathedral differs most dramatically from their Continental counterparts, those of Italy in particular. Despite the fact that armed civic strife continued in Italy down to the nineteenth century, the Italian cathedral stands open in the heart of the city. Despite the fact that a strong monarch began to impose order in England not long after the Norman Conquest, the English cathedral girt itself around with ever higher, stronger walls. Unlike his Continental counterpart, the English bishop identified himself with his diocese, not his titular city, an attitude which persisted into the twentieth century. 'Many bishops still live miles away from their Family House [the cathedral] and seldom enter it and, until recently at any rate, there have been deans who have blindly and boldly maintained that with "their" cathedral the diocese had nothing to do', said the dean of Chester in 1926. And if the bishop withdrew from the rest of the establishment, the establishment withdrew from the city, creating an inward-looking organization. Time has mellowed the massive gatehouses, the towering walls, conferring on them the glamour of antiquity, but they were the outward sign of the mutual suspicion which at times became actual conflict.

The cathedral of Wells in Somerset contains the most complete set of ancillary buildings and institutions of all English cathedrals. Here is the College of Vicars Choral, still occupied; here is the School still literally under the shadow of its parent building; here is the chapter house, the cloisters. But here too is the building which, more than any other, sums up the role of bishop as baron – the great moated palace whose massive walls were designed as much to protect him from his own clergy as from the townsfolk. Most of the defences were built by Bishop Ralph about 1340. The gatehouse is provided with the usual means of delivering molten lead or boiling oil upon the heads of attackers. The drawbridge was actually capable of being raised and lowered until the 1930s. It proved very useful indeed during the Reform Riots of 1831. The bishops, who were bitterly opposed to electoral reform, became a prime target of the mobs – the bishop's palace in Bristol was burned down and he of Wells must have taken considerable comfort in his raised drawbridge, the last time it was used in action. The bishop had his own private prison for 'criminous clerks' in the north-west bastion and in the now-ruined Great Hall some 400 retainers could be seated. They were not being fed and housed from any sense of charity: in times of need they could provide a garrison equal to that of many a castle.

If the palace of the bishop of Wells is the Church in its embattled phase, then the great Close of Salisbury cathedral is the Church as it drifted into a backwater – mellow, charming, but increasingly irrelevant to the raucous, dusty world outside the walls. Unsurprisingly, it acted as a model for an enclosed, self-indulgent ecclesiastical society for both Hardy and Trollope, the one transforming Salisbury into 'Melchester' the other into 'Barchester'. In keeping with the architectural grandiloquence of Salisbury, it is the largest close in England, Daniel Defoe describing it accurately enough as a city within a city, both from its size and from its inward-turning nature. It is a characteristic it retains still into the twentieth century, being among the very last of the closes with its own guardian force which ensures that the great gates are closed each nightfall, keeping that increasingly violent world at bay.

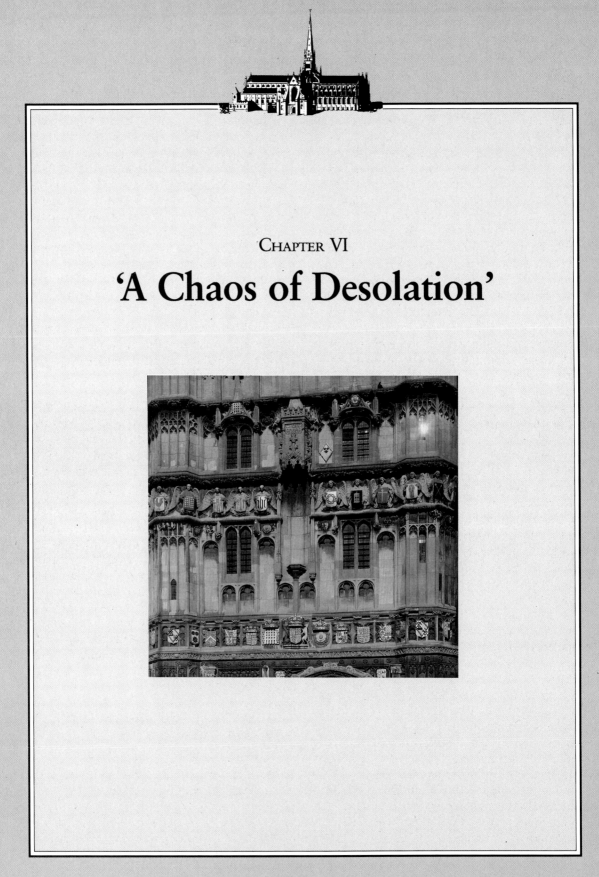

# CHAPTER VI

# 'A Chaos of Desolation'

Since World War II, the British preoccupation with the past has amounted to the obsessional. It is a matter of debate whether this obsession is the result of loss of confidence in the future, or the reaction against a period of climacteric change when customs and institutions that had endured over centuries drastically altered their form, or disappeared totally overnight. Whatever the reason, nostalgia became a boom industry. In the field of historic architecture, the wave of destruction created by 'developers' from the 1960s onward produced a vigorous reaction. At local level there is today no community with any claim to historic interest that does not possess a civic society dedicated to the defence of its physical heritage. At national level, the once reticent Ancient Monuments Division, charged by parliament with the protection and interpretation of the country's major architectural and archaeological sites, has emerged as an independent organization whose glamourized title of English Heritage demonstrates the concept of physical continuity. The cathedrals remain outside this organization but they have benefited from the wave of sentiment, confidently issuing appeals measured in millions of pounds. In the tiny city of Wells, national and local appeals exist side by side: simultaneously with a national appeal of some £3 million for restoration of the west front is a local appeal for £¼ million for the restoration of the tower of the parish church of St Cuthbert's. Preserving the cathedrals and great churches of the kingdom has become both a moral obligation and a financial activity.

It is of relatively recent development. Filson Young's criticism, in 1910, of his fellow citizen's indifference to Manchester cathedral is unusual only in that he deplored such indifference. Prior to his day, the indifference was itself either a matter of indifference, or a matter of actual congratulation. In the mid-nineteenth century, Bishop Blomfield, bishop of London looked critically at St Paul's and delivered himself of a scathing judgement: 'I look at this great Cathedral and think of its large revenues and great responsibilities and ask myself – what good is it doing to this great City, and I feel compelled to answer, not any to a single soul in it'. In the 1830s a canon of the cathedral described its distinguishing characteristics as being 'vast emptiness and encompassing dirt', an opinion heartily

echoed by the parsonical wit, Sidney Smith, who announced that a visit to St Paul's was tantamount to a death sentence through cold.

All over the country, the cathedrals and greater churches could tell a similar story of neglect. Ely seems to have been particularly badly served by its bishop. When the indefatigable traveller Celia Fiennes visited it in 1698, she remarked caustically, 'The Bishop does not care to stay long in this place not being for his health ... all things are directed by the Bishop and it is a shame that he does not see it better ordered'. Daniel Defoe visited Ely about twenty years later and remarked of the cathedral that 'it is so ancient, totters so much with every gust of wind, looks so like decay that whensoever it does fall it will be wondered why it did not do so one hundred years earlier'. William Cobbett passed through Ely on his Rural Rides in 1830 and fiercely returns to the attack on the bishop and clergy: 'They say that this bishop has an income of £18,000 a year. He and the dean and chapter are owners of all the land and tithes for a great distance round: and yet this famous building, the cathedral, is in a state of disgraceful irrepair and disfigurement'. He then goes on to give a detailed picture of the state of the great building on which Alan of Walsingham had laboured for twenty years:

The great and magnificent windows to the east have been shortened at the bottom, and the space plastered up with brick and mortar in a very slovenly manner for the purpose of saving the expense of keeping the glass in repair. Great numbers of the windows in the upper part of the building have been partly closed up in the same manner, and others quite closed up. One doorway, which apparently had stood in need of repair, has been rebuilt in modern style, because it was cheaper: and the churchyard contained a flock of sheep acting as vergers for those who lived upon the immense income, not a penny of which ought to be expended upon themselves while any part of this beautiful building is in a state of disrepair ...

Just as serious as the physical neglect of the cathedral, and a major contributory factor to that neglect, was the way in which it was, by the early nineteenth century, peripheral, not central, to urban society. Its services were conducted in a lackadaisacal manner in echoing emptiness, by clergy mechanically going through a paid occupa-

tion. A seventeenth-century pamphleteer indignantly informed Archbishop Laud of the state of things at Salisbury: 'Of 260 canonical howers per ann, they [congregation] are not 60 in the church: of these 60, not 30 at second lesson: of these 30 not 10 at confession, no not at communion'. Things were far worse by Cobbett's time. On his visit to Salisbury in 1826, he entered the cathedral:

... and was looking about and admiring the columns and the roof [when] I heard a sort of *humming* in some place which appeared to be the transept of the building. Following the sound, I turned in at a doorway to my left, where I found a priest and his congregation assembled. It was a parson of some sort, with a white covering on him, and five women and four men: when I arrived there were five couple of us ... I wonder what the founders would say if they could rise from the grave and see such a congregation as this in this most magnificent and beautiful building ...

But even this was better than what he experienced in Ely: 'My daughters went to the service in the afternoon, in the choir of which they saw God honoured by the presence of *two old men*, forming the whole of the congregation.'

The two causes commonly cited for the decline and fall of the greater churches and cathedrals of England are the anti-monasticism of the sixteenth century and the ferocious iconoclasm of the seventeenth century. Neither were peculiar to Britain. Iconoclasm was very nearly as old as the Christian Church for, from the earliest days, there was expressed disquiet that the paganism and idolatry so recently driven out was returning under the guise of 'reverence' to sacred icons. The split between the Eastern and Western Churches in the eighteenth century was precisely on this issue, when the clergy of Constantinople, alive to the mockery of neighbouring Moslems and Jews at the 'image-worship' of Christians, decreed the destruction of all images. The clergy of Rome resisted, and the split began. On the other hand, even such fanatical Continental reformers as Calvin and Zwingli drew the line at the destruction of those works of art which had expressed the faith of their forefathers.

*Opposite*
William Cobbett, who fiercely attacked the clergy for the neglect of their charges.

Similarly, not long after the monks and nuns of Britain had been driven out of their houses, an anti-monastic movement was developing in the very heart of Roman Catholicism, an Italian writer sourly summing up the life-style of his monastic compatriots:

These wellfed gentlemen with their capacious cowls do not pass their time in barefooted journeys and in sermons, but sit in elegant slippers, with their hands crossed over their paunches in charming cells wainscotted with cyprus-wood. And when they are obliged to quit the house, they ride comfortably on mules and sleek horses. They do not overstrain their minds with the study of many books, for fear less knowledge might put the pride of Lucifer in the place of monkish simplicity'.

It was the misfortune of our cathedrals that the English combined the two elements, anti-monasticism and iconoclasm. And when the religious passion had been spent, the cathedrals had to endure probably an even more damaging experience: restoration at the hands of men who thought they better understood the significance of Gothic architecture than the men who had actually erected the buildings.

The excuse given by the dean and chapter of Westminster Abbey in 1542 for the sale of certain ornaments, that they were 'monymentes of Idolatre and supersticyon', runs through the entire period of the great plundering after the Dissolution. The 1536 Act for the Suppression of the Lesser Monasteries gave the impression that their assets were simply being put to better – but still religious – uses. The reality had been exposed in the Act of Parliament of 1534 which gave the king one-tenth of the Church's income. The taxation inventory of the following year, called the *Valor Ecclesiasticus*, showed that perhaps fifty per cent of all monastic foundations enjoyed an income of less than £200. Conveniently, it was found that these poorer houses were abodes of 'manifest sin, vicious, carnal and abominable living', and they were the first to be swept into the net. Even now it is probable that the government had not envisaged a wholesale destruction of the monastic system but, having tasted blood and exasperated by the rebellion in the north known as the Pilgrimage of Grace, in 1539 it passed an Act for the suppression of the greater

Monastic gateways tended to survive either because they could be re-used or because they added prestige. The gatehouse at Ely (*above*) was successively a prison, chapel, brewery and school while that at St Alban's (*below*) was also used as a prison then as a school. Canterbury's Christchurch gate (*opposite*) undoubtedly survived because of its handsome appearance.

monasteries and eight cathedral-priories fell into Henry's hands.

Hereafter, any pretence that the operation was for any other purpose but the replenishing of the royal coffers was at an end. A certain sum of money was set aside for pensions and the like, some cynically insufficient, some remarkably generous, but from the first the King's commissioners kept the closest possible tally of the negotiable wealth of their victims. Probably the biggest, single prize was that of the shrine of St Thomas in Canterbury cathedral. The most potent of all the pilgrims' shrines, for nearly 400 years it had been loaded with the offerings from great and small. From the moment that the second Act was passed, the valuables belonged to the king: an unfortunate abbot of Glastonbury who attempted to hide some of his abbey's treasures was hanged as a thief. The archbishop of Canterbury therefore took good care that the shrine should remain intact until the coming of the King's commissioners. The bones of the martyr were dragged out of their casket and thrown away, the jewels and precious metals that studded the shrine were prized out, or ripped off and placed into two chests – so large and heavy that, according to contemporary reports, each had to be carried by eight men. It is probably an accurate statement, for the later assessment of the treasures revealed that the chests contained a total of 4,994 ounces of gold, 4,425 ounces of silver gilt and 5,285 ounces of solid silver. Later, twenty-six carts were required to carry away the less concentrated valuables. The immense ruby described by the Venetian finished up in a ring on the king's finger, an unequivocal act of plunder whether or not the overall despoilation was rationalized as suppressing 'monymentes of ... supersticyon'.

Shrines were the primary targets, for not only would they yield an immense loot in the form of precious metals and gems, but they could be shown to be causes and objects of superstition. In ordering the destruction of the shrine of St Richard in Chichester cathedral, the king was able to hide the act of plundering behind a smokescreen of piety:

For as much as we have been lately informed that in our City of Chichester and Cathedral Church of the same, there hath been used long and is used much superstition and certain kynd of idolatry about the shryne and bones of a certain bishop of the same, which they call S. Richard.

Anxious for the spiritual well-being of his subjects, 'men of simplicitie' who, through the blandishments of priests, 'seke at the said shryne and bones of the same that [which] God only hath authoritie and power to grant, the solicitous monarch ordered that the shrine be dismantled forthwith, and that 'all the sylver, gold, juells, and ornaments ... to be safely and surely conveyed and brought into our Tower of London, there to be bestowed as we shall further determine at your arrival'.

Second in popularity and wealth only to the shrine of St Thomas at Canterbury was the shrine of St Hugh at Lincoln. Here, again, King Henry VIII was worried that the 'symple people be moch deceaved and brought into great supersticion' and decreed that this, too, should be destroyed – and as an afterthought added that the valuable objects should be taken to the Tower. The Commissioners recorded the removal of 2,621 ounces of gold and 4,285 ounces of silver, together with an uncounted number of diamonds, sapphires and rubies, presumably prized from out of the shrine.

Gold and silver in bullion and precious jewels in loose form were easily lootable. But the Church held precious metals and gems in a remarkable variety of forms: generally in candlesticks, in censers and reliquaries, and in rings and plate. Hereford yielded up a golden chalice weighing twenty-two pounds nine ounces, a couple of basins totalling 102 ounces and a silver-gilt pastoral staff weighing over eleven pounds. But there were too, the richly embroidered ceremonial robes used by the clergy in their 'popish' masses. Canterbury yielded an incredible collection of 262 heavily encrusted copes, for each 'suffragan' or assistant bishop was by custom supposed to donate a cope to the mother house. The actual fabrics were simply destroyed; the gold and silver thread and the gems so thickly sewn over the fabrics were ripped out to join the growing hoard in the Tower of London.

The monastic libraries, too, suffered badly: the liturgical books were simply ripped apart, the jewelled covers broken up, the gold scraped off the very parchment – which was then sold as waste at so much a pound. Genuine scholars were horrified: John Leland, the topographer, complained to

Thomas Cromwell that foreigners were actually coming to England to buy up the monastic libraries. His friend John Bale later recorded bitterly 'What maye bryng our realme to more shame and reubuke than to have it noysed abroad that we are despysers of learning'. Posterity owes much of its knowledge of monastic life to cathedrals for they were permitted to retain their archives and manuscripts, when those belonging to the ordinary monasteries were dispersed and sold. The king was determined on destroying the monastic, not the episcopal, system on which the administration of the Church rested, and it is due to this dispensation that such priceless records of monastic life as the Sacrists' Rolls at Ely, the Chapter Minutes of Westminster and the Statutes and Customs of Salisbury have survived.

The ancillary monastic buildings of the cathedral-priories, or of those monastic churches which were elevated to cathedrals, survived on a random basis. The prestigious cloister was usually preserved, even though it now had no function, just as a secular cathedral like Salisbury could decide, perversely and entirely for the sake of prestige, to build this characteristically monastic structure. After the Dissolution the cloisters of only Winchester, Ely and Peterborough disappeared in their entirety. Bristol's and Oxford's cloisters survived only in parts but all others remained as a memorial of past life. Some of the more impressive gatehouses also survived, either because they still discharged a function or because they conferred a certain dignified approach to the cathedral. The uses they were actually put to were varied and by no means necessarily dignified in themselves. The massive Porta at Ely became, at various times, a prison, a chapel, a brewery and finally a grammar school. That of St Alban's went through a rather similar experience. Furnished with strong dungeons, it had served efficiently as the abbot's prison for his jurisdiction and after the Dissolution automatically became the town jail. The building was so large that its upper storey could be used for the quarter sessions and later was actually used as a prison for French soldiers captured during the Napoleonic Wars. (It was said that they begged from the townsfolk by letting a shoe down on a length of string.) It was not until 1870 that the building ceased its grim role. It became part of St Alban's School when it was moved from the

'temporary' home it had occupied in the Lady Chapel since 1550 in order to allow the Chapel itself to be restored. The beautiful gatehouse which Prior Goldstone built for Canterbury about 1517 – ironically, less than thirty years before the Dissolution, survived unchanged, even though it bore the heads of Prince Arthur and the youthful Katherine of Aragon, unwitting cause of the vast upheaval in the nation's history.

The domestic buildings of most of the monastic cathedrals survived the centuries to a remarkable extent. Wells still possesses its Vicar's Close, still inhabited by members of the cathedral staff and therefore boasts of being the oldest inhabited street in Europe. Winchester's chapter house survived until 1637 and was then demolished, not for political or religious or aesthetic reasons, but for the humdrum sake of the lead on its roof. But the prior's lodging was happily transformed into the deanery. A similar sequence happened at Worcester. The gatehouse remained, but as late as 1660 the domestic buildings leading off the cloisters were torn down, again for the lead and timber on their roofs. These realized the astonishingly high price of £8,204. Given the steady drift towards puritanism, and the value of building materials, one can only be surprised at how much did indeed survive down into the twentieth century to be cherished at last as 'heritage'. Unfortunate Ely again felt the blows of fate. In 1541, the same year in which the shrine of St Thomas at Canterbury was demolished, the dean and chapter at Ely were given precise instructions as to what was to happen to their monastic buildings. The Bishop's 'mansion house' was to be retained, but the other buildings of the monastery were to be let out to tenants. The chapter was instructed to 'pluck down and sell and reserve for necessary bylding' all other unwanted buildings. Similarly at Norwich the dormitory and infirmary were let to prebendaries and the dean took over the prior's lodging, but most of these ancillary buildings had disappeared by the early nineteenth century.

Looking back at the sequence of events following on from the Dissolution of the monasteries, it is as though one were witnessing a sea wall with a gap that had been torn in it gradually widening, then the wall itself suddenly collapsing as the tide pours in at a geometric rate. Until the death of Henry VIII in 1547 the rate of change was relatively slow, the targets being only the monasteries and the portable treasures of the great churches. But with the advent of the boy-king Edward VII, the area of attack widened as fanaticism grew. In 1548 an Order in Council decreed the removal of all images from all churches, all cathedrals, the first indication of the iconoclasm that would rise to feverish heights in the next century. The Rood Screen of Old St Paul's was torn down – at the cost of two men's lives as they fell from the great height. At Lincoln the bishop and dean personally took part in the defacing of the tombs in their care: at Winchester, Bishop Horne led in the cleansing of the cathedral of 'objects of superstition'.

Casual desecration of the cathedral was a commonplace long before the Commonwealth elevated sacrilege into a moral duty. The laity had always regarded the nave as being 'their' place, an inevitable result of the clergy literally and figuratively withdrawing themselves behind the choir screen. Until the coming of the great railway stations in the nineteenth century, the nave was the largest covered area in the community and was used for a remarkable variety of purposes. Even during the monastic regime, the nave of Ely cathedral was used to set up stalls for St Audrey's fair. There was at least a link, if only a tenuous link, between the commercial and the religious bodies for the 'St Audrey' in whose honour the fair was held was the same St Etheldreda, the Saxon princess in whose honour the cathedral was originally built. (A further, ironic, etymological twist provides the word 'tawdry' from the gewgaws that were sold at St Audrey's' fair.) There was no such link, tenuous or otherwise, at Salisbury where the horsetraders actually held their market in the cathedral itself, and as early as 1358 the dean and chapter at. Exeter actually had to ban drinking parties in the cathedral – and the impression received from their prohibition is that they were content to control, rather than to ban outright. There was, too, an extraordinary custom at Salisbury which seems to have continued right into the nineteenth century, which took place at the Whitsun fair. This was held in the vast cathedral close and, at a certain stage of the proceedings, the entire cathedral was thrown open to the public. The mob, usually far gone in drink, not only surged through the nave but found their way up into the triforium, the roof passages and even the spire. According to an eighteenth-century writer, 'It seems they had certain sports in their passage up and down: viz, those who were the highest had the pleasure of discharging their urine on those below'.

London's St Paul's, in the heart of a great trading city, suffered the widest and most degrading of usages. The fact that lawyers and their clients used the nave for their purposes was a natural and – given other dubious uses – an unexceptional legacy from the time when the great building was used for major councils of Church and State. But from as early as the fourteenth century the nave was popularly known as 'Paul's Walk', an indication of its role. Here prostitutes plied for hire, gratefully nave-walking instead of street-walking in England's unpredictable weather. Here fashionable young men about town swaggered, drank and played at dice and cards. Pornographic prints were openly displayed for sale, activities which rendered relatively innocuous the endless procession of porters carrying market produce between Carter Lane and Paternoster Row and using the nave as a short cut. In 1554 the City Fathers tried to prevent this usage by passing an Ordinance forbidding the leading of mules or horses through the cathedral, a device which would at least limit the heavier traffic such as the transportation of casks of beer. But the need for such a prohibition does give some idea of the bizarre appearance the great nave must have presented. Nor did such activities cease during Divine Service. In 1598, it was reported that not only did 'Porters with Baskettes of flesh and such like' continue to use the nave as a thoroughfare but:

The choristers were eager in search of spur-money [i.e. fining those who entered the church wearing spurs] with such noyse of the children and others in the side chapels at the divine service that a man can scarce be heard. People walked about in the upper choir where the Communion Table doth stand with their hats on, commonly, all the service time, no man reproving them ...

The church itself, according to this report, was filthy beyond belief: 'the sweepings of the church lay in it three or four weeks together till the smell became very noysome; in St George's Chapel lay old stones and a ladder; in Long Chapel old fir poles and other old lumber'. Those responsible for the day-to-day maintenance of the cathedral betrayed their office by making money on the side. Visitors were admitted into the organ loft 'to the decay of the instrument'; the very vaults were let out to a carpenter.

Things were no better at Canterbury: 'Men both of ye better and meaner sort, mechanics, youths and prentises do ordinarily and most unreverently, walk in our church in ye tyme of divine service.' As at St Paul's, the vergers were far more interested in lining their pockets than checking the abuses. The clergy themselves many times 'have been fayne to ryse and go out of our seates to see & staye ye disorders. But I never (to my uttermost rememberance) saw Barfoot ye verger (who sits on my right) to rise at ye greatest noyse'. In 1881 the delightfully named Sparrow Simpson, reviewing the history of St Paul's, wearily summed up the abuses common even before the Puritan reaction:

Alas, we need not end even here. Many another grand cathedral had the same sad tale to tell; the same wearisome story of pluralities and non-residence; of overwhelming greediness and self-seeking; of rampant nepotism; of desecrated naves and deserted choirs; of dignitaries receiving great revenues and rendering no service in return. The way was paved for still greater desecrations, and they came. Horses neighed in canons stalls and Dr Cornelius Burges, with his twenty thousand pounds of plunder, preached in the ruined choir ...

What this catalogue of woe seems to show is that the dynamic had moved away from the cathedral to the parish church. The English cathedral, unlike its Continental counterpart, was rarely identified with its host city and when the cathedral clergy proved unequal to the task of maintaining the great building, there was no body of laity to take their place out of urban pride. But the deterioration of the cathedrals was the result of indifference and indolence, not of outright hostility. There was, as yet, no direct attack upon the very idea of the *cathedra*. On the contrary. In 1561, when the lamentations of moralists were painting a bizarre picture of degradation, there began a major restoration of one of the most venerable of all the cathedrals, that of London's St Paul's. This enormous church (its length of 690 feet exceeds by far the 556 feet of Winchester, the longest surviving medieval cathedral in Europe) was built on the site of a Saxon church towards the end of the eleventh century. In June 1561 its timber spire was struck by lightning and the entire roof destroyed. Some £6,000 was spent on replacing it, but it was obvious that the five-hundred-year-old building was in an advanced state of dilapidation and in 1632 a major restoration was entrusted to Inigo Jones.

Later, no less a person than Christopher Wren was to eulogize Inigo Jones's portico for the west front of the cathedral as 'an absolute piece in itself'. Posterity has only illustrations upon which to judge Jones's work but posterity — certainly late twentieth-century posterity — while doubtless agreeing that the portico was a work of genius 'in itself', would heartily deplore Jones's entire approach to the task entrusted to him. For the great architect and stage designer was in the vanguard of the 'anti-Gothic' reaction. He was a classicist to his finger tips and, as far as he was concerned, the enormous church before him was simply a shell to be decently clothed in the elegance of classic form as swiftly as possible. The description and illustrations of the famous portico leave little doubt of what would have been in store for the cathedral had the entire work come to pass. It was a colonnade 161 feet long and 162 feet high, supported on Corinthian columns, and surmounted by ten statues in Roman costume. Charles I actually offered to pay for the portico out of his own pocket — the two statues which were all that eventually appeared were those of the king and of his father James — and for work on the cathedral as a whole the immense sum of £100,000 was allocated. The work was still in progress nine years later when the Civil War broke out and the monarch was swept on to the rubbish heap of history. The unchecked tide of puritanism now seemed destined to sweep away every trace of the Church Triumphant, as expressed in the stone splendour of its great buildings.

It was painfully symbolic of what was about to happen that one of the first objects to be swept away was the scaffolding Jones had erected for the 'restoration' of the south transept of St Paul's. The men of Colonel Jephson's regiment, clamouring for their pay, were told to dismantle the scaffolding and sell it for what they could get. They did so, destroying part of the walls as they went, a foretaste of what was to come. In 1642 the Long Parliament, with an air of rolling up its sleeves and

getting down to a long overdue task of sanitation, passed the Root and Branch Bill extinguishing the episcopacy. The cathedral, whose entire raison d'être was the providing of a locale for the episcopal throne, became thereby irrelevant and the attack upon it increased in intensity. But there was now a new element: not simply a desire to sweep away an outmoded custom, but a desire to humiliate and degrade. A pregnant mare was dragged into St Paul's and the foal was baptized from a helmetful of urine. An elaborate charade was put on at Westminster. The famous Chamber of the Pyx, repository for the abbey's regalia, was forced open and the poetaster George Withers arrayed himself in the ceremonial robes and regalia, 'Who being thus crown'd and royally array'd (as right well became him) first marcht about the room with a stately garb, and afterwards with a thousand apish tricks and ridiculous actions exposed those sacred ornaments to contempt and laughter'. A few months later the church was taken over by a company of soldiers. They used the communion table as their mess table, eating and drinking and smoking. They dressed up in the canonical robes, playing hare and hounds round the church: 'He that wore the surplice was the hare, the rest the hounds'. Later they turned the abbey into a brothel, 'introducing their whores into the church' and deliberately defiling it, 'laying their filth and excrement about it'.

Canterbury suffered in a similar manner when the nave was used as a barracks. Again an attack was made on the fabric, the valuable lead torn off the roof and sold, the organ destroyed and the high altar overturned. Here, the work of destruction was led and systematized by a priest, a certain Richard Culmer, whose speciality was the smashing of the great glass windows, rejoicing in particular when one of the windows bore the image of St Thomas: he was 'rattling down proud Becket's glassy bones' he announced proudly as the glass fragments fell. Norwich was subjected to an orgy of destruction in 1643 when everything movable was carried outside and thrown upon a sacrificial bonfire. Bishop Hall describes the proceedings in a graphic contemporary account:

*Opposite*
Inigo Jones. Wren described his portico for the west front of St Paul's (*overleaf*) as 'an absolute piece in itself'.

What clattering of glasses! What beating down of walls! What tearing up of monuments! What pulling down of seats! What resting out of irons and brass from the windows and graves! What demolishing of curious stonework! What tooting and piping upon the destroyed organ pipework! And what a hideous triumph on the market day before all the country, when all the organ pipes and vestments together with the leaden Cross which had been newly sawn down from the Green Yard pulpit, and the service books and the singing books were carried to the fire in the public market place.

Norwich's great neighbour, Ely, for once escaped relatively unscathed. Oliver Cromwell, so much more moderate and civilized in this as in so many other matters than his fanatical supporters, placed the cathedral under his protection – perhaps from a sense of piety for this, after all, was his home ground. But even he did not feel equal to the task of keeping the more rabid Puritans at bay and ordered the minister 'to forebear altogether the choir service, lest the soldiers should in any tumultous or disorderly way, attempt the reformation of the Cathedral Church'.

Peterborough, on the other hand, was the object of a particularly savage attack in 1643, an attack recorded in detail by Dean Patrick, who later published a pamphlet entitled 'A short and true narrative of the Rifling and defacing of the Cathedral Church of Peterborough in the year 1643'. The culprits were a regiment of soldiers, stationed in the town for about a fortnight, visiting the cathedral to carry out a systematic destruction. The choir, the very heart of the place, was the first object of attack. Over two days they destroyed the stalls and tore up all the liturgical books, then moved on to the Communion Table and overturned it. No distinction was drawn between 'popish images' and non-representational carvings; anything that smacked of artistic form automatically attracting the soldiers' attention and rage. Dean Patrick was particularly distressed by the destruction of a stone screen behind the altar, 'a curious piece of Stone-work admired much by Strangers and Travellers ... This now had no Imagery work upon it, or anything else that might justly give offence and yet, it was pulled all down with ropes, layd low and level with the ground'. Muskets were discharged at a Christ in Majesty on the ceiling, but

Ecclesia Cathedralis S.
Pauli latus occidentale.

Daniell King sculpsit.

most horrific of all was the destruction of the tombs and their contents. Peterborough cathedral was famous as the burial place of two tragic queens, Mary Queen of Scots and Katherine of Aragon. Mary's son, James I, had moved his mother's remains when he came to the throne but Katherine of Aragon was at the fanatics' mercy: 'They break down the rails that enclosed the place, and take away the velvet pall which covered the Herse; overthrow the Herse itself, displace the gravestone that lay over her body and have left nothing now remaining of the Tomb.' The chapter house fell victim, too, to the soldiers' rage, the records ransacked and destroyed. Windows, memorials, all statuary within reach was attacked: 'Thus in a short time a fair and goodly structure was quite stripped of all its ornamental beauty and made a ruthful, a very Chaos of Desolation and Confusion'.

So the dismal trail spread throughout the country as a healthy reaction to opulence, a revulsion against a mechanistic view of religion, became corrupt in its turn, a mindless rage directed against any attempt to render the incorporeal corporeal, to use physical beauty as a means of expressing a worship. Parliament actually decreed the demolition of Winchester cathedral and though turned from its purpose by the indignation of the townsfolk, unleashed its destroyers upon the interior with drearily familiar results: 'the monuments of the dead were defaced; the bones of the kings and bishops thrown about the church ... the church vestments put on by heathenish soldiers riding in that posture in derision about the streets'. In 1645, when Bristol surrendered to Fairfax, the roof was torn from the bishop's palace in order to get at the lead, even though the bishop's wife actually lay in childbirth. She died as a result of it, her husband and children being turned into the streets. The palace itself was turned into a malthouse and a determined assault launched on the cathedral, the lead being stripped from the roof in preparation for demolition. But again the townsfolk rallied to their cathedral and the wave of destruction passed it by.

Lichfield, in Staffordshire, was not so fortunate: caught up in a battle between Royalists and Parliamentarians it came as close to total destruction as possible. The cathedral was doubly unfortunate in that the clergy were loyal to the king, while the townsfolk were Parliamentarians, and in the fact that the close was a place of considerable military strength. Ironically the siege began on 2 March 1643 – the festal day of St Chad, the cathedral's patron saint. Just a century earlier the commissioners of Henry VIII had destroyed the saint's shrine: now it seemed likely that the successors to those commissioners were about to destroy the cathedral itself. Siege guns were brought up, and the Parliamentarians captured the close after three days. They barely had time to settle down to their ritual work of destruction before they were expelled in their turn by Prince Rupert, the King's nephew. Three years later, the Parliamentarians again took the building after a four-month seige and they remained thereafter in possession. Altogether, it was calculated that 'two thousand shot of great ordnance and fifteen hundred grenadoes' had been hurled against the cathedral. The central spire was totally destroyed, the roof and vaulting broken into, all the stained glass broken. By the time of the Restoration in 1660, the building was virtually a shell, what services there were being held in the chapter house, the only habitable part of the building. Sepulchral monuments had suffered particularly badly. At an early stage of the occupation a soldier had lifted the slab covering the remains of Bishop Scrope and had found a silver chalice and valuable crozier. Excited by the prospect of loot, the soldier's comrades set about the systematic destruction of all other tombs, dragging out the human remains in search of saleable valuables.

But worse, far worse, was to happen to this and other ancient cathedrals as the restorer arrived to 'correct' the devastations of the past.

*Opposite*
Inigo Jones' elaborate design for the west front of Old St Paul's cathedral.

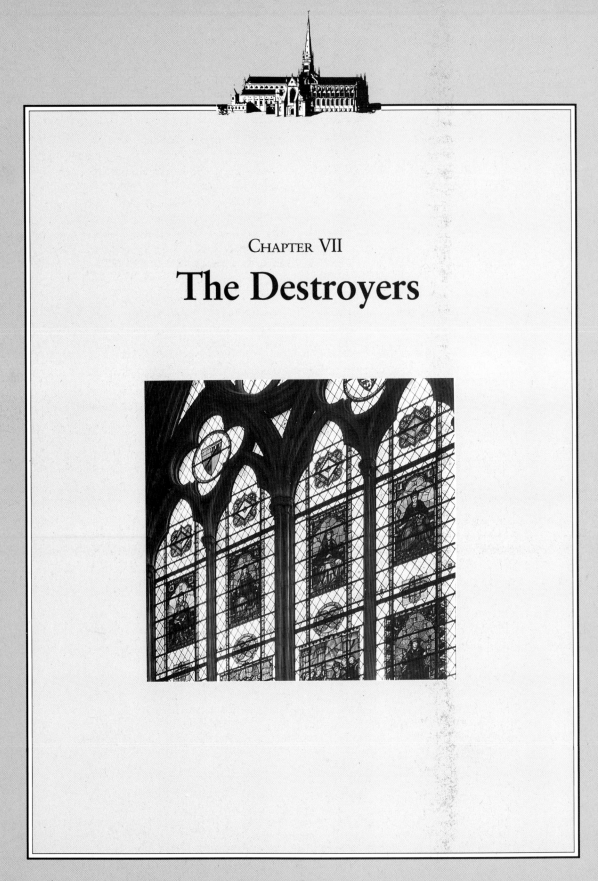

CHAPTER VII

# The Destroyers

Thomas Hardy tells the story of how, visiting an ancient church whose restoration had been placed under his surveillance, he looked for an Early English window whose repair had been specifically requested under the contract:

But it was gone. The contractor, who met me on the spot, replied genially to my gaze of concern, 'Well, now, I said to myself when I looked at the old thing. I won't stand upon a pound or two. I'll give 'em a new window now I'm about it and make a good job of it, howseomeever.' A caricature in new stone of the old window had now taken its place.

Worse was to follow, as Hardy soon discovered:

In the same church there was an old oak screen, very valuable with the original colouring and gilding, though much faded. The repairs deemed necessary had been duly specified, but I beheld in its place a new screen of deal. 'Well,' said the builder more genially than ever 'I said to myself, please God now I'm about it, I'll do the thing well, cost what it will'. 'Where's the old screen,' I said apalled. 'Used to boil up the workmen's kittles – though 'a were not much at that'.

Hardy told this anecdote, doubtless to satisfying gasps of horror, to a small but distinguished audience, the members of the Society for the Protection of Ancient Buildings. Founded in 1877 by William Morris, the Society was a vigorous

William Morris, founder of the Society for the Protection of Ancient Buildings.

reaction against the wave of 'restoration' which was transforming the ancient churches and cathedrals of Britain. Throughout the nineteenth century, disastrously energetic ecclesiastics were ripping out 'debased' architectural forms in pursuit of the pure 'Gothic' which fashion decreed was the only form in which God wanted to be worshipped. Architectural histories have laid the blame on the architects themselves, saddling such a man as James Wyatt with the title 'The Destroyer'; but behind the architect lay the patron, the incumbent of the parish church or the dean and chapter of the cathedral who decreed the change, authorized it and paid for it. The destructive freedom possessed by them was well illustrated by the reported case of the Lincolnshire church 'which was restored throughout in the most approved fashion, except that the very ancient Norman chancel was for a time spared. It remained not long, for the young ladies of the Parsonage could not bear to see it. They found it wholly out of keeping and frightfully disfiguring to the new work and so it was taken down'. To the long list of hazards that faced ancient buildings was now to be added bored young ladies, turning from painting on velvet to architectural criticism.

The problem of insensitive restoration was by no means limited to England: all over the Continent an immensely confident nineteenth century was placing its imprint upon the past, demolishing or 'improving' with a splendid impartiality. Thackeray Turner, one of the first secretaries of the SPAB describes a scene in Venice in 1887 which distressed him to the bottom of his sensitive soul. Work was proceeding in San Marco on a rare and most ancient marble screen:

A workman came in during the dinner hour when the Church was almost empty, and took out of his bag several little marble capitals and other bits of carving, then having found the parts of the screen to which they corresponded he proceeded to cut out with his chisel the ancient details and having made the holes the right shape, he inserted the new work, this he smeared with a little soot or other dirt

'It would have been less injurious to the building if they cut their names in great letters across the front.' The west front of Exeter cathedral as left by the nineteenth-century restorers.

to tone down its glaring whiteness – and behold a restoration.

William Morris witnessed with similar horror another workmen in San Marco who knocked down a large area of mosaic in order to replace a small section of deteriorated work.

The Italian workmen, if challenged, would probably have retorted that they were doing exactly what their grandfathers had done and that the hypersensitive Englishmen were being absurdly idealistic. But Morris and Turner had justification for their apprehension. They were the products of a wealthy, advanced industrial society and were aware of such a society's passion for mechanical neatness, for creating things that 'worked' or restoring things that did not. The SPAB was the first body to recognize that too much money was as great a threat to the well being of ancient buildings as too little. For over four years the Society carried on a running battle with the dean and chapter of Exeter cathedral who were virtually re-carving the great west front. 'The Dean and Chapter argue apparently that the more money expended, the more virtue there is in the work,' the Society lamented, calculating that over £80,000 had been collected and spent in the deplorable activity. 'It would be less injurious to the building, and a less violent exercise of their power, if they cut their names in great letters across the front.'

The process had started some two centuries earlier, the clearest statement of intent coming from Inigo Jones's attempt to turn the 'Gothic' sprawl of St Paul's into a decent classical – ie Renaissance – building. Looking back through the mist of undocumented centuries it is all but impossible to say whether or not a master mason was intent upon following, or rejecting, a predecessor. At Norwich, certainly, there was a conscious attempt, spreading over 150 years from the 1270s onwards, to rebuild the cloister according to one harmonious design, an attempt which must necessarily have involved the conscious use of archaic styles. A similar process was followed at Westminster whose nave appears homogenous, but the work continued for over 200 years: the masons in the latter decades must obviously have been consciously following the design of their predecessors even though, again, that design must have appeared increasingly old-fashioned as the decades went by. But the overwhelming impression conveyed by the work of the medieval masons was not so much an indifference to the past (except insofar as it could provide technical guidance as with the work of Vitruvius) as in a surging confidence in the present. Gervase of Canterbury singled out, with pride, the 'new work' embodied in the reconstructed choir. Later, Alan of Walsingham was to spend the greater part of his life urging through the 'new work' of the lantern at Canterbury. The only completely analogous modern attitude is that which brought the new cathedral of Coventry into being. All the imaginative energy of the master mason was directed towards translating into stone the religious symbolism demanded by his ecclesiastical employers: neither he, nor they, nor the few architectural critics of their day seem to have paid the slightest attention to any question of architectural style as such, or as to whether one style was more appropriate to the worship of God than another.

Certainly all of them would have been astonished to learn that they were building in a 'Gothic' style. By the time Inigo Jones got to work on St Paul's the traditional style was an object of contempt. Sir Henry Wotton who, in 1624, published one of the earliest conscious critiques of architecture, writes of pointed arches, the very basis of the style: 'these, both for the natural imbecility of the sharp Angle it selfe, and likewise for their very Uncomeliness, ought to be exiled from judicious eyes and left to their first inventors, the Gothes, or Lumbards, amongst other Reliques of that barbarous Age'.

But this was an extreme view. John Evelyn, who was at least as widely travelled as Sir Henry, and considerably more flexible intellectually, was enchanted by England's ancient cathedrals. His *Diary* records a tour he made in 1654 during which he explored, with the delight of any modern tourist, those buildings which were earning the contempt of the new generation of classicists. As so many subsequent visitors have done, he marvelled at the detail of Bath's west front, with its stone ladder climbing to Heaven: 'the faciate of the Cathedral is remarkable for its mistical carving'. Salisbury

*Opposite*
John Evelyn, an unabashed admirer of the despised 'Gothic'.

140

cathedral 'was the compleatest piece of Gothic work in Europe, taken in all its uniformity'. Gloucester's Minster 'is indeed a noble fabric'; Worcester's though 'much ruined by the late warrs, is otherwise a noble structure'. York's left him almost groping for words adequately to match its aesthetic appeal. He noted that 'of all the greate churches of England [it] had been the best preserved from the furie of the sacrilegious by composition with the Rebells when they took the Citty .... It is a most intire magnificent piece of Gothic Architecture. The skreene before the quire is of stone carv'd with flowers, running work and statues of the old Kings'. Lincoln's Minster 'is almost comparable to that of York itself, abounding with marble pillars and having a fair front'. He describes with indignation the assault on the cathedral made by the Cromwellian troops: 'The souldiers had lately knocked off most of the brasses from the gravestones so as few inscriptions were left. They told us that these men went in with axes and hammers, and shut themselves in till they had rent and torn off some barge-loads of metall, not sparing even the monuments of the dead, so hellish an avarice possessed them'.

Evelyn was a member of the hastily assembled Commission for the Repair of St Paul's Cathedral which, on 27 August 1666 met in the enormous building to decide what was to be done about it. Inigo Jones's work had been little more than cosmetic (after the Fire it was found that his new facades had not been properly bonded to the old and simply peeled away like a skin). The great cathedral was not simply in an unsightly, but an actively dangerous, condition and, four months earlier, a thirty-four-year-old architect called Christopher Wren had been invited to put forward ideas for its restoration. The Commission met to consider his proposals and, in Evelyn's words, 'to survey the generall decays of that ancient and venerable church, and to set down in writing the particulars of what was fit to be don ...'.

As far as Christopher Wren was concerned, the only fit thing to be done to that ancient and venerable church was to demolish the lot and to start again. He admitted that it was 'a monument of power and mighty zeal in our Ancestors to publick Works in those times when the Citty contained neither a 5th part of the people nor a 10th part of the Wealth it now boasts of', but

further than this he would not go. It was, to begin with 'both ill-design'd and ill-built from the Beginning: ill-design'd because the Architect gave not butment enough to counterpoise and resist the weight of the Roof from spreading the Walls ...', ill built, because the pillars supporting that roof consisted of nothing but 'a core of small Rubbish-stone and much Mortar which easily crushes and yields to the weight'. Like William of Sens at Canterbury so many centuries earlier, he realized that his potential employers would jib at too drastic a plan and therefore reluctantly agreed that it would be possible to 'follow the Gothick Rudeness of the old Design', but he also proposed a startling innovation – nothing less than an immense dome, crowned with a remarkably large and ugly 'pineapple', to be erected over the central crossing. A version of the dome, though happily without the pineapple, was later to appear on his own cathedral. For, just five days after the Commission met, the Great Fire of London broke out and resolved the problems of 'restoration or re-building'.

Evelyn visited the ruins on 7 September and sadly recorded his impression:

I was infinitely concerned to find that goodly Church St Paule's now a sad ruine, and that beautiful portico (for structure comparable to any in Europe not long before repair'd by the late King) now rent in pieces. It was astonishing to see what immense stones the heate had in a manner calcin'd, so that all the ornaments, columns, freezes, capitals and projections of massive Porland stone flew off, even to the roofe, where a sheet of lead covering the great space (no less than six akers by measure) was totally mealted ... Thus lay in ashes that most venerable Church, one of the most antient pieces of early piety in the Christian world.

Wren also visited the ruins and recorded (happily, one suspects) that his earlier plan for restoration was now quite impracticable. 'What Time and Weather had left entire in the old and Art in the new repair'd parts of the great Pile of St Pauls, the

*Opposite*
Christopher Wren. He agreed that old St Paul's was 'a monument of power and mighty zeal' but thought it 'both ill built and ill designed'.

SIR CHR: WREN.
Late Surveyor General of
the Royal Buildings.
He died the 25<sup>th</sup> of Feb<sup>ry</sup> 1723, aged 91.

Wren's classical masterpiece: the west front of St Paul's, London.

*Opposite above*
Guildford's cathedral was built of bricks actually made on site. Designed by Edward Maufe, commissioned in 1930 but not finished until 1961.

*Opposite below*
The great screen at York, with its majestic row of crowned figures, separating the presbytery from the secular area of the nave.

144

*Opposite*
Graham Sutherland's tapestry at Coventry. Basil Spence records that he instantly envisaged an immense tapestry in this position when he first began to design the building.

*Left*
Jacop Epstein's St Michael group flanking one of the entrances to the lobby of Coventry cathedral. The lobby forms a modern link between the ruins of the old cathedral and the new.

*Below*
Basil Spence's practice as a designer of exhibition halls comes out clearly in this glowing study of Coventry's nave.

late Calamities of the Fire hath so weaken'd and defac'd that it now appears like some Antique Ruine of 2,000 years continuance'. But all was still not plain sailing: the commissioners, with the innate conservatism of the English, continued to hanker after restoration, building a new Choir perhaps but patching up the rest where possible. Eighteen months after the Fire, however, Wren received a letter from one of the most influential of the commissioners, Dean Sancroft, generously admitting their mistake: 'What you whispered in my Ear at your last coming hither, is now come to pass. Our work at the West End of St Paul's is now fallen around our ears.' The diehards still resisted, but a little later Sancroft was able to inform Wren that 'My Lords of Canterbury, London and Oxford met on purpose to hear your letter read once more and to consider what is now to be done. They unanimously resolv'd that it is fit immediately to attempt something and that without you they can do nothing'. On 1 July 1668, Charles II signed a royal warrant giving permission for the work of rebuilding. In 1710 the architect, now an old man of seventy-eight and styled Sir Christopher, experienced one of the rarest achievements in architectural history when he contemplated, from within, a cathedral completed to his own design.

Despite his abomination of the 'Rude Gothick style', Wren was the first to survey its historical development and provided a theory for its origins so startling in its perception as to be accepted only in recent times:

This we now call the Gothick Manner of Architecture (so the Italians called what was not after the Roman style) tho' the Goths were rather Destroyers than Builders: I think it should, with more reason, be called the Saracen style: for those people wanted neither arts nor learning; and after we in the West lost both, we borrowed again from them, out of the Arabick books, what they with great Diligence had translated from the Greeks. They were Zealots in their Religion, and where-

ever they conquered (which was with amazing Rapidity) erected Mosques and Caravansara's in Haste ... Their carriage was by Camels, therefore their buildings were fitted for small stones [instead of the huge blocks used by Romans and Greeks] and columns of their fancy consisting of many pieces. And their Arches were pointed without Keystones which they thought too heavy. The reasons were the same in our Northern Climates, abounding in Free-stone but wanting Marble. The Crusado gave us an idea of this Form ....

While the details of Wren's theory might be debated the overall concept was elegantly simple and substantiated by modern scholarship which indeed traces Gothic back to the Middle East.

Wren's immense prestige ensured that the classic form had returned for good – but the despised 'Gothic' was far too lively a form to disappear forever. It went underground, to reappear in so bizarre a form that it might indeed have been better had it gracefully accepted extinction. In reaction to the cool formality of classicism, there began to build up the wave of romanticism, the search for the 'picturesque', for the creation of sham ruins and follies. It began as a private whim, affecting only private residences; by the end of the eighteenth century it would lay its cloying, distorting influence on some of the greatest of England's churches and cathedrals.

If any one man was responsible for the return of Gothic in the form of 'Gothick', that man would be the dilettante Horace Walpole. In 1763, a century after Sir Henry Wotton had inveighed about the 'natural imbecility' of Gothic, Walpole was waxing ecstatic about Bristol cathedral, 'very sweet and has pretty tombs', and 'adorable' Peterborough, while mourning over what the Puritans had done to Canterbury: 'I wish you had seen Canterbury some years before they whitewashed it: for it is so coarseley daubed, and thence the gloom is so totally destroyed, and so few remains for so vast a mass that I was shocked at the nudity of the whole.' His house at Strawberry Hill in Twickenham became a kind of seedbed for the revived style. He congratulates himself on 'imprinting the gloom of abbeys and cathedrals on one's house' and even offered to give a home to the enormous, and overwhelmingly genuine, Gothic tomb of Aylmer de Valence which the dean and chapter of

*Opposite*
This photograph of Salisbury cathedral is taken from the same standpoint as Constable's famous painting; only the rainbow is missing.

Lichfield's west front. Pugin was appalled by what 'The
Destroyer' (James Wyatt) had done to it.

Westminster were anxious to remove from the abbey in order to put up a monument to General Wolfe. But he believed, or affected to believe, that the entire movement was transitory: 'My buildings are paper, like my writings, and both will be blown away in ten years after I am dead. If they had not the substantial use of amusing me while I live, they would be worth little indeed'. It is fair to say of Horace Walpole that he, of all men, would have been shocked to see the effect this 'amusing' style would have upon the historic buildings of England.

In January 1833 a lively young architect of French descent, Augustus Pugin, arrived at Lichfield during the course of a tour of northern cathedrals. He was only twenty-one years of age but he held strong, and unusually well-informed opinions as to what was proper in ecclesiastical architecture. His father, Auguste Charles, Comte de Pugin, had worked as a draughtsman for the great John Nash himself and later published a number of superbly illustrated and knowledgeable books on Gothic architecture. The twentieth century, with its unlimited access to an immense and ever-increasing library of photographic illustrations of historic buildings, has brought the up-to-date visual appearance of every major building to layman and specialist alike. Before the invention of photography, the visual appearance of a cathedral would be familiar only to inhabitants of its host city, unless it were such a place as Canterbury or York where fashion would ensure that some aspect of its contemporary appearance would be sketched or painted or drawn from time to time.

This had apparently not recently happened to Lichfield for young Mr Pugin approached it with the highest expectations. He described his painful experience in a letter to a friend:

From its distant appearance [it] promised great things but what was my horror and astonishment on perceiving the West Front to have been restored with brown cement, cracked in every direction, with heads worked on with the trowel, devoid of all expression or feeling, crockets as bad, and a mixture of all styles. My surprise, however, ceased on the verger's informing me that the whole church was improved and beautified about thirty years ago by the late Mr Wyatt. Yes, this monster of architectural depravity – this pest of cathedral architecture – has been here. Need I say more?

James Wyatt has gone down into history with the label 'The Destroyer' firmly tied around his neck. In Salisbury, certainly, he deserved that label for, in contrast to his disastrous 'creativity' at Lichfield, at Salisbury in the 1790s his activities are indistinguishable from that of the iconoclast. First to go were the two ancient chapels of the Hungerford and Beauchamp families, the tombs ripped out and set neatly between the columns of the nave. The thirteenth century belfry which stood in the close was deemed to be in a dilapidated condition and that, too, was demolished. Arguably, he was acting in the interests of economy in proceeding with these demolitions, but it is almost impossible to account for his onslaught on the stained-glass windows. Until his arrival, they had miraculously survived time, weather and iconoclasts alike: they now went in one tremendous holocaust. A local glazier apparently had the commission, for he was able to write to a customer offering him as much as he wanted, provided he came and fetched it himself, 'as it is a deal of Truble to what a beating to peacis is'. In 1803, an indignant visitor to Salisbury recorded in the *Gentleman's Magazine*: 'The north cloisters is at present of much service in being made the rubbish repository of the religious pile. Here let the infatuated antiquary, like me, pore out for broken painted glass, funeral trophies of helmets, gauntlets and banners; sculptured gravestones, enriched paving tiles and all the off-scourings of the professional "improvers"'. In 1849 a certain C. Winston reported, through the Proceedings of the Archaeological Institute's meetings at Salisbury, how 'an informant' had told him that 'whole cartloads of glass, lead and other "rubbish" were removed from the nave and transepts and shot into the town ditch'.

Wyatt may have deserved the style of Destroyer – but equally certainly some version of that title should have been hung around the necks of the dean and chapter. To do Wyatt justice, it was he who cleared up the filthy condition of Salisbury's close and graveyard. In 1782 a disgusted visitor remarked of it that it was like 'a cow common, as dirty and neglected, and through the centre a boggy ditch'. Another visitor, encountering that 'boggy ditch' in high summer, remembered how it had

'The Destroyer' James Wyatt, who placed his own idea of
'Gothic' upon genuine Gothic buildings.

become 'extremely offensive' in hot weather. Wyatt restored the close to a decent appearance, even though it meant covering all the graves so that they were no longer visible, and his destructive work on the cathedral itself was at the behest of – or, at very least, with the tacit approval of – the dean and chapter. Similarly at Lichfield, the dean and chapter not only acquiesced in the grotesque remodelling of the west front, but ordered their architect to destroy an elegant seventeenth-century reredos and so incorporate the Lady Chapel into the body of the cathedral.

At Hereford, the Destroyer found that a greater destroyer had preceded him: on Easter Monday 1786 the west tower suddenly collapsed, carrying with it all the west front and most of the nave. Wyatt solved the problem by shortening the nave by an entire bay and rebuilding in a style which he evidently believed to be Early English, one of the first examples of the disastrous attempt to 're-create' the past, which was to disfigure so many cathedrals in the nineteenth century. (By a singular irony his west front was demolished and rebuilt in 1908 by yet another architect – Oldrid Scott, son of the ubiquitous George Gilbert – who wrongly believed that he too had the ability to interpret the past.) At Durham the dean and chapter did, for once, stand between their cathedral and the wilder excesses of their hired architect. Among his extraordinary plans was the demolition of the

George Gilbert Scott. 'My report I viewed as a masterpiece.'

exquisite Norman 'Galilee' Chapel or western porch, purely to gain space for a carriageway along the cliff on the western side of the cathedral. He also wanted to demolish Bishop Hatfield's superb forteenth-century altar tomb and the bishop's throne on top – reputedly the highest bishop's throne in the world. All this and much else was prevented, but he still went ahead and shaved some three inches of stone from the entire face of the cathedral – a Draconic solving of the problem of decaying stone.

After Wyatt, the 'restorers' come thick and fast, each convinced beyond peradventure that he, and he alone, had the key to the past and could enter the mind of a medieval mason and recreate what the long-dead hand had brought into being centuries before. Even so great an architect as Christopher Wren was supremely confident of his ability to bring back the past. Commissioned to restore the north transept of Westminster Abbey in its Gothic form, he announced loftily, 'I have prepared perfect Draughts and Modells such as I conceive may agree with the original Scheme of the old Architect, without any modern mixtures to shew my own Inventions'. And if a man like Wren could have so deluded himself, there was little likelihood of lesser men having clearer insight.

Hard on the heels of Wyatt came George Gilbert Scott – literally so, for the four cathedrals that had felt Wyatt's hand – Ely, Salisbury, Lichfield and

Hereford – now suffered the attention of Scott. His comment on Wyatt's remoulding of the medieval figures at Lichfield can stand as example both of Scott commenting on the work of Wyatt, and of one architect commenting pityingly on the work of his predecessor: 'The mutilated work presented the most difficult enigma. I believe that I recovered the design absolutely, but some parts of it were discovered through remains so slight that, though conclusive, their interpretation was of intense difficulty.' Unlike Wren and Wyatt and most of his taciturn predecessors, Scott provided posterity with a copious account of his own doings. Published under the title of *Recollections* in 1879, a year after his death, it breathes with the very spirit of Victorian self-complacency with no hint of uncertainty: 'I made, I believe, a very perfect design illustrated by beautiful drawings .... The pains we took in recovering old forms were unbounded – no restoration could, barring this, be more scrupulously conscientious .... My report I viewed as a masterpiece'.

No man has been more ill served by his autobiography. Judged on the *Recollections* alone, Scott would emerge as a thick-skinned egoist plastering his interpretation of the past over other men's work. He was, in fact, an immensely able and industrious architect: it is, perhaps, his very conscientiousness, his almost painful determination to reproduce past forms, that eventually were to betray him in the eyes of posterity.

A particularly audacious forgery in World War II throws fascinating light on the difficulty – indeed, the impossibility – of creating a copy of a past art form which will continue permanently to deceive. A Dutch artist by name of Van Meegeren produced a number of forgeries of the works of Vermeer which not only totally deceived the collectors acting on behalf of Hermann Goering, but also Dutch art experts after the war when Van Meegeren was accused of collaborating with the enemy. He saved his skin only by painting a new 'Vermeer' before the very eyes of his accusers. A generation afterwards, however, the art historian John Cornforth makes the excellent point that the women in Van Meegeren forgeries look disconcertingly like the great Garbo. Time leaches out the truth in art as in all other fields and despite – or because – of the fact that George Gilbert Scott prepared for his work by closely studying French cathedrals, his

hard, shiny, 'finished' work is almost immediately identifiable.

But at times he could rise above himself, and nowhere is this more clear than in the chapter house of Westminster Abbey. He was appointed surveyor to the abbey in 1849 and retained that post for nearly thirty years until his death in 1878 and during that time made the minutest study of the great building, details of which he published under the rather coy title *Gleanings from Westminster Abbey*. The chapter house has, and continues to have, a curious history. It is quite independent of the abbey itself, today being the responsibility of the Department of State, known as English Heritage, which is responsible for such publicly owned monuments as Stonehenge and the Tower of London. The division came about in the Middle Ages when the chapter house became, in effect, the House of Parliament. After the Dissolution it became a depository for records and began its long decline. The eighteenth century tackled the problem of dilapidation in its own robust way – by demolition: the vault of the chapter house, becoming suspect, was pulled down in 1740 and a flat wooden ceiling put in its place. Meanwhile, in the manner of all bureaucracies, the flood of paper increased, placing the custodians of the chapter house under ever greater pressure to find storage space. They did this by gradually covering the entire walls in wooden shelves and cases, gaining access to the upper half by constructing a gallery, approached by a massive staircase. By the time that Scott tackled the task in 1866, the once exquisite chamber resembled nothing so much as a musty, dusty lawyer's office. Scott ripped out all the woodwork, and what he then saw would have daunted a less confident man: indeed, one may be fairly certain that had this work of 'restoration' taken place a century earlier the entire structure would have been simply demolished. Scott set about restoring it, as far as possible, both to its original dimensions and to its original appearance. By great good fortune he found the original ribs and bosses of the vault that had been ripped out more than a century earlier and, employing an ingenious system of cast-iron ties, used them again

*Opposite*
The chapter house, Westminster Abbey, as restored by Scott.

Lord Grimthorpe, polymath: patron but later bitter enemy of Scott.

as a skeleton for the vault. Westminster chapter house today bears evidence of restoration but it is honest evidence, the original shape apparent again.

Sir George Gilbert Scott, the ebullient, immensely confident architect, met his Waterloo at St Alban's, defeated by an amateur – Edmund Beckett Denison afterwards Lord Grimthorpe. But it is doubtful if any ordinary man could have withstood Grimthorpe, and St Alban's Abbey paid the price of the battle between them. And this must, surely, be the last occasion when a great national monument became the hobby of a rich amateur.

St Alban's, the third oldest of the great Norman churches of England, had felt to the full the melancholy combination of iconoclastic rage followed by clerical neglect. An indication of the fury of the iconoclasts is provided by the fact that the

beautifully carved pedestal which bore the shrine of St Alban was smashed into more than two thousand pieces, which were then used to wall up the Lady Chapel. The shrine itself disappeared totally while the Lady Chapel, after being ritually desecrated, was thereafter used as a school. A public right-of-way was established right through the church between the chapel and the high altar.

But Puritan iconoclasm was far less destructive than sheer indifference. Engravings made as late as the first half of the nineteenth century show the abbey in a condition of picturesque neglect which would have satisfied the heart of any romantic antiquarian. The nave was virtually ruinous and the great central tower was quite evidently not far from collapse. The condition of the abbey was all the more alarming in that there were plans afoot to upgrade it to cathedral status. A meeting was held in St Alban's town hall to discuss both the promotion and the restoration of the abbey. The idea of turning it into a cathedral was postponed, but Scott was appointed as architect for the restoration and an initial subscription raised. And it was at this meeting that Grimthorpe and Scott met.

Grimthorpe tells the story in his abrasive, abusive booklet entitled *St Alban's Cathedral and its restoration*. He was a remarkable man, very much a product of his time in his immense self-confidence, and in the lofty manner in which he ran other people's lives for their own good. The son of a banker and himself a successful barrister, he was just thirty-seven years old when he met Scott and behind him he already had a string of bizarrely differing publications – covering such subjects as the Apocalypse, the perennial debate of marriage with a deceased wife's sister, and on clock and watchmaking – all bearing testimony alike to his wide-ranging interests and his total confidence in pronouncing judgements on anything that attracted him.

Grimthorpe was by no means a charlatan: the still working machinery of Big Ben, which he designed, is testimony to that. It was his aesthetic sense which was at fault and, unfortunately both for Scott and St Alban's, he had a passionate interest in 'Gothic' architecture and had already published two books upon it. According to his own account he turned up accidentally at the town hall meeting. He lived locally, regarded himself as the local potentate and took the abbey under his protection, energetically pushing forward plans for its promotion and also both raising and contributing considerable funds to its restoration.

The work was to take over twenty years. In the first few years Grimthorpe and Scott got along reasonably well, Grimthorpe contenting himself with delivering a series of lectures on Gothic architecture in St Alban's in which he advocated the 'Early English' style of building instead of the 'Decorated' style favoured by Scott. In his *Recollections* Scott gives an account both of the astonishing dilapidation of the building and the measures he was taking to restore it. Not the least of his successes was the discovery of the fragments of the pedestal of the shrine, and with pardonable pride he describes how he, assisted by his foreman, pieced them together so accurately that today one

can still see the depression in the stone made by the knees of pilgrims. Vividly he describes the degradation of the eastern end of the building and the means employed to restore them to dignity:

Previous to the commencement of the present movement, the eastern chapels, so long alienated had been recovered to the church by making over the old gatehouse, long used as a prison, to the grammar school which had hitherto occupied the Lady Chapel. They at present remain desolate and the footpath [through the church] still perforates them, but surely this cannot continue.

He was at least fortunate in seeing this extraordinary thoroughfare, which had been driven in derision through the abbey after the Reformation, closed before he died in 1878.

Until the 1870s work on the abbey seemed to have proceeded on an *ad hoc* basis, money being raised to repair this or that feature as need was required. In 1871, however, the condition of the central tower was so grave that Scott estimated that a sum of at least £50,000 was urgently needed if the church was to be saved. A national appeal was therefore launched, the first of many national appeals for England's cathedrals. Scott undoubtedly saved the tower and, with it, the eight hundred-year-old building: one of the extraordinary discoveries he made was of a hollow space, filled with combustible material, under one of the piers – presumably an attempt, by some person or persons unknown, to burn down the tower.

It was shortly after this successful rescue operation that Grimthorpe moved in personally on the work of restoration, instead of directing from a distance. According to his own account, he received an alarming message that stones were actually falling from the south-west face of the building. He dashed to the abbey, realized that urgent measures were essential and, at his own cost, ordered the weak wall to be shored up.

From this point onwards the relationship between the all-powerful patron and the unfortunate architect began to deteriorate. In 1877 the abbey was at last promoted to the status of a cathedral, the seat of the bishop of the new diocese of Hertfordshire and Bedfordshire – but a dean and chapter had not yet been appointed. Lord Grimthorpe, author of treatises on the Apocalypse and on Christian marriage, designer of clocks and

confident interpreter of the intentions of medieval master masons, moved into the gap wielding not a trowel but a cheque book. He had undoubtedly saved a substantial part of the building by his prompt action and now he took advantage of his position by declining to do anything more until a proper committee was established which would have 'power and control over the architect and builder'. He then moved in directly to attack the unfortunate Scott:

The restorations ever since I first knew anything of them would have been done better and cheaper without any architect. Everything he told us, beyond the obvious fact that the church was going to ruin, turned out wrong, and was the result of first carelessness and then wilful refusal to examine it properly when requested.

The core of Grimthorpe's accusation, insofar as it was not based on personal spite, was that Scott acted too late and too timidly. But meanwhile, the wretched architect was under just as fiery an attack from an entirely different quarter – the purists, led

The west front of St Alban's (*above*) before restoration and (*right*) after rebuilding to Grimthorpes design. On the evidence of the nineteenth century photograph there is little doubt but that Grimthorpe saved a substantial part of the building – but his personally executed design was in the very worst form of Victorian 'Gothic'.

by William Morris – for an entirely different reason: he had been too drastic. As he said in his apologia, 'I am in this, as in other works, obliged to face right and left to combat at once two enemies from either hand, the one wanting me to do too much and the other finding fault with me for doing anything at all'. Bitterly, and accurately, he then put his finger on the weakness of Grimthorpe's theory, a theory which was to alter the character of vast areas of the new-born cathedral: '[He] argues that we ought to deal with old buildings as the medieval builders themselves did; in point of fact, to treat them as we should do any modern building, doing to them just what is right in our own eyes'.

Scott died a few months afterwards, the money ran out, and the cathedral of St Alban's was wholly at the mercy of Lord Grimthorpe. Over the next

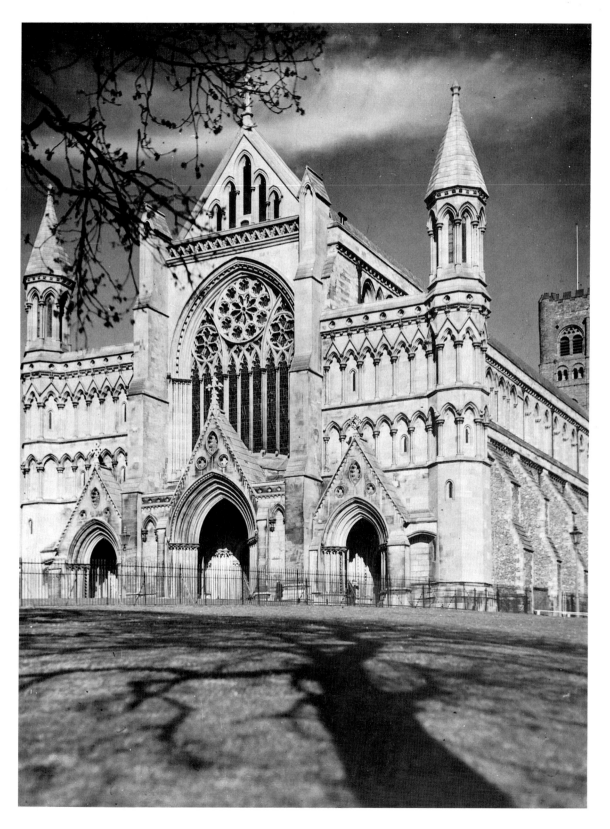

sixteen years he was estimated to have spent at the very least £140,000 of his personal fortune on the building and there is little doubt that without that money at least half the cathedral, from the west front to the tower, would have collapsed. But in return for his money he demanded, and received, total, dictatorial powers. He was not content with overseeing and directing, but personally designing, and designing not simply unobtrusive capitals or arches but entire major areas. 'In the summer of 1879, I made a rough sketch of a new west front and showed it to most of the Committee and sundry other people who all approved of it', he recorded complacently. He describes, just as complacently, how he sent Scott's son packing: 'Though Mr Scott had deprived himself of any claim to be employed, I gave him not only one but two chances of acting as architect – of course under my control. But fortunately for me and the church, he refused'. He records, with relish, his battle with 'that trade union, the RIBA, who thought I could not do without them. They cunningly put a clause to that legal effect in their specifications of contracts which I have taught people how to frustrate in my *Book on Building* – a sort of red rag to those bulls ...'

Grimthorpe's major monument at St Alban's is the appalling west front which resembles, in its mechanical symmetry, nothing so much as a child's box of bricks. Like so many others of his time and taste, he arbitrarily decided that there was only one 'correct' period of Gothic, only one style in which God wished to be worshipped. That style was the so-called Early English and everything that conflicted with that style, and which could be removed without actually weakening the structure, was removed. Inside the west porch he had himself portrayed in the guise of St Matthew. In the transepts the despised 'Perpendicular' windows were ripped out and 'correct' rose windows put in their place – windows of a mechanical design consisting of a large circle with a number of smaller circles, locally nicknamed 'change for a sovereign'. He reconstructed the fourteenth-century piers of the nave and recorded, again with that ineffable complacency, 'It took no small trouble to get the new stones worked as roughly as the old ones, so as to make the work homogenous and bewilder antiquaries'. He inserted a genuine Norman doorway in the south transept, added decorations

to it and thereafter announced 'people wrongly guess which are old and which are new stones'.

It was while Lord Grimthorpe was enthusiastically turning new stones into old and confidently 'recreating' a long-dead past that the Society for the Protection of Ancient Buildings came into being. Its founding father, William Morris, set out its aims and objects in a ringing manifesto, which begins: 'A society coming before the public with such a name as that written above must needs explain how, and why, it proposes to protect those ancient buildings which to most people have so many and such excellent protectors.' Then, in a masterly summary which established the canons of conservation, he achieved one of the most difficult of all critical feats, that of standing outside his own time to distinguish between that which is current fashion and that which is constant function:

The civilised world of the nineteenth century has no style of its own amidst its wide knowledge of the styles of other centuries. From this lack and this gain arose in men's minds the strange idea of the Restoration of ancient buildings; and a strange and most fatal idea which by its very name implies that it is possible to strip from a building this, that and the other part of history – of its life, that is – and then to stay the hand at some arbitrary point, and leave it still historical and even as it once was. In early times this kind of forgery was impossible ... If repairs were needed if ambition or piety pricked on to change, that change was of necessity wrought in the fashion of the time ... But those who make the changes wrought in our day under the name of Restoration, while professing to bring back a building to the best time of its history, have no guide but each his own individual whim to point out to them what is admirable and what contemptible.

The society was inevitably stigmatized – particularly by go-ahead deans and parsons each anxious for his own little piece of immortality – as desirous of 'protecting' ancient buildings, simply by allowing them to fall to pieces. Vigorously, the society rejected this accusation and, in a letter to *The*

*Opposite*
The nave of St Alban's, showing surviving original timber ceiling.

160

*Times*, that ultimate court of appeal, Thackeray Turner pilloried the objectives of the 'restorer'. Discussing proposals to restore the royal tombs in Westminster Abbey, he remarked:

I fear there are those who wish to change the present appearance of the monuments, who believe that it is possible to bring them back to their original splendour. They would, no doubt, replace the vanished mosaic in the twisted columns of the Confessor's shrine, replace the partly perished marble by brand-new slab; do the same by the Purbeck marble of Queen Eleanor's tomb and polish the new work till it shone like glass ... And to what purpose? To foist a patch of bright new work – a futile academic study at best – amidst the loveliness of the most beautiful building in Europe.

To the ear of posterity, Thackeray Turner's outburst sounds perilously near antiquarianism at best and preciousness at worst. But to the ear of posterity he, and Lord Grimthorpe, and William Morris, diametrically opposed though they might be aesthetically, were all speaking with the same enviably confident voice, laying down each in his own way an eternal canon of unchanging aesthetics.

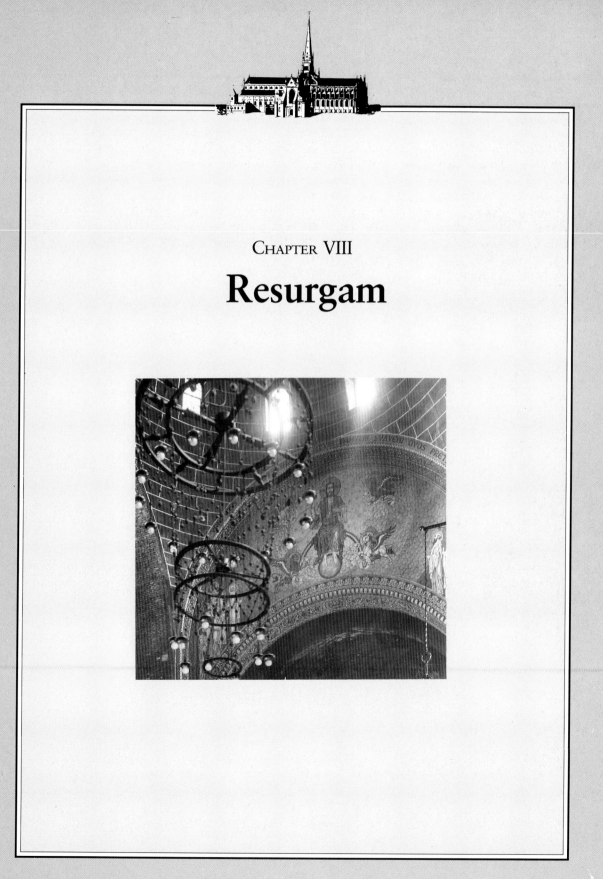

CHAPTER VIII

# Resurgam

On November 14 1940 330 bombers of the *Luftwaffe* raided the city of Coventry for eleven hours, killing 554 people and totally destroying the four hundred-year-old cathedral of St Michael, adding the word 'coventration' to wartime language. St Michael's had been elevated to cathedral status only since 1918, but a committee met almost immediately after its destruction to decide how, and when, and in what form, a successor should arise.

The committee might well have added the word 'if' to their brief for the omens were anything but auspicious for the building of a cathedral in the new world about to be born. It was not the fact that Great Britain was still locked in a life-and-death struggle with a mighty enemy that presented a hazard: all over the country eager civic authorities were drawing up what they called 'blue-prints for the future', laudable and optimistic plans for the brave new world that was going to be, plans which envisaged the sweeping away of the slums that disgraced the ancient city centres, and the building of gleaming new buildings for a thrusting new generation. Could such plans include a stone Titan? Coventry City Council was among those who thought not and Coventry City Council's opinion was important. No longer could a dean or a bishop or even a monarch simply decree that a great building should come into being: now there was the need to thread a path through the labyrinthine ways of town-planning procedures, and to gain the approval of the 'planning authority'. Coventry City Council was the planning authority, and Coventry City Council thought that, in those hard times, a cathedral was an 'unnecessary building'. And if proof were needed they only had to point south, to the town of Guildford, whose new cathedral languished roofless amidst an apathetic townsfolk, or west to the city of Liverpool, where not one but two cathedrals – one of them planned to be the largest in the world – had been a building for over half a century and the end was still not in sight.

In the latter half of the nineteenth century Liverpool was approaching the peak of its astonishing prosperity as Britain's major Atlantic port. The population was expanding at a commensurate rate and, in 1880, the city became a diocese and a competition was launched to chose an architect for a cathedral worthy of the thrusting,

confident city. Initially, it was specified that the design had to be in the mandatory Gothic, but after vigorous protests from architects, this limitation was removed. Designs were submitted by 103 architects: five were short-listed and Oldrid Scott, son of the Scott who had laboured so long at St Alban's, was chosen as architect. He was astonishingly young – just twenty-three-years old – for so prestigious a project, the first on a new site since the Middle Ages, and a joint architect was at first appointed with him. But when the other man died, shortly after work commenced, Scott went on alone.

The site had been chosen, and the competition launched, in 1901. Scott submitted his design in 1903 and work began in 1906. Work was still in progress when Scott died, worn-out and aged seventy-seven, in 1960. He had spent fifty-nine years upon the cathedral, compared with the thirty-five years Wren had worked upon St Paul's – a lifetime during which he had drastically changed his design, endured the problems of two world wars, (work went on through both) during the second of which bombs fell perilously close, and finally saw another cathedral beginning to rise barely a stone's throw away. The site chosen for the first cathedral was dramatic, high on St James' Mount above an ancient cemetery in a quarry, but the limitations of the site forced Scott to break away from the ancient east-west orientation – and thus provided a precedent for what was to happen at Coventry half a century later. Opinions of the vast building, second in size only to St Peter's in Rome, inevitably changed over the decades. For the historian GH Cook writing in the 1950s it is 'a mighty church [of] stern and purposeful restraint'. Twenty years later Nikolaus Pevsner saw it as 'desperately of a past that can never be recovered', though allowing that its titanic tower, higher even than Canterbury's Bell Harry 'might become the venerated last resting-place of romantic architecture'.

A few hundred yards away from the Anglican cathedral of Christ, the Roman Catholic cathedral of Christ the King belongs to another age. Turning to it after contemplating its Anglican sister, Pevsner

*Opposite*
Coventry cathedral, the morning after the raid, 1940.

sums up the two: 'If the Anglican cathedral on Liverpool's skyline seems an engine of past emotion, the Catholic cathedral may at first seem a cross between cooling tower and circus tent, part power station and part fairground'. Irreverent Liverpudlians, taking into account its shape and the ethnic group predominating in its congregation, nicknamed it 'Paddy's Wigwam'. But its peculiarities are by no means exhausted: what is visible is only a fraction of an intended whole. Beneath is a truly gigantic crypt, meant to be the underpinning of the world's largest cathedral, not simply bigger than its rival down the road, but bigger than St Paul's in London and bigger than St Peter's in Rome, its dome surpassing – in size at least – even that created by Michelangelo. It was to be the trumpet call of resurgent Roman Catholicism after centuries forced underground.

But English Roman Catholicism already had a trumpet call, not so strident perhaps but clear and authentic, in the form of the cathedral of St Chad built by Augustus Pugin in Birmingham.

The Catholic Emancipation Act of 1829 allowed Roman Catholics the right of again freely practising their religion. Suppression had not been total: in Birmingham as in other cities there had been Catholic chapels where the old rites had been conducted with a certain amount of discretion. A masshouse was built by a Franciscan in 1688 (its site recorded, if no more, by Masshouse Circus on the Ringway) and though this was later destroyed by a Protestant mob, a chapel was eventually built, in 1808 on the site of what was to be the cathedral. In 1834, however, a group of Catholics decided that it was 'highly desirable that a commodious and splendid church be erected in the town of Birmingham, a town which for the numbers, the wealth, and the spirit of its inhabitants is justly termed the metropolis of the Midland district'. Thomas Rickman – the same who devised the 'styles' of architecture – was appointed as architect, but fortunately there was a dispute over the site and the idea was temporarily dropped. When it was revived, the new architect was – Augustus Pugin.

Even now we are perhaps too close to Pugin to do him justice: had he been born in the Middle Ages, which was his spiritual home, then he would be placed in context. As it is, his incredibly crowded short life – he died at the age of forty – resembles more that of the eccentric so cherished by the English than that of the genius. For he was an original: before he was fourteen he had thrown himself into designing medieval buildings: before he was twenty he had gained fame as a designer of operatic scenery. He married twice before he was twenty-one, turned his back on architecture, then picked up again. Unlike such pedestrian natures as Scott and Rickman he did not so much copy Gothic styles as recreate them: a Pugin church is instantly recognized as a church of the nineteenth century, yet is infused with that design associated with the so-called 'Age of Faith'.

The cathedral of St Chad achieved two notable 'firsts': it was the first cathedral to be built in England since Wren's St Paul's of 170 years earlier and it was the first cathedral of the Roman Catholic rite to be built since the Reformation. Lack of money and an understandable caution had led to an uncharacteristic austerity in the few Roman Catholic chapels and churches that had recently been built: Pugin decided that this first-of-all new Roman Catholic cathedrals should reflect the richness and splendour of earlier centuries. He would ensure that the casing was rich: patrons would have to contribute to the furnishing. He was fortunate in gaining the support of the wealthy and artistically discerning Earl of Shrewsbury who gave, among much else, the pulpit, throne and canon's stalls, all of fifteenth-century Flemish workmanship. The bones of St Chad completed their long odyssey in the handsome chapel specially built for them and Pugin himself gave a splendid organ in 1846. The consecration on Monday 21 June 1841 was a splendid affair, the Roman Catholics of England indulging in colour and sound after the long years of austerity: no less than thirteen bishops were present in the sanctuary when Bishop (later Cardinal) Wiseman preached.

It was an unprecedented occasion which created an explosion. Until 1850, English Roman Catholic bishops had taken their titles from uninhabited sees in Turkey and North Africa, to avoid exacerbating British feelings. The bishop whose *cathedra* was in this Midland town bore the exotic style of bishop of Hetalonia. In 1850, however, Pope Pius IX

*Opposite*
Coventry cathedral, cleaned up, but before rebuilding, 1946.

established a formal hierarchy in England and Wales and the bishop of Hetalonia took the less glamorous, but rather more accurate title of bishop of Birmingham. It caused an explosion of rage in a country where religious feeling still ran high. *The Times* hurled its thunderbolts against 'this latest act of papal aggression'; protest meetings were held all over the country and addresses of loyalty made to Queen Victoria as though the Armada were again sailing up the Channel and the British throne was in need of protection. Parliament even passed an Act in 1851 stating that only Anglican bishops could use English titles, but the civilized Gladstone repealed it twenty years later. As a matter of courtesy and common sense, Roman Catholic bishops do not use the same territorial titles as their Anglican counterparts: when the church of St John in Norwich was elevated to the status of a cathedral its bishop took the style of bishop of East Anglia, from that long-forgotten pre-Conquest diocese whose cathedral had been at North Elmham, in order to distinguish himself from the Anglican bishop of Norwich.

By a quirk of history there was to be a kind of apostolic succession between the cathedrals of Birmingham and Liverpool. The Roman Catholic diocese of Liverpool came into being in 1850, thirty-eight years before the Anglican and three years later a cathedral was actually begun in one of the northern suburbs, the architect being none other than Pugin's son. The project languished, however, only the Lady Chapel being built until, eighty years later Edwin Lutyens was commissioned to build a church to rival the Anglican monster. Lutyens was then at the height of his fame and his gigantesque approach was exactly that which appealed to the Roman Catholics of Liverpool. The building was going to be somewhat shorter and narrower than St Peter's in Rome, the largest church in Christendom, but it was to be far higher and the immense dome, with a width of 168 feet was actually planned to be thirty feet wider than Michelangelo's, and forty-two feet wider than Wren's St Paul's. Work started in 1933, continued with immense dash, and then was suspended – forever, as it turned out – in 1940. Only the crypt was completed and, in describing it, Nikolaus

The Anglican cathedral, Liverpool, 'last resting place of romantic architecture'.

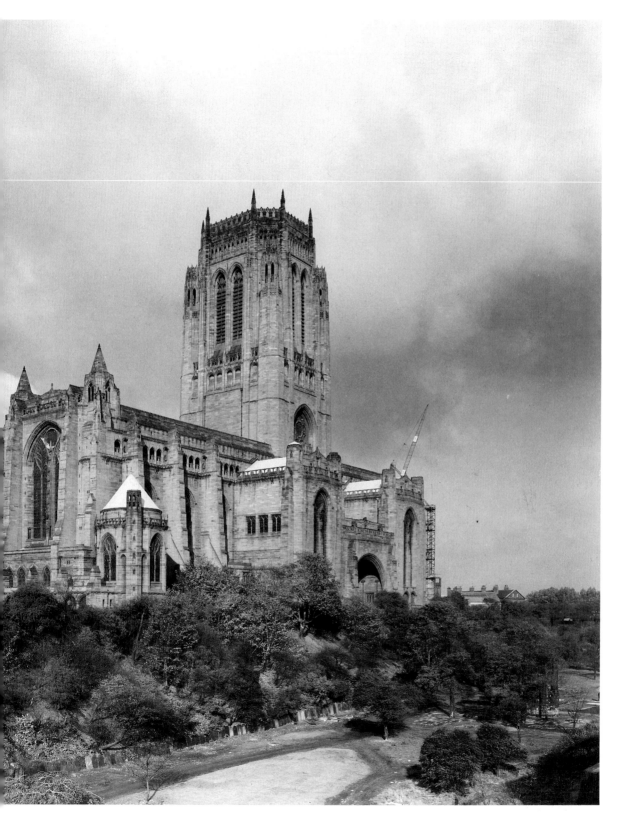

Liverpool Roman Catholic cathedral.
(*Left*) exterior; (*above*) looking down on the circular nave from the corona.

Pevsner's usually restrained style borders on the lyrical: 'But what a crypt! For comparison one can only think of that of St Peter's, and in addition of the substructures of such a Roman palace as that on the Palatine, or better still Diocletian's at Spalato'. It is a debatable point whether this Titan would, or could have been completed even if there had been no war, but it was obviously wholly impracticable in the austere post-war years. In 1959 a competition was held seeking solutions to the problem. It was won by Sir Frederick Gibberd who, taking advantage of the wind of change sweeping through the ecclesiastical world, a wind which swept away the concept of priest and laity occupying different worlds and physically brought them together in the church, he designed the circular building on part of the site. The actual construction took just five years – but it had been 114 years since Liverpool had first decided it needed a Roman Catholic cathedral. Subsequently, that length of time had almost been equalled by the mother church of Roman Catholicism in England, the Metropolitan cathedral of Westminster. Begun in 1896, the actual fabric was completed by 1903. A Byzantine style was chosen, in order not to compete with the genuine and superb Gothic of Westminster Abbey at the other end of the street, but as a matter of deliberate policy, the rich mosaics and marbles cladding the interior have not been completed in order not to put too great a financial burden upon the present generation. The marble cladding of the walls goes up about halfway, leaving the remainder of the twelve million bricks employed in the building uncovered, and uncovered they will remain at least during the present century.

Throughout the nineteenth century, and increasingly in the twentieth, there began to be expressed by both major denominations of the Christian Church of England something of doubt as to the need or, indeed, the propriety of diverting Church funds to these superb but horrifically expensive expressions of the Christian faith. When Westminster cathedral was first proposed Archbishop (afterwards Cardinal) Manning, while encouraging the idea, insisted that the first need of the diocese was the provision of schools and orphanages so that, while a site was obtained for the future cathedral, actual work was deliberately postponed. In 1905 Birmingham joined the ranks of cities elevated to that of a diocese and it might have been confidently predicted that big, brash Birmingham would have built the world's biggest, brashest cathedral. Instead, the new bishop had to content himself with the exquisite, but small, eighteenth-century parish church of St Phillip. Birmingham, however, was the very cradle of dissent, a city constitutionally unlikely to have much sympathy with such High Church falals as cathedrals, and the question as to whether or not the twentieth century needed cathedrals, or approved of the money diverted to their construction was postponed. It became a matter of vigorous, indeed, acrimonous debate twenty years later when the first proposals were mooted to build a cathedral in Guildford, the first – apart from Liverpool's – planned for a new site since the Reformation.

The commissioners of Henry VIII had recommended that, in addition to the five new dioceses planned for England, provision should be made for the creation of 'suffragan' bishops – a peculiarly English measure which enabled any bishop to nominate 'two honest and discreet spiritual persons', one of whom the crown would chose as his assistant, with the style and dignity of bishop. It was a far-sighted awareness of the growth and shift of population. Guildford was chosen as title for a suffragan, but the slow growth of population in Hampshire and Surrey made it long unnecessary for the bishop of Winchester actually to appoint an assistant. It was not until 1874 that the long dormant provision of Henry VIII was activated and a bishop of Guildford was at last appointed as suffragan to Winchester.

The suffragan status lasted for fifty years and would probably have continued for even longer had it not been for the phenomenon of the population explosion in the south-east. Surrey's population began to move towards the half million mark as the development of the railway brought in new blood. A condition that had lasted unchanged for 800 years was drastically altered within half a century and in 1923 came the proposals to divide the ancient diocese of Winchester into three parts, still retaining Winchester as the heart of the mother diocese but erecting Portsmouth and Guildford into the dignity of full bishoprics. Both the new bishops had to make do with a parish church as their cathedral. Portsmouth's old parish church of St Thomas was large enough and dignified enough to serve as the bishop's seat with a certain amount of enlargement, but in Guildford the old parish church of Holy Trinity was held to be too small and too shabby to serve in perpetuity as a cathedral.

Tentative plans were put in motion. The diocesan authorities would, in effect, be forced to prove in the middle of the twentieth century that the forces which had created the medieval cathedrals were dormant, not dead. And those forces found expression not only in design but also in the humdrum, but vital, ability to provide the money to execute the design. The age of princely gifts was past: the bulk of the money would have to come from an anonymous laity increasingly described as indifferent, if not actively hostile, to established religion. In May 1928 the Diocesan Conference courageously decided that the age of faith did not necessarily lie in the past and resolved to build a new cathedral. A local magnate, Lord Onslow, gave a virgin site of 6 acres on the edge of the town and an appeal was launched. It was estimated that the cost of the cathedral would be £250,000 – a figure which was to be more than trebled by the time the last brick was in place a generation later.

The appeal could not have been launched at a worse time. In November 1928 there began that economic collapse which has now entered history as the Depression. In England, the numbers of unemployed climbed into their tens of thousands, then into their millions. The economic powers of those who would be called upon to contribute to the building of the new cathedral declined sharply; simultaneously, the growth of population in Surrey placed an impossible pressure upon existing ecclesiastical facilities. What money was available

*Above*
The skyline of Norwich is dominated by the ancient Anglican cathedral (commenced in the eleventh century) and the modern Roman Catholic cathedral, (commenced in the nineteenth century).

*Below*
The Erpingham gateway, leading into the strongly walled close of Norwich cathedral.

should be devoted to building new parish churches, it was argued, and not squandered on grandiose, outdated concepts. The most telling aspect of this attack was that it came from the heart of the Church itself, launched by practising Christians who were at least as dedicated to the Church as the defenders of the cathedral concept. In June 1935, after the appeal had been launched, the architect chosen and the first work commenced on the site, the local paper published a long letter from a correspondent who signed himself simply 'An Observer' but whom the leader page described as 'written by one actively engaged in Church life in the diocese'. Citing his experience in other cathedral cities 'Observer' described the average cathedral congregation as being composed of people who came for the music and roundly attacked cathedral clergy as 'a snobbish race apart. The Bishop foresaw crowds of nice, decent people coming into the diocese. Do they frequent the present cathedral now? No.' Finance was one of the barriers between the clergy and the laity: 'The minds of the clergy seemed to be so saturated with thoughts of how they were going to meet parish expenses that they seemed incapable of speaking with enthusiasm on any other subject ... Now, in addition, they are urged in pious language to find money and more money for a cathedral.'

The letter triggered off a massive reaction, the heavy correspondence that followed being almost equally divided between opponents and defenders of the idea. The bishop entered the controversy to deny the charge that a kind of palace was being erected at the cost of parish work: 'No one proposed to erect a cathedral with a dean and chapter and full staff. What was contemplated was a new cathedral of a new kind, with a provost and

*Opposite above*
The Roman Catholic cathedral at Liverpool, a compromise building sitting on its enormous crypt.

*Opposite below*
Detail of the richly sculptured screen at York Minster.

one or two clergy. The idea of a complete cathedral establishment was wholly misleading.' The statement was uttered in good faith, but time was to make it as innacurate as the early optimistic estimates of cost.

The effect of the controversy was to cool down even further an initially lukewarm impulse. Lord Onslow had offered the site on only one condition – that the offer be taken up within three years. Nearly four years later the site was still virtually untouched. In 1932 he wrote an impatient letter to the Lord Lieutenant of Surrey, chairman of the Appeal Committee. Did the diocese want a new cathedral or not? In his turn, the Lord Lieutenant wrote to the Mayor of Guildford. Did Guildford itself want a cathedral? It had been expected that the town would cordially welcome the prestige, 'But this has not been the case. So far as any general expression of opinion has been given we have rather met with discouragement. The question will be fully decided at the coming Diocesan Conference on December 6 1932. The want of interest may prove to be a deciding factor'. The Mayor could only give a negative assurance at best: 'The idea has never been present in the minds of Guildford people that we should NOT have a cathedral'. Once the work was well and truly started he had little doubt but that the townsfolk would become wholehearted in their support. It is doubtful if the conference was finally persuaded by this heavily qualified local support, but work began in December 1933.

Two years earlier, the Cathedral Council had announced an open competition. The spirit of the cathedral builders was undoubtedly not dead, for 183 architects submitted designs of whom five were invited, for a retainer of 500 guineas each, to prepare detailed plans. The Council was still groping for a precedent: an unabashedly traditional Gothic seemed out of keeping but there was a reluctance, too, to countenance any drastic departure from tradition. A generation later and the changes of thought produced by a global war opened the path for Basil Spence at Coventry: in 1930 continuity seemed both logical and desirable. The chosen design, by Edward Maufe, neatly bridged the gap between the equally uncertain innovators and traditionalists. In the architect's own words, it was 'a design definitely of our time and yet in line with the great English cathedrals; to

build anew on tradition; to rely on proportion of mass, volume and line rather than elaborate ornament'. The cathedral itself was literally to grow out of the hill upon which it was built, for it was to be constructed of bricks which were themselves to be made of the clay actually on the site. In the post-war years the design was inevitably criticized by a generation which had come to believe that tradition provided a shackle rather than an impulse, but contemporary opinion was enthusiastic. Charles Reilly, Professor of Architecture in the same city where the other great Anglican cathedral was so slowly rising, compared Guildford's favourably with Liverpool's: 'Mr Maufe's building is monolithic in appearance compared to that of the old Gothic structures. The rectangular masses will at Guildford be much plainer and more solid looking even than they are at Liverpool.'

Edward Maufe was inevitably involved in the local controversy as to cost but fought back by pointing out that the tower alone of Liverpool cathedral was equal in cost to the whole of Guildford's. He estimated that the work could be completed well within five years, but three years and two months after the archbishop of Canterbury laid the foundation stone, World War II broke out. Work ceased during the war and in the austerity years that followed continued only haltingly: at one period there were only half a dozen men working on the site. It seemed likely that Guildford's cathedral would suffer the same fate as Liverpool's, if indeed it were ever completed, proving unequivocally that the age of faith was indeed past.

Salvation came from a completely unexpected direction – not from the nation, but from the small town which, before the war, had appeared to be entirely apathetic about the project. The provost of the parish-church cathedral attacked the Town Council, and by implication the citizens of Guildford, for their apathy. The Mayor reacted as vigorously, specifying an interest in Church affairs. His motivation was civic pride rather than religious emotion but it proved to be an adequate trigger.

Again an appeal was launched, a massive pilgrimage initiated, some £42,000 collected and building gathered impetus again. The cathedral was finally completed and consecrated in May 1961.

Looking back down the perspective of the twentieth century, and contemplating the experiences of their cathedral-building predecessors, the mixed body of laity and ecclesiastics who met in 1947 to consider how and when the new cathedral of Coventry should come into being must have felt some uncertainty about their chances. They were, however, spared one problem – that of raising the money, or, at least, a very substantial part of it. The cathedral had been destroyed by enemy action and they were therefore entitled to funds under the War Damage Compensation Act. In retrospect, it is curious that Coventry's was the only cathedral destroyed in Britain during the war: not only were most cathedrals in the heart of major cities, but some had been the deliberate targets for aerial attack during the so-called Baedeker Raids of 1942. Launched by the *Luftwaffe* in retaliation for RAF raids on historic German cities, the raids had for their targets the historic towns of Britain and during them a number of cathedrals received severe damage, Norwich and Exeter among them. One of the most famous photographs of the London blitz shows St Paul's engulfed in fire and flame, the great dome alone soaring above the smoke: the extent of devastation around it makes its survival all but incredible. But only Coventry's was damaged so badly as to make repair out of the question. The architect would be given a clean slate upon which to design a building of the post-war world.

On D plus 2, June 1944, I was dug in just off the beaches of Normandy. An army friend, also dug into the ground for protection, asked me just before we fell asleep what my ambition was. The circumstances were such as to set one thinking about such mortal longings. I said 'To build a cathedral'.

Such is Basil Spence's opening of his lively, highly personalized account of the rebuilding of Coventry cathedral which, aptly, he entitled *Phoenix at Coventry*. He was already an architect of standing, with a growing practice, but his experience and flair lay in the designing of exhibition areas and the like – a fact which was to be of very considerable importance for the Coventry cathedral of the

*Opposite*
Pugin's Roman Catholic cathedral in Birmingham (the screen has since been removed).

Westminster Roman Catholic cathedral: (*left*) exterior; (*above*) interior showing
unclad brick. Although conceived at the time when
Gothic was in high fashion, a Byzantine style was chosen as counterpoint to the
genuine Gothic of Westminster Abbey further down the street.

future. As early as 1944 Oldrid Scott had taken time off from his life's task at Liverpool to design a cathedral for Coventry but it had been turned down: 'Conflicting requirements of the clergy made impossible demands on the architect', was the sympathetic assessment of his fellow architect. In 1947 the Harlech Commission was set up, which recommended that, though an entire new cathedral should be built, it should be in the 'Gothic style' a recommendation which was fortunately dropped. In June 1950 competition conditions were issued. The competition was opened to all architects not only from the Commonwealth, but also from the Republic of Eire. Considering that Eire had studiously avoided assisting its sister state during the recent troubles, even sending a message of condolence to the German Embassy on the death of Adolf Hitler, this was a remarkably generous gesture, in keeping with that spirit of international reconciliation which was to be the new cathedral's inner and outer characteristic.

In their preamble to the Schedule of Requirements the Reconstruction Committee outlined a noble ideal: 'The Cathedral should be built to enshrine the altar. This should be the ideal of the architect – not to conceive a building but to conceive an altar and to create a building'. But the Committee was aware, too, of the need to maintain some form of continuity in that period of social fragmentation and traumatic change and emphasized that at least the tower and ancient crypts of the old cathedral should be saved, leaving it to the architect's discretion as to how much he would save of the remainder. The Committee further laid down requirements for three unique and poignant symbols: the Charred Cross, the Cross of Nails and the Chapel of Reconciliation. On the morning after the air raid a workmen in the still smouldering ruins had come across two charred beams, one of which had fallen across the other to make a cross. Impulsively, he picked it up, bound the transverse piece to the taller length and set it up. The Cross of Nails was made out of nails twisted by heat (later scores of these Crosses would be made and sent overseas). As for the Chapel of Unity, the Committee said that it was 'probably the most difficult thing we set before the architect: we regard it as one of the most important'. The chapel would belong to both the Free Churches and the Anglican Communion and the problem, as the Committee

saw it, was to give 'weight' to this separate and relatively small building in the shadow of the cathedral.

Basil Spence states that the instant he visited the ruins he saw exactly how the new cathedral should look – even down to the fact that a great tapestry must appear above the altar. There would be endless refining of detail but the grand concept presented itself in an instant. As for the ruins, 'As soon as I set foot on the ruined nave I felt the impact of a delicate enclosure. It was still a cathedral. Instead of the beautiful wooden roof it had the skies as a vault. This was a Holy Place ... whatever else I did I would preserve as much of the old Cathedral as I could'. The Committee, following the precedent established in Liverpool, had dispensed the architect from following the traditional east-west orientation of a church and this dispensation allowed Spence to evolve the boldest concept of all, using the ruins of the old as a vast porch for the new. Here, in the heart of the old cathedral, beneath that vault of the sky, was set up a replica of the Charred Cross, above an altar made of the old stones carved with the two words 'Father Forgive'.

The competition had attracted scores of entries, among them one which included a cross hundreds of feet high and another, going to the other extreme, proposing a building that would be entirely underground 'because of the atomic bomb'. Edward Maufe, architect of Guildford's still unfinished cathedral, was one of the three assessors who finally chose the design presented by Architect No. 91 because it had 'qualities of spirit and imagination of the highest order'. Initially, the general public disagreed violently with this assessment. Backed by an imaginative and loyal Reconstruction Committee, Spence went on an extended tour to 'sell' the design, including a three-months' tour in Canada and the USA. In Montreal, a formidable dowager took him to task about the flèche he had added to the cathedral, a traditional French flourish: 'I advise you to remove that radio pylon. What use is it anyway?' The architect's patience had grown thin and he snapped back, to the delight of the pressing crowd, 'Madam, it is there to receive messages from heaven!' At Calgary,

*Opposite*
The nave, Guildford cathedral.

St Paul's during 'the Blitz'.

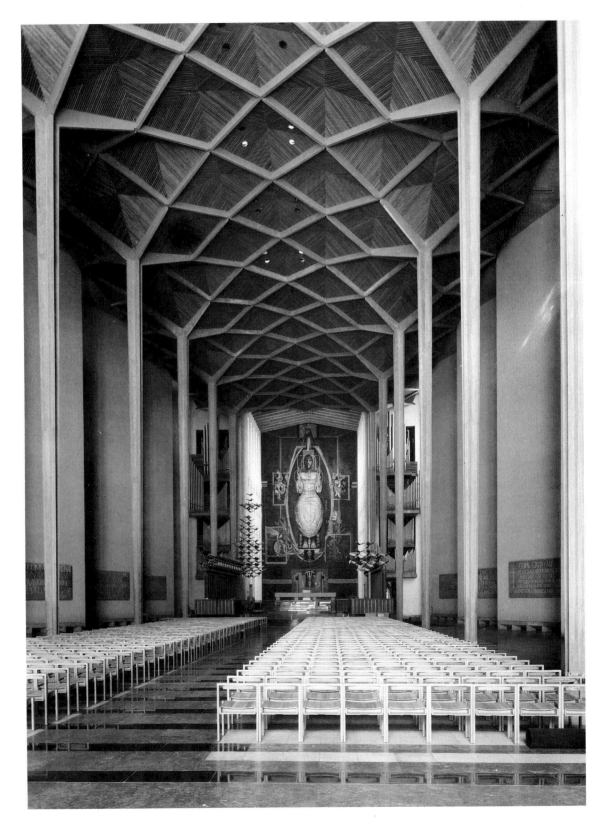

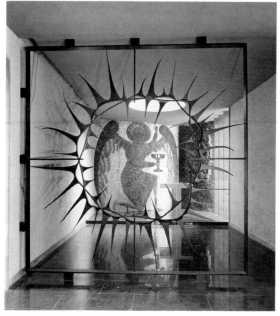

Coventry cathedral: (*opposite*) the nave showing Sutherland's tapestry as originally conceived by Spencer; (*above*) the baptismal font from Bethlehem; (*left*) the Gethsemane chapel, the architect's gift to the cathedral.

he was assailed by a prominent citizen with the remark, 'So you're the perpetrator of that concrete monstrosity'.

But the hostility of distant critics paled before that of the local community, as reflected in the City Council. They held the trump card of planning permission and argued that at this time of great shortages, social buildings were more important than ceremonial. There was, perhaps, justification in their argument, but when they actually went on to claim that not just houses but also new law courts, a police station and even public swimming baths took priority, one can only wonder at the motivation. The Council actually sent a deputation to the Minister to put their case against the cathedral but they were overruled and, in due course, on 5 May 1954, Building Licence No. 9/0/14822 was granted, giving permission for 'building of new Cathedral at a TOTAL COST not exceeding £985,000'. By an irony of history, twenty years later when the economic depression struck Coventry with particular force, a leading trade-union official in the city urged the provost of the cathedral to exploit its tourist potential and so bring in much needed income.

Coventry cathedral took just six years to build, the foundation stone being laid on 23 March 1956 and the building consecrated in April 1962. It is thus completely homogenous, one linking human mind drawing together the scores of separate actions, the master mason in the twentieth century. In his lively account Basil Spence brings out the fact that the architect of a cathedral had to know a little of a great number of trades. He had to be a good enough artist to sketch out the idea of a tapestry for Graham Sutherland to develop in detail; a good enough sculptor to provide Jacob Epstein with a starting point; and above all, a diplomat to bring together the various, frequently conflicting objectives. This comes out clearly in the heated exchange, over the matter of the choir, which took place between Bishop Gorton and Sir Ernest Bullock, Professor of Music at Glasgow University whom Spence had called in as consultant. The bishop's attitude was summed up by his remark that the choir boys should be kept out of sight as they were usually fidgety and scruffy. Bullock also wanted the gap between the two sides of the choir to be made narrower to increase the musical effect. The Bishop said this would hide the altar: music was secondary in importance to communion – a remark which very substantially increased the temperature of the debate. Spence solved the problem by making choir stalls of movable units. But above all, Spence demonstrated that in the last analysis a committee, no matter how distinguished, could not design a great building: in the last analysis the architect had to have the courage of his own convictions. He, personally, had chosen Jacob Epstein as sculptor for the great statue of St Michael binding Satan that is the dominant motif of the cathedral. 'When I mentioned Epstein to the Reconstruction Committee there was a shocked silence, at length broken by the remark "But he is a Jew" to which I replied quietly "So was Jesus Christ".'

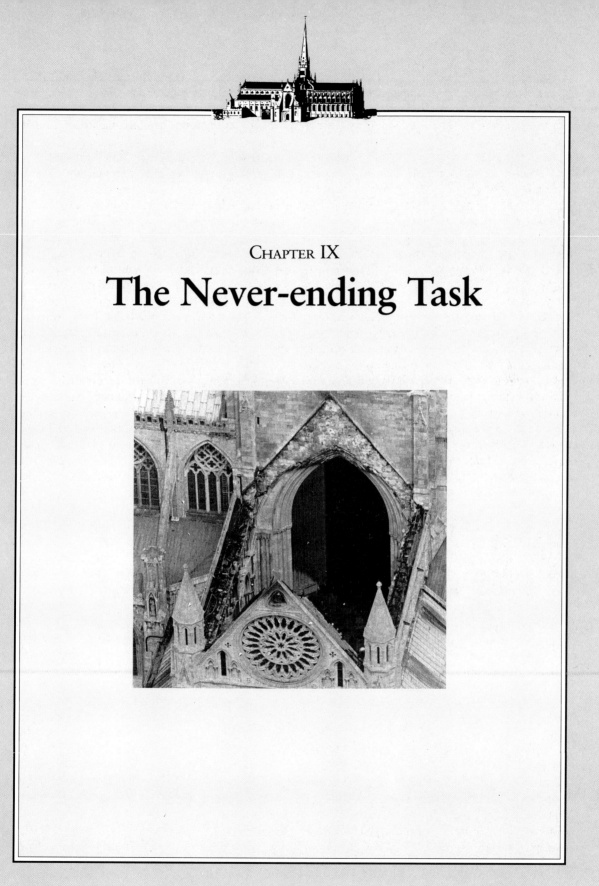

CHAPTER IX

# The Never-ending Task

It was a bitterly cold day with a knife-edged wind keening across this sky-city of stone but the young man wore only a thin shirt beneath his overalls: 'You get used to it: I've been working on this section for eight months now, since May'. The lift rose, juddering; there were no sides so vision was unimpeded, giving a rather alarming impression of being suspended in mid-air. Behind us was the nine hundred-year-old stone of the abbey, honey-coloured where work had been completed, blackened and streaked with water elsewhere; in front, the 'Gothic' fantasy of the Houses of Parliament. My guide and companion was the foreman of the tiny gang of men cleaning the exterior of Westminster Abbey: they, or their predecessors had been at it for years and they, or their successors would be there for years yet. Were they proud 'Yes and no. It's fiddly, tedious. We use only water for the delicate bits, sand and water for the rest.' How does the foreman recruit? 'We all know each other.' His brother recruited him to the gang, he recruited his brother-in-law, who brought in a friend, the group instinctively recreating the medieval guild system.

The lift groaned up past the great Rose Window. The foreman had spent six months, alone, cleaning the elaborate stonework, six months at the end of which he was almost mindless with boredom: 'I used just water and a brush – a toothbrush sometimes. Going over and over the same bit, teasing the muck away. The times I felt like putting a hammer through it. One way to go down in history, I suppose!' Unconsciously he echoed the arsonists of Ephesus.

The lift came to the top. There was another world here; a stone forest with the great buttresses soaring even higher, and in this sky forest there was a builder's yard: planks, cement, barrows, sand, men bustling back and forwards. The lift descended rose again bearing a great stone carved in the likeness of a greyhound. We watched as it was delicately manhandled across the planks and into its final position. Nearly 300 feet above the ground and more than a dozen feet in, no one would ever see this little masterpiece – except another mason working up here some time in the future. It replaced another which had worn away and that in turn had probably replaced another, an impressive example of integrity. Nearby were a number of small carved heads – portrait busts, in effect: 'Him over there – that's the foreman of the masons. That one – he's a priest or something. There's an American somewhere about. He made a big donation.' There was no deliberate attempt at antiquarianism: the faces were modern, yet they fitted into their background.

We picked our way across the bustle to a vast, blackish-grey buttress that had been picked for a demonstration. Already waiting was a man dressed like a space-walker in heavy green overalls and helmet, holding a massive hose. My guide nodded, a switch was thrown; far below a powerful compressor began throbbing and a tawny stream of sand and water gushed out and hit the buttress. Magically a date appeared – 1705 – as the blackish deposits melted before the impact of sand and water. There was a heavy damp mist all around but, contradictorily, a taste of dust in the mouth. We stood well back. 'A mate of mine had contracted silicosis – and he's never been down a mine in his life. It must be this – the sand.'

Stone cleaning began after World War I, the first tentative reaction to removing the layer of carbon that the Industrial Revolution had laid over all great building in urban areas. But not until the smoke-control Acts passed by Parliament in the post-World War II years was there any point in cleaning buildings on a large scale. The gang I met at Westminster Abbey belonged to a small, close-knit group of stone cleaners who work high above the heads of the public in city after city. Westminster Abbey was merely another point on their endless round, another place to be cleaned. But they were aware of the nature of the building, of their relationship to those who had gone before and those who would follow. They carved their names or devices in discreet corners: 'All the lads do it, all the masons particularly. Carve their initials and the date. The architects get furious and call us vandals! They do it of course – but that's called signing their work. With us its vandalism!'

I met the remainder of the gang in a hut on a level with the Rose Window. Inside it was odorous, fuggy but blessedly warm after the piercing cold of the upper levels. Two other young men were already there, drinking tea. I was introduced and conversation became technical, reminiscent. They swapped stories of other cities, other buildings, ticking off the great monuments of London. One of the gang had discovered that the angels of St Paul's

The Dean of Wells (Patrick Mitchell) standing in for a vanished forerunner.

were crying: 'Nobody knew that till we cleaned the muck off'. They enjoyed their work, but tended to be bitter about their relatively low status. As it happened, in 1971, a livery company of cleaners was established complete with Latin motto, the equal of such centuries-old aristocrats as Merchant Taylors and Vintners and the like, entitled to their own hall and their own banquets. But these men who clambered up and down the faces of our great buildings, revealing them again as though they were drawing a veil aside, contrasted their status with the aristocrats of the profession, the masons: 'They'll scarcely give us the time of day. But without us ...'. Stone cleaners do not create: their value is the negative one of removing unwanted matter. But their role is vital, for sandblasting is not simply for cosmetic reasons: the powerful jets cut away corroded material so that, when cleaning is completed, the masons can see exactly what is to be replaced. 'We're the first ones on the scene. You get a cleaner who doesn't give a damn, or is bloody-minded – he can do a lot of damage. But you don't get them on this kind of job. We're nuts! Dennis over there –' he nodded at a massive young man placidly drinking mahogany–coloured tea from a massive mug – 'he wouldn't have any help when he was cleaning the arch on the north door. So he could say he did it all himself. Nuts!' Dennis grinned sheepishly but did not deny the charge. Running a master mason to earth on site is not like contacting a chief clerk in his office. 'Mr Rice? Try the south cloister.' The south cloister is empty except for some headless torsos, a couple of bodiless heads, a hand or two and a foot. The lower half of a clawed monster writhes around a fragment of pillar; a small cherub smiles up at the freshly painted ceiling – centuries old fragments from the parent building.

The mason's yard? I hurry across the open stretch of ground which is so immensely popular with tourists in the summer. But there are no tourists now: even the swans that lord it over the moat are huddled up in the protection of the gatehouse as a snow flurry howls across. In a bare wooden hut in the yard, a girl is working with meticulous care on the body of an angel, teasing out the muck that has accumulated in the folds of its robes, bringing out traces of the soft blues and greens that have survived seven centuries. She has been working on this single small figure for two

months, and will continue doing so for as long again and no one will ever see her work in detail, for it will go back again high up on the west front. 'Mr Rice? He said he was going up the south tower.'

My heart sinks. The top of the tower is all but obscured in the blizzard, the scaffolding looking horribly flimsy. In answer to my call a head appears. 'Come on up.' The actual ascent is not as bad as it looks for the ladders, zig-zagging backwards and forwards like those on a Snakes and Ladders board, are comfortingly solid. But their wooden rungs are already slippery with the snow trodden in by the masons working at the top and, apart from an occasional piece of scaffolding placed at a strategic point, there is nothing whatsoever between climber and distant ground. Slowly one of the most exquisite panoramas in Western Europe unfolds veiled in snow flurries: the great cathedral church of St Andrew in the city of Wells in its green setting. The bishop's palace comes into view, surrounded by its moat, fed by the springs that gave the place its name. The city itself is a tiny, enchanting toy, its ancient heart occupying little more space than the enormous cathedral and its attendant buildings.

The master mason is waiting at the top, smiling encouragingly: 'Come and look at this'. 'This' is a carving of a seated man, about two feet high, holding something in his hand. 'We think it's the chap who built this tower. Look what's in his hand.' The seated figure holds a miniature version of the formalized foliage that decorates this part of the tower. The two masons regard each other across the centuries, and then the one of flesh and blood takes me on a tour. David Rice walks as casually as though he were in his sitting room: he has, in fact, probably spent more time high on this

*Opposite above*
Exeter cathedral, conforming to the English preference for length over height. One can be within a few yards of the great building and yet be unaware of its presence.

*Opposite below*
The cloisters at Worcester, once a passage and working area but now an integral part of the cathedral.

*Above*
The unmistakeable profile
of Wren's masterpiece, St
Paul's cathedral. Compare
this tranquil picture with
that taken at the height of
the Blitz (page 182).

*Below*
The Fox and Beaufort
chantry chapel at
Winchester.

Winchester cathedral crypt during one of its frequent floodings.

horrible contraption than he has spent in that sitting room.

Work on the great west front of Wells cathedral began eleven years before and was scheduled to finish in the summer of 1986. Long before work started, and throughout the years of work, the project was the centre of a lively and at times heated controversy. Iconoclasts of the seventeenth century and restorers of the nineteenth century had both laid their hands on the front but this peerless relic of the thirteenth century had survived remarkably well. A strong body of opinion held that work should be kept to the absolute minimum of cleaning. In 1972, new heads were proposed for a decapitated group, a proposal which aroused a storm of protest from purists. According to the 1975 Report of the Restoration Committee, 'The

fuss had the effect of drawing attention to the apalling condition of these statues and others were examined from scaffolding. This group was found to be split in five pieces. To prevent further damage by frost, the group was boxed-in throughout last winter and finally given a shelter-coat mainly of lime'.

There then rose the inescapable question: what to do next? A specialist sub-committee, whose members were drawn from a wide range of disciplines, was set up and the dean and chapter, in consultation with this committee, came to a compromise decision. There would be no 'restoration' whatsoever – certainly not in the form that Wyatt or Scott would have recognized. There would be total replacement of any important and badly deteriorated sculpture and conservation of the rest. The dean of Wells, Patrick Mitchell, had been familiar with the west front for over thirty years. In 1984 he took a sabbatical leave in Oxford, researching into the probable shape and iconography of the missing figures at the top of the

The Restoration of the west front, Wells Cathedral.

*Opposite*
An assistant cleaning sculpture with a toothbrush. The lime poultice clads the lower half of the sculpture.

*Above*
Cleaning a sculptured head with a spatula.

*Right*
Cleaning a figure from the Resurrection tier with mist sprays and handsprays.

*Overleaf*
The Clerk of Works and members of the staff of the mason's yard steady the central section of a replacement sculpture during its installation.

central pediment, the most important place of all, which included the great Christ in Majesty which held the whole concept together. In the event, there were seven major replacements – including the central Christ, by David Wynne, and an untold number of minor repairs and replacements ranging from the substitution of a plain, worn-out block to the recarving of a finial.

The mason's yard of Wells cathedral, that had echoed to the sound of chisel and mallet for at least 700 years, was closed after work on the west front ceased. The reason, for once, was expansion not decline. Early in the long-drawn project the dean and chapter made the decision that the workforce should be kept together. Usually, after a major restoration, the workforce is dispersed with consequent loss of expert workers most of whom, in the medieval tradition, go again on their travels. At Wells, two separate bodies were set up: the Wells Conservation Centre and Wells Cathedral Stonemasons. Each is an independent commercial organization, going out to get work for itself. But each works with the other and both give priority to cathedral work – and the cathedral, indeed, gets a share of the profits for future restorations. The Conservation Centre concentrates on the kind of work that goes on in museums: the girl working so painstakingly on the angel's robes was on contract to the Centre. The Stonemasons moved out completely to Cheddar where modern machinery has largely taken the place of tradition. But traditional techniques still survive: one of the masons was engaged in a task which Adam Lock would have immediately recognized seven centuries before: making templates for blocks to be used in a restoration for a bridge in another part of the country.

Almost as soon as they were completed, cathedrals presented a major problem of maintenance to their custodians, as Bishop Roger de Mortivale's injunction, written within a generation of the completion of Salisbury cathedral, makes clear. As the slow centuries pass, the problems grow greater, the solutions more drastic. And of all the solutions, that which took place in Winchester at the beginning of the twentieth century must surely rank as the most unusual, for the major work was undertaken by a deep-sea diver.

The problem at Winchester began when the thirteenth-century retro-choir started to sink almost as soon as it was constructed and to break away from the earlier, Norman part of the building. Two centuries later, the cathedral was further weakened when the monastic structures on the south side were demolished at the Dissolution. Winchester is honeycombed with springs and streams, the great cathedral lying in such a position that the crypt is periodically flooded, rising and falling according to the season. (One of the oddest notices to be seen in any cathedral is that at Winchester which states, as a matter of routine, that the crypt is closed due to flooding.) In 1905, great cracks appeared in the east end. Subsequent investigations showed that the builders had constructed their walls not on solid foundations but on a raft of logs which, in turn, lay upon a peat bed. This peat bed had contracted over the centuries so that a gap of nearly three feet now existed between the bottom of the walls and the peat bed, the whole being below the permanent water level.

The problem could be solved by placing concrete blocks and bags of concrete in the gap and to do this a deep-sea diver, William Walker, was brought on to the restoration team. For five years, he worked in black darkness below the foundations, placing an estimated 25,800 bags of concrete and 114,900 concrete blocks alone, unaided, in position. An additional hazard was that of infection, for he was working in a graveyard. Years later his assistant who operated the air-pump, described in a BBC interview how Walker believed that his pipe was an adequate prophylactic: 'He was fond of a smoke and when he come up somebody told him about germs, which didn't worry him. And he'd say "Where's my pipe"? Just sticking out from the drift there might be a stone coffin. He said, "This is one solid mass of germs down there".'

The 'drift' to which the assistant referred was the area of peat which the diver cleared away – and which would frequently disclose a burial. Each 'drift' was a tunnel of up to twenty feet and in this tunnel Walker would stack the bags of concrete, bonding them as though they were a wall. They set in about three hours, water was pumped out from behind them and the wall completed, to join the base of the cathedral wall itself. In 1912, Walker received the Royal Victorian Order from the hands of George V, and in 1964 a statue was raised to his memory.

Attended like a medieval knight, diver William Walker prepares to descend below Winchester cathedral.

Bronze statue in Winchester cathedral commemorating the diver William Walker.

The major restorations undertaken in recent years using advanced technology have, as a byproduct, through archaeology, thrown considerable light on the early history of the great buildings. There was dramatic evidence of this in York Minster when, in 1967, work began underpinning the central tower which had been weakened by a similar sequence of events as had happened at Winchester. The Normans had placed their foundations on a raft of great timbers but as the water table fell, so the timbers rotted. Slowly the 16,000 tons of the central tower were subsiding into the void and, to create the essential strengthening, it was necessary to excavate to a greater depth, and over a wider area than had ever been excavated before. An undercroft has now been created whose floor is at Roman level so that the successive stages of development can now be clearly seen. No trace of the original Saxon cathedral was found, the assumption being that the Roman basilica was still in use at the time the Saxons began to build their

own church. What is visible below the cathedral is the headquarters building or *principia* of Legio IX Hispana and its successor Legio VI Victrix.

The work of shoring up the tower was planned: unplanned was the need to re-roof the southern transept, destroyed by fire in 1984. Already this fire is the making of a myth for it took place the day after the consecration of the unorthodox bishop of Durham who had been the centre of fierce controversy over his views on Christian doctrine. Explanations for the fire are varied, from the flat 'No one knows' of the master mason, to the opinion of a policeman's wife, 'My husband was first on the scene. It was a hot sultry night. They said the passage of so much traffic had built up static', and to the guarded reply by the chancellor of the Minster: 'We've eliminated arson and technical fault. The probability – the eighty-five per cent probability – is that it was lightning'. The unexplained fifteen per cent has provided the very stuff of legend, from the finger of God rebuking the archbishop of York for installing an heretical bishop, to the action of extra-terrestrial visitors. No one reading accounts of the fire at York Minster that have appeared in both the popular and the serious press can doubt but that religion – or at least, the supernatural – is still very much a live issue in Britain today.

But that same event, too, showed the very real place that the cathedral played in the community – the world-wide community, and not simply that of the United Kingdom. In 1985 an exhibition of letters about the fire was placed on display in the new undercroft. They came from all over the world: from Toronto and from Zanzibar; from Chicago and from Cyprus. They came from scarcely literate people, enclosing a pound note, to typed official letters enclosing cheques for hundreds of pounds. Most remarkable was the reaction of children. The dramatic possibilities had fascinated them and the display included drawings ranging from crude crayon sketches with lurid flames to sophisticated collages made by a class. Among the letters was one from a six-and-a-half-year-old boy, addressed to the archbishop. 'Here is £1 to mend the Minster. I'm glad you lived in the Palace and not the minster or you would have got burnt.'

York Minster's established team of masons and carpenters were capable of dealing with the results of the fire. But the unexpected event added that much more to the financial burdens of Minster, just as the effects of time, with the concomitant metamorphoses of the stone and glass and wood, inexorably adds to the financial burdens of all other cathedrals. Ever since that first national appeal for financial help for St Alban's in the nineteenth century, national appeals for one or other of our cathedrals have become part of the way of life. The appeal for funds for the restoration of Westminster Abbey, launched by Sir Winston Churchill in 1954, had for objective the all-but-incredible sum of £1 million. The very size of the sum – an almost magical figure – took the public fancy: the Abbey, too, had a very special place in the hearts of the British. St Paul's belonged to London, Canterbury to the Anglican community as a whole, or to the historian, but Westminster Abbey, with its monuments ranging from the grotesque to the sublime, with its tombs of the kings and of the Unknown Soldier, its Poet's Corner and Coronation Chair, belonged to what used to be known as the British Empire and still had its enormous pull on the millions who had once regarded the few hundred square yards around it as a loadstone. The £1 million was raised. A generation later and that sum is regarded virtually as a preliminary: Canterbury appealed for £3.5 million, much of it earmarked for the restoration of the stained glass; Wells initially appealed for £1,300,000 simply to restore the west front and that sum had escalated threefold before the work had finished.

Traditionally, the building and maintenance of the cathedral was one of the first charges upon its parent community, yielding precedence only to defence. The means of financing the work might vary from country to country, from city to city, but essentially such financing was possible only because of a passionate public desire. It might be the grandiloquence of a guild, desirous of expressing its wealth and power by adding a chapel or donating a window; it might be an individual's terror of death, or gratitude for deliverance, or desire to express personal splendour. Whatever the cause, the money came from scores of tributaries to swell the great stream necessary to maintain the building.

In our own time as, ironically, the cost of maintenance rises, income descends. Primarily, the cause is the weakening of the religious impulse, coupled with diversification of financial demands and objectives. The rich man today is far more likely to endow a university chair or a charity than to build a chapel or insert a window in a cathedral; the trade union, lineal descendant of the guild, ploughs spare cash back for pensions and future strike funds rather than donating it to the repair of an ageing building. Appeals can, and do, bring in large sums from individuals but these tend to be once-for-all gifts, whereas the needs of the cathedral not only continue but escalate as another month, another year, another decade is added to its age and the stone crumbles a little more and the glass deteriorates and a wooden beam at last gives way. Then another appeal is necessary, twice the size of its predecessor, for workmen's wages and the cost of materials have soared in the interim.

'And for what purpose? To allow tourists to wander around – tourists who may be Hindu or Moslem or atheist, actively hostile to what we stand for.' So said one dean. His task, as dean, is to keep the centuries-old fabric of his cathedral in being: 'To do that I've become a shopkeeper, a restaurant owner, a cadger, a cajoler. Is this what I was ordained for, to keep a tourist attraction going?' He does his work well. Scaffolding endlessly makes its appearance here and there round the great fabric; new wood appears; there is an excellent restaurant which visitors much appreciate and which yields a comfortable profit — a profit promptly absorbed in the never-ending task. 'And to what purpose?' More and more Christians echo him. They are the ones upon whom falls the full burden of maintaining a beautiful dinosaur and some feel that the money they raise is better devoted to a spiritual use. 'There are new estates in this diocese that don't have a church. We can run up a pre-fab for £50,000 or so. But we don't. Why? Because we need £100,000 to repair the cathedral roof and after that there's the tower.' But if maintenance money is devoted to 'spiritual uses' what will happen to the cathedral. 'That's up to you, up to the government, up to the Tourist Boards. Just how long are we supposed to prop up this monster? Another century? Two centuries? A thousand years? Or until it just crumbles away. I'm no iconclast, but it's just worth remembering sometimes that Christ taught in an open field.'

Some twenty-years after the consecration of Guildford cathedral, however, the then Dean of Guildford, Antony Bridge, in an essay entitled 'Cathedrals, Worship and the Arts' raised the question of the propriety of diverting church funds to artistic purposes. 'The maintenance of cathedral choirs and the sustaining of liturgical and ceremonial splendour in the state to which elitist congregations of cathedrals have become accustomed, with an expensive *corps de ballet* of Deans, Precentors, Canons, Succentors, Priest Vicars, Servers, Taperers, Crucifers, Thurifers and Virgers, supplemented from time to time by the appearance of such guest stars as Bishops and Archbishops with minor parts to play in the regular choreography of the place, costs a great deal of money.' What, asked Dean Bridge, was its justification? He had himself been a professional artist before taking Holy Orders and was therefore able to answer the question from a deeply informed basis. The arts 'have provided us with the most profound kind of language at our disposal: or rather they have provided us with a series of languages capable of great profundity — greater, indeed, than that of

everday speech'. From a twentieth-century standpoint, therefore, he reiterated the argument put forward by the twelfth-century Honorius of Autun, that a cathedral was one great symbolic act of worship, substantiating that argument with evidence taken from modern evolutionary theory: 'All animals communicate primarily by symbolic movement'. It was impossible to isolate any one facet of the multi-faceted cathedral and say that this was 'religious' or simply 'art': the whole combined into a unity transcending its parts.

So who pays? Tourists is one obvious answer. In 1985 there were more than twenty million visitors to the national cathedrals. They ranged from school children doing 'projects', to aesthetic atheists, with every degree of religious and cultural impulse in between, a financial reservoir that is only slowly being tapped. Cathedral accounts in the past have been handled in what can only be called an amateurish manner. One lay administrator found, when he took over the accounts of a northern cathedral five years ago, what he called a 'cocoa-tin' system: 'You know — a tin for lighting, a tin for heating, a tin for rainy days. There were thirty-five separate accounts.' The tendency is to think of the Church as being immensely wealthy, with endowments accumulating vast sums over the centuries. The relatively newly established Roman Catholic cathedrals have, from their very foundation, realized that their income must be derived from current sources: even the doyen of them all, Westminster cathedral, lives on this hand-to-mouth basis. This is to be expected — but it comes as a surprise to discover how much the ancient, historical cathedrals also depend upon casual gifts. Salisbury calculates that thirty-eight per cent of its income is derived from visitors' offerings, Coventry fifty per cent; even Canterbury admits that without this revenue its financial situation would be parlous.

The main financial debate in the closing decades of the twentieth century, is about the propriety of charging for entrance. In 1926 the dean of Chester congratulated himself and his chapter on freeing themselves from the shackles of 'the obnoxious

*Opposite*
Aerial view of the burnt-out roof of the south transept, York Minster.

sixpence' – the then frequently made charge for entering a cathedral: 'I do not think myself that a cathedral can even begin to do its proper work until it has replaced visitors' fees by pilgrims' offerings'. Four other cathedrals – those at Bristol, Ely, Salisbury and Worcester – had followed Chester's lead, the dean said, 'and in every case, I believe, pilgrims' offerings have exceeded the sum previously received through fees'. Sixty years later, by one of the ironies in which history delights, it was Salisbury who pioneered the way for the introduction of charges by placing an unabashed box office in the only entrance into the cathedral. In theory, the sixty pence donation was still voluntary but it would take a very strong-minded person to push past without paying. Canterbury continued to refuse to make a fixed charge: 'It constitutes a contract and so changes the relationship between visitor and cathedral'. Most others contented themselves with a compromise: instead of a modest box tucked away in a corner, they provided a large chest with some spectacular sign such as, 'This cathedral costs 50p a minute to keep open. Please contribute'. The results varied: Lichfield found that donations increased five-fold when they introduced the system; St Paul's found that donations dropped. In 1986 Ely grasped the nettle, re-introducing the charge it had dropped half a century before – but now it was one pound fifty pence, not sixpence. Other cathedrals wait in the wings to see the result.

Coventry, designed by Basil Spence as much as an exhibition area as a place of worship and with a heavy financial burden inherited from the prodigal 1960s, has gone in openly for the tourist trade, with four shops and 'heritage' displays reminiscent of Madame Tussaud's. But all cathedrals now seem to be dependent on tourists in some degree. At peak period, more than 2,000 people an hour will crush into the four most popular – Canterbury, St Paul's, York and the aberrant Westminster Abbey. Their very presence may threaten the physical building, as thousands of feet wear away stone and the exhalation of countless breaths dim and corrode ancient paint and metal. At Canterbury, the nave has again been given over to quasi-secular purposes as it was centuries ago: at Westminster on the other hand a complex crowd-control system creates a kind of flood and ebb tide corresponding to the opening and closing of sacred services.

Psychically, the cathedral seems able to cope. Most have adopted a simple but effective device to combat the increasingly showground atmosphere. At certain fixed periods a loudspeaker will click on and a crisp, authoritative voice requests everyone to stand where they are. Brief, unaffected words of welcome follow and then, usually, the Lord's Prayer. And, as the ancient prayer unwinds its charged length, so the atmosphere changes perceptibly, as the Christians are reminded of their faith and the alien and the atheist reminded of other frames of reference. The loudspeaker clicks off and everyday life resumes, but at a more subdued and thoughtful level. The cathedral, it seems, can adapt to twentieth-century mass tourism, even as it has adapted to other threats down the long centuries.

*Opposite*
Art in the service of the Church: the John Piper tapestry in Chichester cathedral.

# Bibliography

Anderson, M D, *History and Imagery in British Churches*, 1969

Andrews, F B, *The Medieval Builder and his Methods*, 1925

Barley, M W and Hanson R P C (eds), *Christianity in Britain 300–700*, 1968

Bennett, F S M, *The Nature of a Cathedral*, 1925

Benson, E W, *The Cathedral*, 1878

Biddle, M, *Excavations at Winchester 1962–71*,

Biddle, M, *St Alban's Abbey: Chapter House Excavations 1978*, 1979

Bond, F, *Gothic Architecture in England*, 1905

Bridge, Antony, *Cathedrals, Worship and the Arts*, nd

Briggs, M, *The Architect in History*, 1927

Briggs, Martin, *Goths and Vandals*, 1952

Butler, Lionel and Given-Wilson, Chris, *Medieval Monasteries of Great Britain*, 1979

Capes, W W, (ed.), *The Charters and Records of Hereford Cathedral*, 1908

Chapman, F R, *Sacrist Rolls of Ely*, 1907

Clarke, B F L, *Church Builders of the Nineteenth Century*, 1938

Colchester, L S and Harvey, J H, 'Wells Cathedral', *Archaeological Journal*, 1974

Colchester, L S, *The West Front of Wells Cathedral*, 4th edn 1974

Cook, G H, *The English Cathedral through the Centuries*, 1960

Cook G H, *Medieval Chantries and Chantry Chapels*, 1947

Cranage, D H S (ed.), *Thirteen-Hundredth Anniversary of the Diocese of East Anglia: Official handbook*, 1930

Deansley, M, *A History of the Medieval Church 590–1500*, 1976

Dobson, R B, *Durham Priory 1400–1450*, 1973

Dodwell, C (ed. and trans.), *Theophilus: De diversis artibus*, 1961

Eastlake, C L, *A History of the Gothic Revival*, 1872

Edwards, K, *The English Secular Cathedrals in the Middle Ages*, 1967

English Tourist Board, *English Cathedrals and Tourism*, 1979

Foster Peter, *Ten Years' Restoration of Westminster Abbey*, 1985

Frankl, P, *The Gothic: literary sources and interpretations through eight centuries*, 1960

Goodman, A W, *Chartulary of Winchester Cathedral*, 1927

Gould, J, *Lichfield: Archaeology and Development*, 1976

Harvey, J H, *Gothic England: a survey of national culture 1300–1550*, 1947

Harvey, J H, *Cathedrals of England and Wales*, 1956

Harvey, J H, *The Medieval Architect*, 1972

Haskins, C H, *Studies in the History of Medieval Science*, 1924

Haskins, C H, *The Renaissance of the Twelfth Century*, 1928

Hewett, C A, *English Cathedral Carpentry*, 1974

Hope-Taylor, B, *Under York Minster: Archaeological Discoveries 1966–7*, 1971

Hudson, Henry A, *The Medieval Woodwork of Manchester Cathedral*, 1924

Jope, E M (ed.), *Studies in Building History*, 1961

Kendrick, A F, *The Cathedral Church of Lincoln*, 1899

Knoop, D and Jones, G P, *The Medieval Mason*, 1967

Kraus, Henry, *Gold was the Mortar*, 1979

Lang, J, *Rebuilding St Paul's after the Great Fire of London*, 1956

Lethaby, W R, *Westminster Abbey and the King's Craftsmen*, 1906

Lethaby, W R, *Westminster Abbey Re-examined*, 1925

Malden, R H, *The Growth, Building and Work of a Cathedral Church*, 1944

Miller, E, *The Abbey and Bishopric of Ely*, 1952

Morgan, F C and P, *Hereford Cathedral Chained Library*, 1980

Morgan, M H (trans.), *Vitruvius: The Ten Books on Architecture*, 1960

Nicholson, C B, *England's Greater Churches*, 1937

Panofsky, E. (ed.), *Abbot Suger on the Abbey Church of St Denis*, 1946

Pevsner, Nikolaus and Metcalf, Priscilla, *The Cathedrals of England*, (2 vols) 1985

Prior, E S, *A History of Gothic Art in England*, 1900

Prior, E S, *The Cathedral Builders in England*, 1905

Remnant, G L, *A Catalogue of Misericords in Great Britain*, 1969

Rickman, T, *An attempt to discriminate the styles of architecture in England from the Conquest to the Reformation*, 1835

Salzman, L F, *Building in England down to 1540*, 1967

Scott, G G, *Personal and Professional Recollections*, 1879

Tudor-Craig, Pamela, *One Half of our Noblest Art*, 1976

Whittingham, Arthur, *Norwich Cathedral Bosses and Misericords*, 1981

Wright, G A A and Wheeler, W A, *Mason's Marks on Wells Cathedral Church*, 1971

# Picture Credits

# Index